Light beamed down on my tunnel that led to Lynx Canton. The half an hour train ride seemed to last an eternity. I was the only one in the train car. I had no other passengers to pass the time with to ease my nervousness. I was filled with nerves, confusion, and rage on the inside but kept an emotionless composure on the outside. Emotions were my enemy. I had known that since day one.

The Academy of Anguish was an all-male war academy. The word academy is just another way of saying canton without making it political, but everyone knows Academy of Anguish is a lifestyle not an educational system. The males left the walls of the academy, conducting themselves in a variety of ways, often in a warrior way. When they caused trouble, they weren't questioned by the law, simply returned within the walls to receive whatever punishment was deemed necessary, if any. This is why no female would be foolish enough to subject her body to the agony, torment, and suffering that may wait within those walls. With the academy, there was no guarantee of survival.

The academy reached out past their walls to the Nevan government, because they wanted a female test subject not of Lynxan blood. It was decided that I would be the one to go in exchange for a political alliance agreement. My father had selfishly signed my fate away to the unknown and with only a care for their people in mind.

The academy provided an outfit before my departure. Black pants, black boots and a black tank top. I was told I would not need to bring anything with me. I was to simply get on the private train at the Nevan train depot and everything else would be taken care of. My father tried to hug and kiss me goodbye, but I ran to the arms of my mother, who kissed me swiftly and whispered, 'I love you'. I found the strength somehow and walked out the door. I never looked back.

Now, here I am sitting on a train to doom and not a friend in the world. Most females would be bawling their eyes out in my current situation, but I knew better. Even when you felt like no one was watching, there was always someone watching. And I refused to be seen as weak.

The train finally reached the end of the tunnel and the glow of lights from the academy walls could be seen. The Academy of Anguish was much bigger then I had imagined. It looked like a fortress that went on for miles and miles. The train began to slow down, as I continued gazing out the window in amazement. My focus came back to the train when I was jarred forward as it halted. I stood up from my seat and looked at the exit doors. I knew once those train doors opened, there was no turning back. I'd be forever marked.

Chapter One
The Plunge

I stepped off the train and spied a tall male wearing black workout pants and a white sleeveless shirt. He was leaning against the wall, but stood up when I stepped off the train. He appeared to be possibly ten years older than me, had golden hair, and a scar above his right eyebrow. His skin was olive color, his arms were very muscular, and he was easy on the eyes. He showed no sign of emotions because I could not see his eyes.

"Kaitlyn Armistice," he asked in a deep and husky voice. Not an unpleasant deep but a manly deep.

"Yes," I said with my head high and eyes on his. He grinned.

"Let's get you to Anguish." We walked down the dark empty streets in silence. We finally reached the academy. It was bigger than I had imagined. He opened the doors. I followed him inside the walls and did my best to keep my composure when the doors closed behind me. There was nowhere to run back to now.

I kept my pace with the mystery greeter, as he walked us through different corridors. The academy was dimly lit, but I was still able to make out paintings on the wall and luxurious statues. We came to a stop in front of metal doors with a key pad next to it. He entered the code and the doors opened. It was an elevator. We stepped inside and the doors quickly closed. The floor shifted, and we were on our way down. I kept my eyes focused on the metal wall in front of me.

"You never asked me my name," he finally said. I turned my head to face him.

"If I was meant to know it, then you would have told me," I turned my head forward but not before catching a smile.

The elevator pinged notifying us of our arrival at our destination, and then the doors opened. I was instantly hit with the sound of chaos. The sound of males laughing and shouting could be heard. We stepped off the elevator and made our way toward the chaos. There was another door. Within, I could see a room full of males - hundreds of them. They were all dressed in black and sparring. My escort once again entered a code and the door opened. The room instantly fell silent and all eyes were on us.

"Your room is over there. The one with the orange light," he pointed to the far end of the room. "Welcome to Anguish," he said with a chuckle and stepped off the platform and in to the crowd, leaving me by myself to be gawked at by a room full of men. My heart began to race, as I stared back at all of them. I took a calming breath and rolled my pony tail up in to a bun. It was now or never.

I looked around me and there were steps leading down to the floor where they stood. I should've chosen that way, but instead I jumped off the platform like mystery greeter had done. A few males moved out of my way, but for the most part they stood their ground. I said nothing. Simply kept my head held high, eyes front, and walked towards my new room.

They weren't making it easy on me. Most of them I had to shoulder by to make them move, but I finally made it. When I approached the door, a blue beam scanned me and the door opened. I stepped inside and the door closed. The room was spartan. It looked very much like a cubicle for a detainee. There was a single bed connected to the white walls. On the bed were a white pillow and a black blanket. I examined the room more closely and there were drawers built in to the walls. I pulled them out and they were filled with black articles of clothing to include black under garments. In the corner, there was a desk with a black folder. I grabbed the folder and reluctantly sat on the bed. It was as hard as a rock.

I opened the folder and began reading over the contents. There were pages and pages of instructions. There was a set schedule of when I was to be at certain places and allotted times for hygiene and down time. There was also a map of the compound, as the page called it. The map highlighted the dining hall, training area, restrooms, and bathing quarters. I was assigned a set time to use the bathing quarters and if I missed those times then I would have to wait until the next assigned time. I was to use any restroom marked with an 'A'. My hair could be worn in any style I wished, but no makeup and no perfume. All hygiene products were located for me in a locker with my name on it. The code for the key pad was my birthday.

It seemed like they had everything down to the most minute detail. It even included biweekly health exams and weigh-ins. There was no doubt about it, I was their test subject.

Chapter Two
Welcome to Anguish

I fell asleep shortly after the males outside my room went to their respective rooms. I woke up startled by a banging on my door. I quickly sat up and looked at the window on my door. It was mystery greeter whose eyes were staring back at me. I rose out of bed and made my way over to the door. The blue beam scanned me and the door opened.

"Get ready, your training begins," I nodded my head and stepped back into the room with the door closing inches from his face. He seemed annoyed, which made me smile on the inside. It's the least I could do to him, since he left me by myself in the lions' den.

Without paying any mind to him staring in at me, I stripped down and put on a clean uniform and laced up my boots. I used the small mirror on the wall to fix my hair and I was ready to go. I had used the restroom in the middle of the night, so I didn't have to worry about voiding before beginning my unknown day.

I stood at the door and it opened once more. Mystery greeter looked me over from head to toe, smirked and began walking. I caught up with him and walked beside him. Many of the males were coming out of their rooms and stopped when they caught glimpse of me. I paid them no mind and continued walking.

"Not being vain will get you far in here," mystery greeter whispered with his eyes still forward. I didn't bother replying because I knew it wasn't an opening for a conversation.

He led me to the dining hall, which was already half full of men dressed in all black. Silence fell over the dining hall as we walked in; seemed like I was a conversation stopper. We stood in line and received our food, if that's what they called it. It was loaded down with meat galore. My stomach churned as I stared down at my meat covered tray.

I took a deep breath and followed him to a full table. When we approached two males were gestured by him to give up their seats. They did so without argument. He took his seat and I remained standing. He looked up at me.

"You may have a seat," I took a seat and they all began eating.

"What's her name," a male with dark skin, shaved head, and a body the size of a truck asked.

"Her name is Armistice," mystery greeter said continuing to eat. The male nodded his head in approval.

"Peace," he said looking at me. The rest of the table seemed confused. I smiled and nodded my head.

"Peace," I said and he smiled. He went back to eating and I stared at my tray of carnage.

"Do they not eat meat where you are from," my escort asked, gaining the whole table's attention.

"Meat is not something my body requires," I said simply.

"You will need meat in order to survive training and to keep your energy. You need to eat," he said firmly. I nodded my head and cut a piece of meat. I took a bite and did everything within my power not to heave.

"Five leros says she blows chunks everywhere," the male with red hair said laughing. The whole table erupted with laughter except mystery greeter, who was looking at me with a 'don't you dare' look on his face. I took a deep breath and swallowed. They were all staring at me.

"She will be fine," mystery greeter said and went back to eating. The others continued to stare at me, while I took my next few bites. The meat was not settling in my stomach agreeably. I kept taking deep breaths between bites and before swallows. I wasn't even in full training and already had met my match.

The men devoured their food and stared at me while I attempted to finish half of my tray. Each one of them kept a grin on their face.

"Stop, Armistice," mystery greeter said and stood. "Let's go."
I stood up and grabbed my tray. We disposed of our trays and
he led me out of the room and down the hallway. He stopped
at a restroom marked with an 'A'. I quickly looked at him.
"Go puke, but at lunch, your task is to keep it down." I didn't
bother saying anything, just nodded my head and ran into the
bathroom.
I barely made it to the toilet before I threw up. I held my hair
back out of my face and continued to void my stomach of the
repulsion. I found toothpaste and a toothbrush in one of the
open lockers. I didn't care whose it was at that moment, I
needed a clean mouth. After washing my face and brushing
my teeth, I made my way out of the bathroom. He was leaning
against the wall across from the restroom waiting for me.
"Impressive. Figured you'd be in there at least five minutes,"
he grinned. "And I see you found the toothbrush we put in
there for you," he winked and began walking down the
hallway. I was once again forced to catch up with him.
Everyone we passed came to a halt, moved out of the way and
gave a greeting to him. I was slowly gaining intel about who
he was. So far, I gathered that he was not only a training
officer, but a Captain over Diablo Regiment. His last name
was Taylor and he grinned every time he didn't know what to
say. Everything else would come in due time.
"Are you even listening, Armistice?"
"No," there was no point lying. He stopped walking and faced
me. I figured he would yell at me for intentionally not paying
attention, but he grinned. He kept his eyes on me for quite
some time.
"What were you thinking about," he whispered.
"Just observing the things around me," he frowned.
"But ignoring the task in front of you?" I shrugged my
shoulders.

"You were talking about how there were three rules to being Anguish. One never shows your opponent weakness. Two never run from a fight. Three never quit." He seemed surprised by me recalling his words.

"Thought you weren't listening?"

"I wasn't."

"Then how did you know what I said?" I shrugged my shoulders. "You have a copy memory. "I wasn't sure if it was a statement or a question. He finally smiled, which let me know that it was a statement. "I'm impressed, Armistice." We continued walking once more until we reached training arena 12. The doors opened and we entered. The room was completely red. There was currently no training going on. All the males were sitting on the floor looking at us.

"Here at Anguish we don't believe in baby steps," he said looking at me. I nodded my head. "To the center of the mats and remember what I said the rules were." I nodded again and took my place in the center of the mats. "Matthews, you're up!"

Matthews was a pale white man, who was almost one and half feet taller than me, outweighed me by at least two stone, and looked like he could eat me for breakfast. On the inside, I wanted to find a weapon to give me an advantage to this fight.

Matthews walked to the center in front of me. Much to my surprise, he seemed reluctant.

"Sorry," he whispered.

"I am honored to fight you," I bowed my head slightly. He in return bowed his head to me.

"Enough dancing," Taylor shouted, "fight!"

I don't know why I thought that Matthews would go easy on me. His first move was a kick to my stomach. I flew halfway across the mat and landed on my back. I slowly rolled over and stood up. He was already closing in on me and fast. I repositioned myself, trying to place plenty of room between us. No matter where I stood, he closed the gap swiftly.

"Armistice, make a move," Taylor shouted catching me off guard. I took my eyes off Matthews for one second and this time received a hard blow to my left cheek. I fell to the ground. My stomach and face were both throbbing. I held back the tears and stood wobbly back up. "Give up?"

I didn't bother giving him an answer, I charged Matthews full force and slammed him to the mat. The room filled with uproar. I began punching Matthews in the face. He grabbed me by my wrists, twisted and flipped me on to my back. He was now on top and choking me. I began to see stars dance and my vision darken. He was not giving up. I could see Taylor out the corner of my eye looking at me with disappointment. I racked my brain for an option to get myself out of this mess.

"Sorry," I said to Matthews with a hushed voice.

"For wh…" before he could finish asking me, I kicked him as hard as I could in the groin. He fell off me grabbing himself in the affected area. The room filled with cheers. I knew the fight wasn't over and there was no way my tiny hands were fitting around his neck. The only choice I had was to wrap my legs around his neck and choke him. I lunged at him, brought my right leg around his neck, locking it with my left leg and fell on to my back. He was instantly trapped in my hold. He tried standing up with me, but I tightened the hold. He grabbed at my legs and no matter how painful it was, I didn't let him go. I arched my back and tightened even more. Finally, he went still between my legs and the room filled with cheer.

I quickly released him and climbed around him. His face was dark red. I placed my head on his chest and checked his breathing. He was still breathing, which eased my heart. I smacked his face and still he didn't move.

"He'll be fine," Taylor said standing over me. He extended a hand to me. I reluctantly took it and he lifted me on to my feet. He raised my hand into the air and the males were on their feet cheering. Taylor let go of my hand. "Not bad, Armistice," he said. "Bain. Leonard. Take Matthews to the infirmary."

Two guys were already on their feet and approaching the mat. They were both the same size as Matthews. They lifted Matthews and carried him out the door. I couldn't help but feel bad.

"He will be okay, Armistice. Trust me," I looked up to lock eyes with Taylor. I nodded my head. "Let's go get you checked out in the infirmary too." I shook my head.

"I'll be fine," I walked off and took a seat against the wall. Without argument, Taylor went on to call pairs to the mat. The fights were gruesome but at the end there were no hard feelings. I could only hope there would be no hard feelings between Matthews and me. When an intense fight was going on between Knox and Reagan, I took the opportunity to sneak out and head to the infirmary. I slipped through the infirmary door and found Matthews. He was awake and hooked up to monitors.

"You," he said firmly when he saw me.

"Hey."

"You got one hell of a leg lock, kid," he said laughing. My heart dropped in my chest and a huge weight lifted off me.

"What? Thought I was going to hold it against you?"

"Yes."

"Naw. I will have to hear shit from the others, but hey, an opponent is an opponent, regardless of their gender," he took a deep breath, "Just sucks that I got knocked out by a girl." He laughed and a chuckle escaped my lips.

"I have to get back, but I wanted to make sure you were okay." He sat up in the bed.

"You didn't ask for permission to leave," he seemed amused.

"They won't even notice I'm gone. Knox and Reagan are fighting," he nodded his head.

"Those two never hold back punches," he laughed. "Well, thanks for checking up on me, kid." I smiled and made my way out. Taylor was leaned up against the wall with his arms crossed waiting for me.

"Oh," I said as the door closed behind me.

"Oh?" I nodded. He flew off the wall and stood inches from me. "You do realize that you are in a compound full of only males. They may seem like they wouldn't harm a woman, but trust me, looks can be deceiving. Yeah, you held your own with Matthews, but what would you do if there was more than one guy? You barely survived Matthews. You are not to walk the halls unchaperoned. Do you understand?" He was beyond angry with me. I nodded my head. "Do you understand?" He shouted at me again.

"Yes, sir," I said and walked off from him.

"Armistice," he shouted behind me. I didn't bother stopping, simply went back to the arena. All eyes were on me. I stood in the middle of the mat and said nothing. Taylor entered the room and his eyebrow rose. "Armistice?"

"I want to fight two males this time," the room filled with laughter. "Any two," I snapped at Taylor.

"Not two, just one," he removed his jacket and stepped on to the mat.

"Oh, shit. He never fights lower level Anguish," someone attempted to whisper.

"You are going to learn that there are rules here for a reason," he said smirking. I removed my boots, then my shirt and tossed it on the mat. The room filled with cheers. I was now only wearing pants and a leisurewear bra. Taylor cocked his head to the side and raised an eyebrow.

"You have your means of fighting. I have mine," I hissed. This he must have found amusing because he laughed. He removed his shirt and tossed it to the side. The males laughed. Taylor was built like a deity. His muscles were well defined and tattoos marked his body. I was now regretting removing my shirt.

"All is fair in war," he winked. Next thing I knew, he grabbed me and flipped me onto the mat with great force. The wind was instantly knocked out of me. He was standing over me with a cocky smirk on his face. "Give up?"

"Never," I spat. I flipped on to my feet and kicked him in the face. He stammered a few steps back, held his face then glared at me.

"Fine. Let's go." From that point on, he showed me no mercy. We went blow for blow. My body was in so much pain, but it was my stubbornness that refused to let me throw in the towel. After several minutes of fighting, I was exhausted. "Give up?"

"No," I said breathing heavy. My head was pounding and I felt like passing out. I wiped my face and blood covered my hand.

"Give up, now?" I shook my head and charged him once more. He grabbed me by the waist, lifted me into the air and slammed me on to the mat. Cracks were heard throughout the room and so were gasps from those watching the spectacle. I bit back a scream of pain. My eyes filled with tears. He kneeled next to me. "What about now?" I shook my head. I thought he'd finish the fight, but instead he stood up. "This is someone with an Anguish heart. Smit, take her to the infirmary and report back to me."

A tall man built very much like Taylor approached us. He bent down to pick me up.

"No," Taylor and Smit looked down at me, "I'll walk." Taylor nodded his head in approval and Smit offered me his hand. I gladly accepted his hand and he pulled me onto my feet. The room cheered. Smit and I walked out of the room. The minute the door closed behind us, I collapsed, but before I hit the ground Smit caught me. He cradled me in his arms.

"It's okay. I gotcha," he said walking quickly through the halls. "I'm Kurtz."

"Nice to meet you Kurtz, I'm Kaitlyn."

"Pretty name," he said smiling. He held me against his chest and carried me through the hallways. We finally arrived at the infirmary. The infirmary doors opened and the infirmary team approached us.

"Oh wow. Who got a hold of her?" A man with jet black hair and a name badge reading 'Jeffrey Thomas' asked.

"Taylor," Kurtz grumbled.

"Taylor did this?" Kurtz nodded his head and set me on a table. My bones cracked to the pressure and I bit back another scream. "Taylor never fights Anguishes who are levels beneath him, let alone a female." It seemed like everyone was shocked.

"Don't worry, Taylor will be in later for a checkup. She beat his ass pretty good." Kurtz laughed and looked at me. "You did well, Kaitlyn." I nodded my head.

"Let's get her hooked up and examined. You may leave Smit," Thomas said gesturing at the door.

"I am to stay here until she has been examined then report back to Taylor." Thomas nodded his head. They wheeled me in to a glassed room and shut the door. They began hooking me up to the machines. I tolerated everything pretty well until they began the actual exam. I did my best not to cry or scream. Kurtz even held my hand, though I protested. Finally, Thomas pushed on my stomach and a scream from hell escaped me.

"Not looking good," Thomas said shaking his head. He waved an ultrasound tablet over me and it scanned my organs. "Shit." He pressed a button on the wall. "Get the surgeon in here!"

"What's going on," Kurtz asked standing.

"She has internal bleeding. You need to leave now." Kurtz didn't get a chance to argue. After he was pushed out of the room, I was given a shot and must have passed out, because next thing I knew I was waking up screaming. Thomas was standing over me. "It's okay, Armistice. You're in the recovery room."

I took a deep breath and looked around the room. My heart was beginning to slow down. I glanced down at my stomach. I was bandaged up pretty good.

"You should be healed in a few hours." I nodded my head. "Would you like some water or soup?"

"Both...please." I replied. He nodded his head and walked out of the room.

It was only day one and already I had made a choked one guy out, got beaten to a pulp by my trainer, and needed emergency surgery. They sure picked a fine test subject.

Thomas returned with water and soup. I slowly sipped on both. It felt good to eat something without chunks of meat in it.

"When can I go to my room?" He seemed surprised by my question.

"Don't want to heal up first?"

"I will be fine. I already feel better."

"Don't want to wait a day or two so the bruises go away?" He held up a mirror and showed me my face. I barely recognized myself. I looked like a battered woman. Well, to be fair.

"I'll be okay," I said forcing a smile.

A few hours later, he released me from the infirmary. It was lights out so I didn't have to worry about running in to anyone. I slipped inside my room and laid down. The second my head hit my pillow, tears flowed down my cheek. Even with the meds, I was still in severe pain. I pulled the blanket over my head, in case there were cameras in my room, and cried myself to sleep.

I woke up feeling like I had been hit by a train. I quickly slipped out of my room and made it to the bathing quarters just in time to shower and freshen up. My face was still a disaster, but I had no way of hiding it. After all, make up was forbidden.

The hallway was still empty as I made my way back to my room. I readied for the day's adventure. When the men began to stir, I made my way to the dining hall. All eyes were on me. They must have thought I was weak and looked like a hideous monster. Next thing I knew, some were banging their hands on the tables and chanting my name; an odd display of celebration. I said nothing and made no gestures, but on the inside my heart swelled. I was honored. I grabbed my tray and found a table by myself in the corner. I sat with my back to the room and the chanting slowly died out. I slowly began eating the rubbish. A shadow lingered over me.

"Mind if we sit here," I looked up to see Kurtz and Matthews. I shook my head and they took a seat across from me.

"Morning," Matthews said grinning.

"Morning," I said softly and took another bite of food.

"How are you feeling," Kurtz asked sympathetically.

"About as good as I look," I said smirking. Neither one of them laughed. "It's a joke, guys."

"I know. I just feel bad. If you hadn't come to see me, then none of this would've happened," Matthews proclaimed.

"I'm a firm believer that everything in life happens for a reason." They nodded their heads and began eating.

"How many of the guys have tried to approach you," Matthews asked with a mouth full of food.

"None," I replied.

"I find that hard to believe," Kurtz said laughing.

"Why's that?"

"Look at you," Matthews said pointing at me. "You're tall, curvy, tan complexion, black hair that waves like the ocean, and eyes the color of emeralds." Kurtz and I just stared at him. "Are you a lady, Matthews?" Kurtz asked, jabbing Matthews in the side. That made all of us laugh. We went back to eating our food. Taylor walked into the dining hall as we were finishing up our breakfast. He wore a shiner and busted lip. I couldn't help but smirk at knowing that I had done that.

"Care to escort me to the training arena? Apparently, I'm not allowed to walk anywhere by myself."

"Not at all," Matthews said standing. Kurtz followed suit and we made our way to the trash bins. Taylor spotted me and the look of horror covered his face. I didn't bother stopping. I disposed of my tray and we went to the arena.

I sat and listened to the two of them small talk about life while we waited for the training to begin. Taylor was the last one to show. He began pairing up people. By the end of the training session, I still hadn't been called.

"Who is left," he asked. I stood up.

"I haven't been called yet."

"And you won't," he growled.

"Why not," I snapped back.

"Because you're in no condition to fight."

"Doesn't mean I can't." There was no way I was backing down on this. I began walking over to him.

"You will not be fighting until you are fully healed, Armistice. And that's final."

"Cry me a river," the room fell silent. "Afraid that this time I'll kick your ass?" The room filled with laughter.

"Armistice, don't-cross that line."

"Or what?"

"Everyone out!" The room quickly cleared. I began following the others out the door. I was almost to the door, when Taylor grabbed me and spun me to face him. He was now standing inches from me. His breath was ragged and his eyes intense.

"You think this is a game?"

"I thought I would be treated like everyone else here."

"And you are," he said stepping closer. I could feel the heat of his body. I was now aware of the fact he was still holding my wrist.

"What do you have against me?"

"Nothing," he said gently. "I just don't want to see you hurt."

I laughed at his words.

"Was that before or after you challenged me?"

"Look, I'm sorry," I looked him in the eyes and saw sincerity. "I should've kept my cool and not stepped on the mat."

"It's over with, now if you'll excuse me, I need to get to my warfare class."

"Not until we are done talking."

"What's there to talk about?"

"I need your forgiveness," he whispered.

"Fine," I stepped away from him. "You're forgiven." With that I walked out of the door and to my next class.

Over the next few weeks, Taylor and I didn't speak again. We would simply glance at one another when we were in a room and he did his best not to call on me during training. I stuck to my routine and spent most of my times with the 'twins', as I liked to call them.

Rumors began to spread about Neva and Lynx Cantons soon going to war. Emperor Gable was threatening to end the peace treaty and attack Lynx. His words made my life a nightmare. The other trainees had already hated me, but now they had a real reason to hate me - I was of Nevan blood.

Most of the males made my life hell, exposing me to extreme physical pain. Whenever possible, Kurtz and Matthews stuck up for me against those who had become my abusers. Matthews and Kurtz were becoming two people I could rely on.

Chapter Three
No Pain, No gain

Each day after physical training, I attended my warfare and leadership classes. I was excelling in the leadership classes; however, the warfare classes were a different story. It was difficult to understand the subject matter. In fact, I was failing miserably. I had no clue what they were talking about and my scores were proof. I began spending countless hours in my room and in the Academy library studying. My scores soon began to show it.

"Armistice, how about you tell us what battle plan you would pursue, since you are so quick to rebut Harrison's battle plan," Commander Trials said. Everyone's head turned.

Commander Trials was like Commander Taylor. He was tall and muscular. His skin was a shade lighter than mine. He wore his black hair short. His eyes I was never able to see up close, but they appeared hazel from a distance. And anytime he was mad a vein in his neck became visible.

"Sir, I just feel that his battle plan to attack by land is… premature." The room filled with laughter.

"How so?" Commander Trials asked leaning against the desk.

"The York Canton is known for their skill at land attacks, but also known for their lack of success on the water. That is why an amphibious attack is more appropriate, sir."

"I see," Commander Trials nodded his head. "Well done, Armistice. Maybe females have a brain after all." The room filled with laughter at my expense. Commander Trials began teaching once more. The doors opened and War Councilman Tibbot entered the room. He whispered something in Commander Trials' ear and they both turned to me.

"Armistice, come with me," War Councilman Tibbot said.

"Yes, sir." I stood and gathered my things. I followed him out of the room and down the hall in silence. He took me to the simulator. I hadn't been in a simulator before. I had only heard rumors as to what it was, but everyone who spoke of it said it was excruciating. It was like being tortured mentally. "You know what this is?"

"Vaguely, sir." He nodded his head and faced me.

"This machine simulates being tortured. We will give you a piece of information and then test to see how long you can withstand keeping this information from the machine." My heart began to pound. I glanced in the window at the machine. It seemed like just a plain white chair that was cushioned and in a recline position, but now I knew that it was so much more. "Do you understand?"

"Yes, sir." He handed me an envelope and I opened it. Inside was 'Mission Bravo execute at 2200 hrs.' I put the paper back in the envelope and gave it to War Councilman Tibbot. "Understand?"

"Yes, sir." He opened the door and took my belongings from me.

"Good luck," he said with a smirk. I said nothing more. I walked through the door and he shut it behind me. I walked further into the room towards the chair. I was terrified of what this machine would do to me. I could easily run out of the room, but then what? Where would I go? My father would not let me return home and the Lynxian would shun me for running away from their beloved Academy.

I took a deep breath and sat in the chair. Slowly I leaned back and positioned myself comfortably in the chair. The lights turned off and my heart was once again racing. I heard a hum on both sides of my head and a blue light pulsed from dim to bright. Was this the torture everyone spoke of?

I heard a door open, the shuffling of feet. Something heavy was pulled into the room, and then the door slammed again. Right then the lights in the room came back on. Across from me was a tall pale man with a bald head and a beard. It was unusual to see a man with facial hair. He was standing in front of a table that had a variety of weapons and tools laid out. In his right hand was a gun.

"What information were you told?"

"Nothing," I said. He smirked and opened the door. He bent down, picked up a white puppy, and closed the door softly. I always had a weakness for animals.

"What information were you given?" He said again, more sternly now.

"Nothing." He shot the puppy and blood splattered. "No!" He laughed as he dropped the puppy to the ground. He set the gun down. I tried to jump out of the chair and attack him, but I was strapped down. "You are sick!"

"So, I've been told," he grabbed a knife. "What information were you given?"

"Nothing," I screamed at him. He opened the door and an elderly man was standing there. "No. No. No." I knew what would happen next if I did not give the information. I couldn't let another life end. A tear slipped down my face.

"What information were you given?" The elderly man looked at me with pleading eyes.

"Nothing," I whispered as the man sliced the elderly man's throat and his limp body slumped to the ground. I tried to turn my head from the scene, but it wouldn't move. I watched as the blood gushed from the elderly man's throat and he fell to the ground on top of the puppy's corpse. I could feel cool spots on my arm where his blood had landed.

"What information were you given?" He asked setting the knife down and grabbing a hacking tool.

"Nothing." My voice was no longer recognizable. It was hushed and ragged, terror coursing through it. My mind seemed to be straining against my skull at the thought of what could possibly come next. He opened the door and a priest was ushered in. I shook my head. "No. Please."

"What information were you given?" I shook my head, as tears poured down my face.

"Tell him, child." The man of the cloth pleaded softly.

"I can't. I'm so sorry," I said with my eyes closed. My eyes opened.

"What information were you given," the torturer asked, his voice becoming eerily quiet.

"Nothing." He lifted his arm as high as it could go and slammed it down on the clergyman. The man screamed out in pain as his arm fell to the ground.

"What information were you given," the torturer shouted.

"Nothing!" He began hacking away at the man in cloth. I didn't bother closing my eyes. I knew it wouldn't change anything. Finally, the torturer was done and the priest was laid on top of the puppy and elderly man.

"Shall we continue?"

"Just kill me already," I spat. He quickly looked at me.

"What did you just say?"

"Just kill me already! I'm not telling you shit!"

"No, you are going to do it." He grabbed the gun and walked over to me. "You are going to end your life."

"No!" I said. Suicide was against the Nevan belief. Suicide was a damnation of the soul.

"Do it or I will continue." He adjusted the straps to where my elbow was bent and hand up towards my head. He placed the gun in my hand. I once again tried to move it but it wouldn't budge. The door opened and a girl no older than three was standing there. "Do it, and I shall spare her."

"I can't." Tears were streaking down my face. He laughed.

"Because of the Nevan belief of the dishonor in suicide."

"Yes," I whispered. He strode toward the little girl. "Wait!" He turned towards me. "Do you give your word?" His eye brow rose.

"Do I give my word?"

"That you will not harm the child."

"I give my word." The door closed and opened again. The little girl was no longer standing there. "Should I call her back?" He said with a grin. I closed my eyes and pulled the trigger.

I opened my eyes and the room was empty. There were no corpses, no torturer there was no desk. Only me.

The door I had entered opened.

"You may come out, Armistice." I looked down at my arms and they were no longer bound. I slid out of the chair and made my way to the door. I looked around the room once more to make sure the bodies weren't somewhere else. I stepped out into the hallway and War Advisor Jennings was standing there with the rest of the War Council.

"Gentlemen," I said. Not a single expression was visible on any of their faces. Had I failed the test miserably?

"You dishonored yourself," War Advisor Jennings said firmly.

"Yes. I did, sir."

"Even though you would damn your soul?"

"Yes, sir."

"Would you do it again?"

"Yes, I would, sir." I said with my head held high. I knew my decision, although morally compromising, was the right decision.

"Just one caveat, then." The War Advisor stared at me pointedly.

"Yes, sir?" I couldn't fathom what might have changed the outcome of that whole simulation.

"Never," Jennings replied, "rely on the honor of your enemy. It becomes a bargaining chip."

My eyes hit the floor. "Yes sir."

"Come with us," he said. I followed behind them as we walked through the halls. I hadn't been on this side of the academy. I looked around as we walked. We finally stopped in front of a room. "Do you know where you are, Armistice?"

"No, sir."

"This is the next level of the simulator."

"Oh," I said looking through the window. I hadn't expected to reach the next level of the simulator so soon. The first simulator had played tricks on my mind, making everything seem so real. I could only imagine what the next level would do to me.

"Are you ready," War Advisor Jennings said snapping me out of my drift.

"Yes, sir." The door was opened for me.

"Same as before, just have a seat and the machine will do the rest." I nodded and made my way into the room. The door shut behind me. The room was white like the other simulator, with another plain white chair, reclined and cushioned. I sat in the chair and made myself comfortable, relatively speaking. This room had a set of lights on a circular track above the chair.

The room lights shut off and I was swallowed by darkness. I could hear a hum that surrounded me. Bright lights flashed in my face and began to strobe. I tried to close my eyes, but even with them closed the lights shined through. I opened my eyes and faced the lights once more. They began spinning on the track slow at first, but building up speed to where the lights became one bright flashing light.

I began seeing glimpses of my past. Terrifying glimpses. I saw my father execute my puppy. I saw my father cut the throat of one of my nannies. Everything I saw was my father killing something or someone. I tried to close my eyes, but they were drawn to the horror.

The glimpses continued to flash around me. Soon whispers began to echo through my mind.

'You'll never live to be empress.'

'You are nothing to me.'
'I will kill you and your mother.'
'You will die.'
Over and over the whispers repeated. They were taunting me.
Reminding me of everything my father had told me as a child.
Soon the glimpses vanished and only the whispers and
pulsing lights remained. A blinding light flashed and the
glimpses returned.

My mother was hanging over the edge of the banister. I
screamed as I watched her dangle with my father at the top of
the stairs laughing. They vanished and I let out a breath. The
light blazed again and my mother laid on the bathroom floor
with her arms and legs around her. Her eyes were missing
and her mouth sewn shut. Blood pooled beneath her body.
Tears slid down my face and my throat closed as I watched in
horror. She disappeared once more.

"Tell us what information you were given and we will end
this," a male voice said. I just shook my head as the tears
continued to flow.

The light flashed again and my mother was now sitting in
front of me. She was tied to a chair by her wrists and feet.
Above her was a bright light and darkness around her.

"Kaitlyn, help me," she whispered.

"I can't," I said with regret. She closed her eyes and sobbed. I
opened my mouth to explain why I couldn't help her, but
before the words left my mouth, her left hand was freed and
placed on a table. "No...no...don't!" My words didn't matter.
Her hand was cut off. We both screamed; her from the pain
and me from the terror of watching it.

"Tell us what information you were given and we will end
this." Tears burned my face. I shook my head. Her other hand
was placed on a table.

"Mother," I whispered. She looked up at me. Her face was
pale and blood was running from her severed wrist.

"Please, Kaitlyn," she pleaded, "Tell them."

"I can't," it barely came out as a whisperer. Another whack and her other hand fell to the floor. She let out a scream that fried my nerves, short circuiting my brain. I gaped in shock. "NO!"

"Tell us what information you were given and we will end this."

"I can't!" The sound of a blade cutting through the air echoed and my mom's eyes widened. "Mother?" She didn't say anything. She couldn't. Her head slid off her body and she was dead. I had killed my own mother to protect the information that was entrusted to me. The lights shut off and I sat in the darkness sobbing. I was my mother's murderer.

Chapter Four
Water Tank

I don't know how long I was in the simulator or how long I sat in the darkness crying. I heard the door open and I wiped my eyes. I turned my head in the direction of the light and saw War Advisor Jennings standing there.

"You may exit, Armistice." I slowly moved off the chair and made my way out of the cursed room. They were all staring at me. "What information were you given, Armistice?

"Nothing, sir," I said facing the wall in front of me.

"I will not ask you again, Armistice. What information were you given?" With my head held high and eyes puffy, I turned my head and faced him.

"Nothing, sir!" His face grew angry.

"Final answer?"

"Yes, sir."

"Take her to the water tank," he growled. Two of the councilman took me by my arms and walked me down the hallway, with War Advisor Jennings and other councilmen following behind. I didn't say anything, because I honestly didn't care what they had in store for me next. They had subjected me to watching the one person I loved most be tortured.

They walked me through the dining hall and the room fell silent. I caught Trials looking at me in horror, as I was led through the room. He began to rise from his chair, but Aiyetoro held him in place.

We walked through the doors and down a set of stairs. They opened a door marked 'Tank' and pulled me through it. In the corner of the room was a giant glass tank with stairs leading up to the top of it. The two councilmen released my arms.

"Up the stairs, Armistice," War Advisor Jennings said. I didn't argue, simply walked up the stairs like a robot. The top of the tank was open. "Into the tank, Armistice!" I climbed into the tank without dispute. A lid lowered from the ceiling and fastened down onto the top of the tank. "What information were you given, Armistice?"

"Nothing, sir."

"Armistice," he warned, "If you fail to tell me, the tank will begin to fill with water."

"So be it." I turned my back to War Advisor Jennings and the councilmen. The tank began filling with water. My feet were soon submerged, then my waist. Finally, it reached my neck. "Tell me the information you were given."

"No." The water continued to rise and soon was up to my nose. Water trickled into my nostrils. I tread water to keep my nose above the surface. There were only a few inches between the water line and the lid. I continued treading water. Right as the water was about to engulf me, I took a sharp breath in and held it. I turned so the councilman could see me.

"What information were you given," War Advisor Jennings shouted. I shook my head no. I could feel my lungs tightening and my body wanted to take a deep breath. I had never been one for underwater swimming, so I knew my lung capacity was not my strong point. "What information were you given?" Again, I shook my head.

I could feel myself getting lightheaded and my vision blurred. The room began to spin. My pulse was pounding heavily in my skull. War Advisor Jennings and the councilman soon vanished from my view. I let go of the world around me and was taken by the darkness.

I woke up being carried in someone's arms. I opened my eyes slowly. I was being carried through the dining hall and once again everyone was staring. Water dripped from my body and splashed as it hit the floor. I could no longer hold my head up. My head fell back and blackness prevailed.

Chapter Five
Secrets make friends

I woke up in a room with my head pounding. I looked around and spotted the window on the door. I was in my room. I couldn't move. I ached from head to toe. I just laid there and tried to drift back to sleep. I was unsuccessful.

I rolled on to my side and hit the light on my clock. It was 1400 hrs. I had been out of it for almost an entire day. I sat up slowly and forced myself to get up. I had already missed half a day of training.

Once I was dressed and prepared, I made my way to my 1400 class. All eyes were on me, as I walked in to Commander Trials' class. I walked to the back and took my seat.

"So, glad you could grace us with your presence, Armistice," Commander Trials said making the room laugh.

"Sorry, I was preoccupied with other things, sir," I growled. Commander Trials was taken aback by my words, but he chose not to continue our exchange. Class dismissed an hour later and the students began filing out.

"Armistice," Commander Trials said without looking up from his desk. I stopped walking and turned to him. "Not like you to have a temper towards senior officers. Everything okay?"

"Yes. I apologize for my loose tongue, sir." Much to my surprise he laughed and looked at me.

"No need to apologize. I have seen you crack through your shell more and more as the time passes by. This is a good thing." He nodded his head. "Word is you went to the water tank."

"Yes, sir."

"I see. Is that why you were not in any of your classes, and why you almost missed mine?"

I nodded my head. "Yes, sir."

"It's a hell of a hangover," he winked. "You are dismissed." He gestured for me to leave. I turned and headed for the door. "Armistice?" I looked over my shoulder. "What information were you given?" He laughed and I grinned.

"Nothing, sir."

I went to the rest of my classes and kept to myself. I wasn't in the mood, so I sat with my tray in front of me, while Kurtz and Matthews ate.

"You going to eat anything," Matthews asked. I shook my head and pushed my tray to him. "Thanks." He began eating from my tray.

"So, what happened to you, yesterday? You looked pretty messed up," Kurtz said looking up from his tray.

"Just a little good ole' Anguish fun," I said grinning. They both laughed and that was the end of that conversation. A shadow hovered over the table.

"Armistice," I turned around and Taylor was standing there. "Got a minute?" I wanted to tell him to 'shove off'.

"Yes, sir," I said not budging from my seat.

"In private," he said.

"Fine, sir," I looked at my tray.

"I'll put it up," Matthews said. I nodded my head.

"Thank you." I stood up and followed Taylor through the dining hall. Males were staring and whispering. I could only imagine what they were saying. Probably thought Taylor was going to kick my ass again. We finally made it out of the dining hall and he continued walking. We walked through the halls to the regiment corridor and finally into the Diablo Regiment area. The room was empty. Taylor shut and locked the door.

My heart began to race. I was in serious trouble and no one would be a witness to what happened to my body. I had done my best over the weeks of being here to stay out of his way, so he really didn't have a reason to be angry.

He turned and faced me slowly. His face was hardened and he seemed to be struggling with an inward battle. He reached for the door but pulled his hand away.

"You've been avoiding me," he finally said.

"At all cost, sir." He looked up and glared at me. I finally realized his eyes were emerald green.

"No need for formalities in here." I nodded my head. "Why have you been ignoring me?"

"You've made it quite clear that a female doesn't deserve to be here and that you don't care for me, so why wouldn't I avoid you?"

"Because I am your training officer."

"Who hates me and doesn't wish to see me succeed."

"Why would you say that?"

"It's written all over your face anytime I'm within a hundred feet of you," I growled.

"It's not like that," he growled back.

"What is it like then?" I placed my hands on my hips.

"You wouldn't understand."

"Fine," I walked towards the door and reached for it. He placed his hand on mine and I quickly looked at him.

"I wish I could tell you," he whispered.

"Tell me what," I snapped. Next thing I knew, he had me pinned against the wall and his lips were on mine. I didn't do anything at first, but seconds later my lips parted. He kissed me gently and caressed the side of my face.

I had never been kissed before. Part of me wanted to stop and admit this to him, but he didn't seem to mind the way I was kissing. Why was he even kissing me?

The kiss finally ended and he rested his head on mine.

"I'm a man of actions not words," he said with a chuckle.

"So, I see." I couldn't help but laugh at the entire situation. Since day one of me arriving at Anguish, Taylor and I had been mortal enemies. Now, here we were kissing behind closed doors.

"I didn't mean to offend you," he said standing up tall and looking down at me.

"You didn't," I said smiling. He returned a smile and moved a strand of hair from in front of my eyes. He gently tucked it behind my ear.

"It isn't easy being around you." I frowned, which made him laugh.

"Why's that?" I asked, crossing my arms. He laughed more.

"It's not how you think. Let me finish," he said holding his hands up in a surrendering fashion. A smile broke across my face and my arms settled at my waist. "You are a spitfire. And you like to push buttons." He paused a beat. "Especially when it comes to me."

"Well, if you hadn't kicked my ass so bad that I had to have surgery, perhaps I'd be nicer," I said laughing. I looked up to see remorse and self-loathing cover his face. "I'm just kidding."

"No, you are right. I took it too far and I've felt horrible since that day. I'm hoping I can make it up to you."

"All is forgiven, Taylor."

"Nick," he corrected me. "As long as you are at Anguish, I will prove that I am not a bad guy."

"I know. You were just teaching me a lesson."

"A lesson that wasn't for me to teach," he said releasing a sigh. I shrugged my shoulders. "I suppose I should return you to your peers. I'm sure they are wondering where I led you to."

"They probably think you are burying my body." He frowned at my words. I laughed and shook my head. "I am kidding again, but it is well known that you don't like me." He raised an eyebrow.

"Trust me, I like you," my heart skipped a beat and I looked up at him. He grinned, gave me a swift kiss and unlocked the door. "If anyone asks, I was disciplining you for being late to class." He smirked and opened the door.

"You purposely told me that class time had changed," he winked and gestured for me to leave. I laughed and rolled my eyes. He was a very confusing man.

I stepped out into the hallway and it was empty. I began walking and he didn't follow. He just stood in the doorway watching. I continued walking and soon he was out of view. Once I reached the sleeping bay, I opened the doors and walked in. Very few stopped what they were doing to look at me. I had become just another one of the trainees, no longer the lost female amongst them.

"Armistice," Matthews called from the center of the room. He was sitting at a table with Kurtz, Hawke, and Smith. I made my way through the room and sat down next to Kurtz. They all looked at me.

"What?"

"Well," Hawke asked.

"Well what?"

"What did Commander Taylor have to say?"

"Oh," I laughed. "As usual, I was in trouble; this time for being late to training."

"But he told you the wrong time," Matthews pointed out. I shrugged my shoulders.

"It's whatever. Not everyone wants me here," I muttered trying to play it cool about the whole Nick thing.

"You got that right," a voice came from behind me. I turned in time to see Jared Hampton reach toward me. He grabbed me tightly, picked me up out of my seat and tossed me into the table next to us. The room filled with chaos. The table where I sat at was already up on their feet and coming towards Hampton. I held up my hand and they stopped.

"What the hell, Hampton?" I stood up.

"You don't belong here. This little charade has gone on long enough!" A few people in the room cheered at his words. A crowd began to form. "You need to pack your stuff and leave!"

"And if I don't?" I stood defiantly, arms loose but ready for combat.

"Then I will make you." He moved in close, trying to intimidate me.

"I'd like to see you try," I growled. He took half a step toward me. I hopped back onto the bench of the table behind me. It took half a second to gain my balance, and then I kicked him straight in the face. He staggered back. I didn't wait for him to approach again. I dove at him, landing full on his chest, and slammed him against the table behind him.

The room was filled with clamor, but I ignored it. I began punching him in the face, with all the power I could muster. He blocked most them, but that didn't stop me from fighting. He grabbed me by my hair and stood up. He punched me in the face, as I kneed him in the stomach. He quickly released my hair. In return, I kicked him in the side as hard as I could. It hurt my foot like crazy, but I didn't care. I was sick of the hateful quips, the venomous glares and now his physical assault. I finally lost my mind. I grabbed his head, yanked it down towards the ground, and slammed my knee home, crushing his nose with a wet crunch. He slumped to the floor and the room filled with cheers.

"I have as much damn right to be here as your sorry ass," I screamed still trying to catch my breath.

"What in the hell is going on in here," a voice shouted from across the room. We all turned, frozen in the moment. It was Commander Walter Heat. I knew his full name, because the door to his office had the whole thing printed out in tight, military print. I had been in his office more than once trying to explain how I had ended up locked in his classroom closet. As I said before, not everyone appreciated me being here. Hampton stood up and wiped the blood from his nose. Without a single word, he punched me in the face and all hell broke loose. I'm not sure how it happened but I was back on top of him and hitting him in the face with a Tactical War book.

"I'm tired of being disrespected by you," I hit him as hard as I could with the book, as I was yanked off him. I tried to break free to resume my attack, but I was being held tight. It was Kurtz and he was carrying me over his shoulders away from Hampton, who was out cold on the floor with his face bloodied.

"If he comes near me again, I will kill him." My warning echoed throughout the room. Commander Heat was standing on the platform with a unique look on his face. It was a cross between anger and amusement. Kurtz finally set me down.

"You have to calm down, Kaitlyn," he whispered. I took a deep breath and nodded. My hair was a mess and there was blood on my hands. I fixed my hair and wiped my hands on my pants.

"Armistice," Commander Heat yelled. I looked over in his direction. "Over here, now!"

"Hampton started it," someone shouted.

"Armistice," Commander Heat warned. I walked passed Kurtz and over to Commander Heat. I stood at attention.

"Want to explain to me why you just attacked a fellow trainee?"

"No, sir."

"No?"

"I didn't attack him, sir."

"What would you call it?" His eyes were hot, but his voice was restrained. I looked him in the eyes.

"Survival, sir." He thought long and hard. He looked in Hampton's direction and shook his head. He looked back at me.

"I didn't see anything," he grinned and walked out of the room, leaving me with my mouth wide open.

Chapter Six
Missing in Action

The next morning, Hampton didn't show up to training or any of our classes. Rumor was that he was still in the infirmary. I don't know if I was told in hopes that I would say I was sorry for taking a book to his face, but I wasn't going to apologize. Hampton had deserved it. I only hoped that his friends wouldn't retaliate when I least expected it.

Commander Trials' class ended and I began to walk out the door.

"Armistice," I stopped dead in my tracks and turned.

"Yes, sir?"

"Shut the door," I closed the door and made my way over to the front of his desk. "So, I hear that there was a," he rubbed his chin, "mishap in the sleeping bay."

"Mishap, sir?"

"Yes. Apparently, a book fell on Trainee Hampton's face," he laughed "more than once."

"Oh. Sounds horrible, sir." He nodded his head.

"I visited him this morning and his face was pretty messed up. Far worse than yours was when you went up against Commander Taylor." He laughed again and leaned back in his chair.

"Sounds like someone should bring him some flowers, sir," I said coldly. He laughed even more.

"Well, don't look at me. I hate that kid. He has been nothing but a pain in the ass since he arrived; however, since his father is a Lynxan official, we had no choice but to tolerate him." I nodded my head.

"I see, sir."

"You have definitely come out of your shell, Armistice."

"Thank you, sir." He smiled.

"Next time, one of these boys thinks they are brave enough to take you on, you give me a call and I'll come down and handle it." I looked at him and his face was solid. He wasn't kidding. "A few of us commanders are rooting for you and have your back. We refuse to see you kicked out of the academy because of a fight. Understood?"

I nodded my head. "Yes, sir."

"Good," he smiled, "you are dismissed." I began making my way to the door. "Oh, Armistice?" I looked over my shoulder. He began to open his mouth.

"I'm still not telling you, sir." I grinned. He was still laughing when I closed the door and walked down the hallway.

Chapter Seven
Family Secrets

After six weeks since the fight with Taylor, I was beginning to
look like a human again and not a monster out of a children's
tale. I stepped out of the bathing quarters and Taylor was
leaning on the wall across from the door. He looked at me in
my towel and frowned.

"You always leave the bathing quarters like this?"

"Yes," I whispered trying not to alert anyone to my
whereabouts. "I need to hurry and get back before the others
wake up." I said laughing.

"Okay," he grinned and gestured for me to walk by. I began to
walk passed him and he grabbed my wrist. He handed me a
black cloth bag and I grabbed it with my other hand.

"Have a good day." He kissed me gently and slowly pulled
away. He grinned and left without saying another word. I
made it back to my room and changed in to my uniform
before opening the bag. Inside the bag was the black that
smelled like him, an Armistice guardian charm, and a letter.

Kaitlyn,
Thought of you.
N

I folded the letter and tucked it away in the bottom of my
drawer. Something about his words pulled at something deep
within me. After our fight, I didn't think he and I would ever
talk one on one, let alone kiss; now, he was giving me gifts.
I slipped the charm on to my necklace and sat on my bed with
his shirt against my face. His smell was intoxicating. Never
had I been so drawn to an aroma. I heard the others stirring so
I folded the shirt and placed it in my drawer with my other
shirts.

I made my way out and to the dining hall. After I grabbed my tray I went and found the twins. Much to my surprise they were sitting with Taylor and his group. Kurtz saw me and waved me over with a huge smile on his face. I slowly walked over. Taylor moved his jacket from a seat next to him and began eating again. I slipped into the chair and began eating. "We were just discussing the Warfare and leadership exams. We are quite pleased by how well you are doing on them," Kurtz laughed exposing the food inside his mouth. I shook my head and laughed.

"You know you could've waited to tell me that until after you were done chewing." he frowned, shrugged his shoulders and laughed.

"I'm not here to learn to be a gentleman. I'm here to be a warrior!" The whole room seemed to hear him and began chanting the Anguish motto. I could only shake my head with a smile and continue eating. When the room settled down the males went on having a conversation. Taylor's hand softly brushed my hand under the table. I froze in place. I tried to breathe slowly through my nose.

Taylor continued eating like it was no big deal, while his other hand touched my hand intimately. I had been touched by a male before but never in such a gentle, intimate way. I felt like melted butter.

"Kaitlyn, do you think so?" I brought my attention to Matthews.

"I think that Neva should be included in the boundaries of Lynx." They all stared at me. "Our men are just as strong, and our women are as well." They laughed at my words, which made me frown and pull my hand from Taylor.

"Neva is a place of peace. Thus, your name, right," the dark-skinned male who had first spoken to me said. I nodded my head.

"What is your name," I asked. He smiled and extended his hand to me.

"I am Dimitri Aiyetoro." I smiled at his name and shook his hand.

"We fall from the same tree, sir," his smile widened.

"It would appear, my friend." The rest of the table was clueless, except Taylor who nodded and took a bite of food.

"What the hell was that about," the red-haired male asked.

"Our last names are both translated into a form of peace," Dimitri said smiling.

"Oh, that's lame," the red-haired guy said laughing.

"And, what is your name," I asked.

"You have never heard of Conner McMaster," the whole table laughed.

"Oh, you're the bitch of the family?" I asked cocking my head to the side. Conner's mouth fell open and the rest of the table was rolling laughing. Conner, after digesting what I said, smiled.

"You're okay, Armistice. You're okay." I smiled and took a bite of food.

"I don't know how you guys eat this," I pushed my tray towards Kurtz who was notorious for finishing my plate for me. It was happily accepted and devoured.

"Tastes fine to me," he winked at me and went about eating.

"Ugh," I groaned and drank the rest of my water.

"Has anyone heard anything more on Hampton," Nick asked, causing all eyes to settle on me. I looked at Nick and he busted out laughing.

"I hear he was attacked by a book," Dimitri said laughing.

"Anyone want to tell us what really happened," Nick asked looked at all the trainees, including me, but none of us spoke.

"It's a mystery, sir," Kurtz said shrugging his shoulders.

"He just fell to the ground and his face was busted up, sir," Matthews chimed in.

"Oh," Nick asked. "He said a person did it, but refuses to give a name."

"That's probably for the best," Dimitri said looking at me.

"He says that Commander Heat witnessed it," Nick said looking at me.

"I don't remember seeing Commander Heat there, sir. Do you guys?" I looked at Kurtz and Matthews. They both shook their head so I shrugged my shoulders and looked at Nick.

"Commander Heat said the same," Nick grinned and went back to eating. The remainder of the conversation was focused on all the trainees graduating and finding out their new duties. I was just hoping to graduate. I didn't think they would assign me a duty. I would probably be handed back over to my father, since the experiment would be over. Commander Trials walked by the table and stopped.

"Nick. Dimitri," he said acknowledging the fellow commanders at the table. Nick and Dimitri both nodded their heads. "Armistice," I looked up and he grinned, "are you finished eating?"

"Yes, sir."

"Good," he smiled, "come with me."

"Where is she going," Nick asked before I could stand up. Commander Trials laughed.

"Relax, Nick. I will have her returned before your class starts." I stood up and grabbed my cup. Nick didn't look happy at me leaving. I paid him no mind and followed Commander Trials. Once our items were disposed of, we walked out of the room.

"We will go into my room and talk."

"Very well, sir." We went into his room and he closed the door. He offered me a chair and I took a seat. He soon sat down and looked at me.

"I was asked by War Advisor Jennings to do some digging about Emperor Gable, because of the rumors surrounding the emperor."

"Oh."

"Yes. I was asked to give a briefing on his life, including his family," he was staring at me. I knew where this conversation was going. I took a deep breath. "I have a friend in Neva, who is very informative with matters concerning Emperor Gable."

"I understand, sir."

"He tells me Emperor Gable has a daughter." My heart began to race. My secret would soon be around Anguish. "He tells me Emperor Gable's daughter was traded for a peace treaty. Have you heard of this rumor?"

"Rumors aren't always true, sir."

"You feel that my friend may have been mistaken," his eyebrow rose.

"Perhaps, sir," he dug in his desk and pulled out a photo. He slid it across the desk towards me. It was a family portrait of my mother, father, and me taken last year. "His daughter looks a lot like you."

I let out the breath I had been holding and placed my face in my hands. I was told that not many people would know who I was. Hardly anyone knew because they feared what Lynxans would do to me, if they discovered the truth. With my father threatening war on the Lynx Canton, I would be executed to prove a point. Hampton was right, I was part of a charade, but not the one he thought. I was ready for the charade to end.

"Yes, I am her, sir," I said removing my face from my hands and looking him in the eye. He nodded his head.

"You are ashamed?"

"Who wouldn't be ashamed of being the daughter to a man who has lost his mind, sir?" He nodded in agreement.

"Then you do not agree with him?"

"No, sir."

"What will you do when you are discovered as being the princess of Neva?"

"I honestly hadn't thought of that, sir. I was just trying not to die at Anguish." He laughed and shook his head.

"You are too strong to have your life ended here."

"Thank you, sir."

"I have not shared this information with anyone."

"What," I was shocked.

"You get hassled enough by just being here. You do not need to be subjected with threats or worse. You have proven to be an able body, a soldier, and a true Anguish." I smiled at his kind words.

"Thank you, sir." He nodded his head and leaned back in his chair. "Emily speaks quite frequently of you." He looked at me. Emily became my mother's aide when I was still a child. Over time, Emily became my confidant.

"Emily?"

"Yes, Emily," I said smiling. "She keeps a picture of you in her room. I would recognize your face anywhere." He laughed.

"What are the odds?"

"Very slim, sir."

"She told me to take good care of you or I would have to deal with her." We both laughed.

"That sounds like her, sir." I replied. He smiled at a thought he had.

"I just wanted you to know that I knew, and that your secret was safe with me." I smiled once more.

"I appreciate that, sir."

"You are dismissed, future empress," he laughed at his words and I grinned.

"Thank you, sir."

Chapter Eight
Loose Tongue

I walked out of Commander Trials' room and Nick was standing across from the door. I laughed when I saw him. He had his usual pose of holding up the wall. He stood up when I walked out of the room, and then gestured for me to follow him. I said nothing simply followed him through the hall. I was getting used to being escorted to random rooms without prior knowledge of where I was going.

We finally ended up in the Diablos Regiment once again.

"Everything okay?" I nodded my head. "You sure?" I laughed.

"I'm fine."

"Mind telling me what he wanted to talk to you about?" My heart began to race. I didn't feel comfortable enough sharing my personal information with Nick. A few stolen kisses were one thing, but I didn't think I could trust him just yet.

"Nothing of importance."

"You can tell me."

"I'd much rather not."

"Why?"

"Cause I'd much rather do this," he looked down at me as I reached up and kissed him. He turned the kiss in to a passionate one within seconds. He pinned me against the wall and let his hands roam down my sides. He pulled my body against his. His hands began roaming lower and I brought his hands back up to my waist.

His watched beeped. He groaned and ended the kiss. I couldn't help but laugh, he was pouting. His hands were on my waist and he was staring at me.

"We're going to continue this conversation," he whispered. I rolled my eyes and laughed.

"We shall see," I said winking. He was now the one rolling his eyes.

"Think you can get your way with me?" He asked. I nodded, coaxing a smile from him. "I suppose you are right." He kissed my forehead and held me against his chest. "We should be getting to training."

"I suppose," I said against his chest. He smelled wonderful and I didn't want us to part, but I knew we had to. We left the room and I went the short way and he walked the long way. I caught up with Kurtz and Matthews.

"What'd Commander Trials want," Kurtz asked.

"I wanted to tell her she's leading in scores," Commander Trials said behind us, scaring all three of us. We all jumped a little and turned around. Commander Trials laughed and continued walking.

"He's like a stealth warrior," Matthews grumbled. We walked into the training area and in the middle of the mats was War Advisor Jennings.

"This can't be good," I whispered. We took our seats and all sat in silence. A few minutes later, before class was to begin, Nick walked through the door. He looked at War Advisor Jennings and raised an eyebrow. He walked over to War Advisor Jennings and they talked amongst themselves. None of us could make out what they were saying, which made the conversation that much scarier. They talked for several minutes. It seemed to get more and more intense as the minutes went by. They weren't screaming at one another but the body language was clear. Finally, they both turned and looked at me.

"Uh oh," Kurtz whispered. "Now what?"

"No telling. You seem to be quite popular here lately, Armistice," Matthews whispered. I nodded my head.

"Armistice," Nick shouted.

"Yes, sir?"

"Front and center," he said. I didn't hesitate and made my way over to them. I stood at attention.

"Armistice, it has been brought to my attention that you are excelling in all of your training."

"I see, sir."

"You excelled in both the simulations and water tank." I never did know how I did on either one of those, but I guess now I knew. "I have also learned that you have had problems with some of the fellow trainees. Is this correct?"

"Negative, sir." War Advisor and Nick both looked at me.

"This is incorrect?"

"Yes, sir."

"Hmmm…. So, you all have gotten along?"

"We get along as well as any other trainees would get along, sir." He smirked at me.

"Well in any case, I have a challenge for you. I was told you were the best fighter."

"I wouldn't say that, sir."

"Commander Taylor says differently," I quickly looked at Nick, whose face was resenting telling War Advisor Jennings about my fighting skills. "And after seeing the damage you have done to him when the pair of you fought, I would have to say you are a force to be reckoned with," he laughed.

"Thank you, sir," I said turning my attention back to him.

"I have selected a trainee from another class for you to go up against."

"Oh."

"Class 32 should be here shortly and then we will begin."

"Yes, sir."

"You may take your seat or prepare for the fight."

"Thank you, sir," I glanced at Nick before I walked off. He was angry with War Advisor Jennings. I walked over to Matthews and Kurtz.

"What the hell is going on, now," Kurtz asked.

"Apparently, I am going to fight someone in class 32."

"What the hell," they both said. Nick made his way over to the group.

"We are about to have a class battle," he said looking around at all of us. "Class 32 will be here and Armistice will be going up against their top trainee."

"How's that fair," someone shouted. Nick held up his hand to silence them.

"This isn't my idea, but we will cheer her on and ensure that Class 32 knows we aren't a class to be taken lightly," he growled. The whole group was on their feet, except me, and doing battle cries. Nick continued to pump them up, while I sat there watching the commotion.

The training area doors opened and Class 32 filed in and took their seats across the room for us. Nick looked at me and gestured for me to follow him. I reluctantly stood up.

"You got this, Kaitlyn," I looked at Kurtz and smiled.

"Thanks," I followed Nick on to the mat. "So, what's the real reason, I whispered, "that I'm fighting this guy,".

"I think he is doing this to get at me."

"Oh?"

"Long story."

"Too bad I don't have time to hear it out," I said rolling my eyes. I was annoyed by the fact that I was being used as a tool in their petty fight.

"Don't be mad at me," he whispered.

"We can discuss this later," I bent down and began unlacing my boots. I tossed my boots off the mat. The Class 32 trainee stepped on to the mat along with Commander Burch, who was known as a hard ass. The trainee looked like a tank. He was the same size as Matthews. "Oh, jeez," I muttered. Nick turned and looked at me.

"You got this," he said placing his hand on my shoulder. "Just go for the kill. This kid is known for his moves standing up. Take him to the mat. Understand?" I nodded my head and he moved his hand.

The trainee walked to the center of the mat. He was dark skinned, thick black hair, and had warrior tattoos on his arms. He had murder in his eyes. He was not going to go easy on me. My body ached just looking at him. This was going to be quite painful.

"Remind me to kick your ass, later," I mumbled to Taylor.

"Armistice," War Advisor Jennings shouted at me. I pulled my shirt over my head and my group went crazy, as usual. Class 32, Commander Burch, and War Advisor Jennings were in shock at my attire. I shrugged my shoulders and walked over to them. "You always fight like this?"

"Yes, sir," I said smirking.

"This is not a fair fight," Commander Burch said, "She is trying to distract him with her womanly form!"

"This is not a fair fight, period. He's three times the size of her," Nick shouted. Nick and Commander Burch got up in one another's faces and began arguing. I thought they were going to start throwing punches. The trainee and I just watched back and forth as our two commanders acted out.

"Fight," War Advisor Jennings said in a low voice. I barely heard him but charged at my opponent. Everyone was caught off guard, as I slammed him to the mat. The room filled with uproar. I began punching him in the face. He was so shocked at first that he didn't do anything, but after the fourth punch, he became irate and began hitting me back. He rolled me over and attempted to punch me. I held up my arms and blocked him. I kicked him between the legs, and as he fell back holding himself, I jumped on his chest, wrapped my ankles around his neck and rolled over. He wasn't easy to roll but I somehow found the strength. He began prying my legs apart but I kept tightening them. I was burning energy fast and wearing out too soon. He was a beast and stronger than anyone I had faced.

My opponent finally realized he wasn't going to get my legs apart, so he grabbed me by my waist and stood up with me. Class 32 was on their feet and cheering. He slammed me onto the mat and knocked the wind out of me. Class 32 erupted with more cheers and battle cries. My opponent had the nerve to stand up and bow to his classmates, while I was on the ground.

I slowly stood up, as he continued to bow.

"Hey, asshole," I screamed over Class 32. He turned and I kicked him straight in the face as hard as I could. He fell to the ground. I waited for him to fly back up, but he didn't. He was out cold.

My group was on their feet and running over to me. Kurtz picked me up and placed me on his shoulders. They began doing our class battle cry and jumping all around me. I looked over at my opponent and he was still out cold. Commander Burch and War Advisor Jennings didn't seem too concerned. I tapped Kurtz on the shoulder and he put me down. I walked over to the guy and bent down.

"Hey, you okay," I asked. He didn't respond. I leaned my head on his chest and didn't hear anything. I instantly began panicking. "Call the infirmary," I shouted and the room fell quiet. I tilted his head and began performing rescue breaths on him and compressions. "Come on! Wake up!" I kept doing breaths and compressions on him.

War Advisor Jennings, Commander Burch, and Nick were now standing over us. I ignored them and kept going. I checked his pulse and it was faint. I kept doing rescue breaths. Time seemed to stand still, as I continued doing rescue breaths. I was getting worn out, but refused to stop. I was running on empty, when suddenly he took a sharp breath. His eyes opened and he looked at me hunched over him. I let out my own breath and sat back on my heels. I was exhausted and wanted to fall out on the floor next to him.

The infirmary staff came in a few seconds later and loaded him on to a stretcher. His head turned and he looked at me. We didn't exchange words, but I knew what he meant. He was taken out of the room and the room was still silent.

"Armistice," War Advisor Jennings said. I looked at him. "Good job." I didn't say anything. I walked past him, Nick, and Commander Burch. I had enough of the games. I grabbed my boots and shirt. I made a break for the door. "Armistice!" I stopped and looked at him. "You aren't dismissed."

"No offense, but unless you are going to hop on the mat with me, I am done here, sir!" I walked out of the room slamming the door behind me. I stomped down the hallway and looked for a quiet place. I turned a corner and ran into Dimitri.

"Trying to run away," he asked laughing.

"Something like that," I muttered.

"Oh. In that case, follow me." He led me down the hallway and to his regiment's training area. They were in there practicing. We walked into the room and sat on the bench. I slipped my shirt and boots back on. "What's going on, Armistice?"

I don't know why, but I felt like I could tell him anything. I opened my mouth and everything came blurting out; from day one all the way to a few moments ago. When I finished, he nodded his head and said nothing. I faced him and he grinned.

"Wish I could've seen the look on War Advisor Jennings' face." We both busted out laughing.

"I'm sure I will get my ass chewed or kicked out when he finds me," I shrugged my shoulders because at that moment I didn't care. I was tired of being the experiment.

"If he wants a strong Anguish, he would not kick you out."

"I don't think he cares whether I'm here or not."

"Well, we can ask him," I looked up and he was pointing at the door. War Advisor Jennings' was standing there and he didn't look happy. He walked into the room and everything came to a halt. He stepped on the mat and threw his jacket off. Why were all Anguish males built like tanks?

"Well," he said looking at me.

"Oh, this isn't good," I whispered.

"Waiting on you, Armistice." I stood up and made my way to him. "Everyone out!"

The room began to clear. Dimitri looked at me one last time and then closed the door.

"I apologize for my rash behavior and loose tongue, sir."

"But did you mean what you said?"

"Yes, sir."

"Then I accept your challenge." I was in for it. He was twice my age, but that just meant he had more training then me. I was beginning to wish that I had kept my mouth shut.

"I can't fight you, sir."

"Why not? You were quick enough to run your mouth."

"And I apologized for that. Put me back in the water tank, but I won't fight you, sir."

"Sure about that?"

"Yes, sir."

"You still stand behind what you said to me?"

"Yes, sir." He crossed his arms and stared me down.

"What information were you given?"

"Sir?"

"What information were you given the day of the simulator?"

"Nothing, sir," I said shaking my head. Much to my surprise, he laughed.

"Still won't tell me?"

"No, sir."

"Commander Trials said you won't tell him. Commander Taylor says the same. Is this true?"

"Yes, sir."

"Going to take it to your grave?"

"At all cost, sir." He smiled and stuck out his hand. My eyebrow rose and I stuck out my hand. He shook it.

"You are not what we were expecting you to be."

"Is that good or bad, sir?"

"Definitely, a good thing," he picked up his jacket and made his way towards the door.

"Is that all, sir?"

"For now," he opened the door and left.

Chapter Nine
Metamorphosis

I stood in the room for some time. I kept thinking about all the situations I had gotten myself into since being at the academy. I had stepped off the train a nervous wreck, unsure of my fate within these walls. I had begun my days at the academy by being sent to the infirmary. Now, weeks later, I was challenging War Advisors to fights. I had a death wish.

I made my way back to the training area and the guys were still in there training. At least they were until I walked through the door. They stopped what they were doing and the door closed behind me. They seemed surprised to see me in one piece.

One person did our class battle cry and soon the rest joined in. They all ran over to me. They were either congratulating me on winning, congratulating me for saving my opponent, or they were congratulating me for going up against War Advisor Jennings.

"Enough," Nick screamed. "Back to the mats." I was no longer surrounded and a few inches from me stood Nick.

"Did he find you," he asked in a whisper. I nodded my head. "And?"

"We talked, he shook my hand, and left." He laughed.

"You have got to be kidding me." I shook my head. "Where did he even find you at?"

"I was in Dimitri's regiment training area with him." He laughed more.

"And War Advisor Jennings just walked in there and asked to talk to you?"

"Oh, no, didn't happen like that all," I said laughing. "He came in to the room, walked on the mats, threw his jacket on the ground, looked at me, and basically challenged me." Nick was laughing so hard he had tears in his eyes.

"I wish I could've seen the look on your face, because the look on his face when you snapped at him was priceless. You are both hotheads." He laughed more and wiped his eyes, but didn't stop laughing. "What happened next?"

"He ordered everyone out, and then continued to challenge me. I refused and told him to put me in the water tank but I wasn't going to fight him. He then asked if I was sure. I said 'yes'. He then asked me what I had been told during the simulator. I refused to tell him. He stuck out his hand and shook my hand."

"Wait, what?"

"Yep. He shook my hand. Told me I wasn't what they expected, told me that was a good thing, and walked out the room."

"Wow," he was no longer laughing. "That is huge, Kaitlyn," he whispered. I shrugged my shoulders.

"I'm just glad he didn't rip me a new one or kick me out," he laughed.

"He wouldn't have done that."

"Why not?"

"He just wouldn't. Now go hit the mat before I kiss you in front of everyone," he whispered. I looked up and he was grinning.

"You wouldn't dare," I said laughing.

"Try me."

"Okay. Okay, I'm moving… sir," I said walking away and laughing. I joined Kurtz and Matthews on the mat. I sat down, while they sparred, and stretched. My body was sore from the past few weeks and I wasn't taking very good care of it. The food tasted like garbage and I was tempted to pretend to be sick, so I could go to the infirmary and get soup.

I continued stretching and meditating. It seemed like training lasted forever. Finally, Nick dismissed us. He looked like he was going to say something to me, but he laughed to himself and walked the other way.

The rest of the day was uneventful. We were all given a pass to go outside of Anguish, but I chose to stay behind. Matthews and Kurtz did their best to try to convince me to go with them. I just didn't feel like walking among people my father was threatening to kill. If someone recognized me, it would be detrimental, to say the least.

I laid on my bed and soon found myself mired in deep thoughts. I wondered how my mother was holding up to me being gone, and my father on a rampage. Hopefully, he wasn't being harsh on her. He should be occupied with starting a war and ignore her all together. I only hoped that was the case.

So much had changed in the past few weeks. I had learned so much about myself and the world around me. I was knowledgeable in many things that I didn't even know I cared to learn. I could hold conversations on war and battle plans. I could hold my own against males twice my size. I wouldn't have ever thought any of this would be possible, but Anguish had made it possible. In a way, I needed to thank my father when this was all over.

My mind soon drifted to the thought of leaving Anguish. What would I do once I graduated? Graduation was a few days away. Would I return home, or be given a chance to stay at Anguish? I knew there were still some males here who did not want me around any longer than I had to be. However, I wouldn't mind the opportunity to stick around. It would be nice to be around people who understood me. Be nice to see Nick more. I didn't have a clue what was going on between us, but I hoped it was more than just a few devious kisses.

Chapter Ten
Round One…Victory

A knock at my door made me quickly sit up. I looked at the door window and standing there were Nick and Dimitri. Not who I was expecting to see at my door. I walked over to the door and it opened.

"To what do I owe this pleasure, gentlemen?" They both laughed.

"You're coming to hang out with us," Nick announced.

"Hang out with you two, sir," I leaned against the doorway and crossed my arms.

"Yes, we are having a commander get together and you are invited," Nick said grinning. I rolled my eyes.

"Why would a trainee be invited to a commander get together, sir?"

"Because you're with us," Nick said gesturing between him and Dimitri. I still wasn't budging from the doorway. "Oh, come on, Kaitlyn." Dimitri quickly looked at Nick and then at me. Nick just laughed.

"Such informalities," Dimitri said grinning.

"So, it seems, sir," I said turning to Nick and glaring.

"Oh, come on. Dimitri is my best friend," Nick whispered. Dimitri just looked at me and grinned. I rolled my eyes and continued standing in the door way. "I think she's scared, Dimitri."

"I believe so, Nick." They both looked at each other. They were antagonizing me, but I'd go along with the charade.

"Scared of what?"

"The commanders get together. We have it every time the trainees aren't in the academy. We heard that you were the only one who stayed behind, so we thought we'd change up our rules and invite you to attend," Nick said in one breath. They both looked at me and I didn't move.

"You get to shoot Nick with a microwave beam," Dimitri said.

"I'm in," I said turning around to grab my jacket. Microwave beams were guns that didn't shoot bullets, they shot waves that knocked you on your butt. We'd used them in training a while back. I think I'd rather have been shot with a bullet. "What the hell," Nick said laughing. I walked out the door with my jacket in hand. "You would shoot me?" I shrugged my shoulders.

"No one is safe from me."

"I like her," Dimitri said laughing.

"I like you, too," I said smiling. Dimitri held his hand up and I gave him a high-five. Nick laughed.

"Now you two are teaming up on me?"

"I'm always on the winning side," Dimitri said walking towards the exit. I wasn't sure what they had in store, but I followed them like a lost puppy. We took the elevator up and all the commanders were at the entrance way of the academy; Commanders Burch, Trials, Roy, Kit, Heat, Bruce, Milton, Bruce, Convington, Mason, Jordan, Rival, Orion, and Franklin. And now all of them were staring at me.

"Maybe this wasn't a good idea," I whispered.

"About time you three showed up! Let's go," Commander Trials said. I had never realized it until they were all in a room, but the commanders were young and quite attractive. Nick was the most attractive, but it was still hard to keep my tongue in my mouth.

All three of us were handed a microwave beam and a holster. I put the holster on, secured the microwave beam, threw my jacket on and followed behind the pack of commanders. We walked out and the sun hit my eyes. I hadn't seen the sun in weeks. My eyes were having a hard time adjusting. Nick made me stop and slipped his sunglasses on me. I smiled and we continued walking. As we walked down the streets, people moved out of the way and watched as we walked by. Whispers began when they saw me among them.

"There is a female," someone said laughing. That caused all the commanders to stop and look at the male. The male was quick to stop laughing.

"I guarantee this *female* could devour you in a heartbeat," Commander Trials growled in my defense.

"You will pay her respect or you will be dealt with," Commander Heat said stepping towards the male. The people around the guy moved away from him. I could tell the male was terrified and regretting saying anything.

"I apologize," the male said nervously.

"No, you will apologize to her," Commander Heat said pointing at me. The male looked at me.

"I apologize for my remarks." I nodded my head. Commander Heat pointed at the male.

"Next time, you won't be so lucky. Understood?" The male nodded his head and we continued walking. Once we rounded the corner, they all laughed.

"He almost pissed himself, Walter," Dimitri said patting Commander Heat on his back.

"He is just a measly rat," they laughed more and we continued walking. All the commanders small talked, and I hung in the back gazing upon Lynx Canton. There wasn't much difference between Lynx and Neva. The view of the mountains that divided us was the only big difference.

"It's locked." Dimitri said. I looked up and saw a gate in front of us.

"Can be opened from the other side," Commander Burch said. Then they began arguing over who was going to climb over and unlock it. I stood away from the group and listened to them argue. They reminded me of a group of schoolgirls. Not that I would tell them that. They were still my superiors.

I laughed to myself and ran towards the corner of the gate. I climbed up and over. I pushed the 'open' button and the gate slowly opened. They were all staring at me.

"What," I asked with a smirk. They walked through the gate and I hit the button to close the gate.

"You are very resourceful," Commander Burch said laughing as he walked passed me. Dimitri gave me a smile of approval and I followed behind the group once more.

"The rules are simple. If you get blasted, you are out. Last one standing wins," Commander Roy said. I hadn't had much contact with Commander Roy. I just knew by rumor that he came across shy, but was not the one to make mad. He apparently broke one of his trainee's arms because the trainee sucked his teeth at him.

"Are there teams," I asked, which must have been a stupid question, because every single one of them laughed at me. I took my microwave beam out of my holster. "What level are these set on?"

"Afraid of too much pain," Commander Mason said grinning. I shook my head. "Come on, this is Anguish. They are on level four." In training, we only went up to a level two and that left a mark for a few days. Level four was something that I did not want to experience.

"Oh."

"Oh?" Commander Franklin laughed. "You tell her it's on level four and all she has to say is 'oh'." They were laughing again. It was strange seeing them all laugh. They were usually frowning, growling, or throwing things. I hadn't seen them really smile or laugh.

"And there aren't any rules, correct, sir?"

"Correct, Armistice," Commander Bruce said growing annoyed by me.

"Then I am sorry, gentlemen." They all looked at me and I opened fired on all of them. The ones who weren't shot ran for cover, while Bruce, Burch, Trials, Dimitri, and Kit fell to the ground in pain.

I took off running. I had never run so fast in all my life. I couldn't help but laugh as I ran. They hadn't been expecting me to shoot them. I felt bad for shooting them, but I wasn't much for losing. I quickly found shelter in a sewage tunnel. The smell alone made me want to heave, but I know they wouldn't expect me to be in there.

I heard two blasts and two yells. Apparently, two more people were out which left eight more. I just stayed put and waited most of it out. I heard another blast along with more yelling; now seven were left.

I heard footsteps coming my way. I pointed my microwave beam in the direction of the noise. It was Commander Jordan. I know this because he stopped in front of the tunnel I was hiding in to catch his breath. I felt bad because he didn't suspect a thing, but I blasted him anyway. He screamed and fell to the ground. I ran passed him. He shot me a death look, but I kept running.

I heard another blast, yelling, and it wasn't too far away. I heard running footsteps so I leaned against the wall casually. Commander Orion came around the corner. He stopped when he spotted me.

"You guys don't play fair," I growled.

"We don't," he walked over to me laughing. "Why do you say that?"

"I at least shot them when they were facing me. I wasn't a coward who shot them in the back!" He laughed more. "And, level four is a bit much, don't you think?" He continued laughing.

"I don't know, I've never been shot with level four." I blasted him. He screamed and his knees buckled. I didn't get a chance to see his face because I ran in the opposite direction. I ran down two blocks and heard two more blasts. The blasts were getting faster and closer to me. I fired my microwave beam in to the air and screamed at the top of my lungs. I fell to the ground holding myself.

I heard another blast, then one more a few seconds after that. There was only one more person left. I continued holding my stomach. I heard voices approaching.

"That was sneaky, hiding in the dumpster, Nick," Commander Mason said. Mason and Nick laughed. I couldn't make out who the third person was.

"I won, didn't I?" Nick was now laughing. Their footsteps got louder. "Kai...Armistice, you alright?" I heard him running towards me. I rolled on to my side, lifted my microwave beam and shot him. He fell to the ground in pain. Mason and Franklin both busted out laughing. I stood up and walked over to Nick, who was holding his chest.

"Sorry," I said bending down and offering my hand to him. He shook his head and continued holding his stomach. I covered my mouth and turned my head so he wouldn't see me laughing. Mason patted me on the back.

"Good job." Franklin bent down and pulled Nick up by his arm. Nick was still holding his stomach and glaring at me.

"It was just a game, Ni...sir," I was really trying hard not to laugh.

"You shot me," he growled. I laughed more.

"You should've seen your face," I covered my mouth, but I couldn't stop laughing. Nick let go of his stomach and began walking towards me. He looked like a predator about to attack its prey. I held my hands out in front of me. "No. Don't. Don't you dare," I couldn't help but laugh.

"I'd run if I were you," Franklin said grinning. I took his warning and took off in a dead sprint. Nick may have just been blasted with a level 4 but he was still fast. I got maybe a block down the street before Nick grabbed me. I screamed, but it was a cross between a scream and a laugh.

"Put me down!" I laughed more.

"And if I don't?" He was now laughing.

"I will be forced to fight you." He didn't let go of me.

"You are mine, later," he whispered into my ear and I melted. He released me. "But not until after we shower, because we both smell horrible." I looked down at my clothes and I looked a mess. He didn't look any better, and we both smelled. We walked together back to the gate. Everyone else was already there.

"You do not play fair," Orion said grinning.

"I was told there weren't any rules, sir," I shrugged my shoulders.

"You did tell her that," Dimitri said in my defense. He was soon laughing.

"She is the trainee. Yet, she made it look like child's play," Kit said.

"She used all means necessary. She even shot Taylor," Franklin was laughing as he said it. For some reason, they all found that funnier than anything else.

"Yeah, yeah, eat it up," Nick said shaking his head. "She'll be running extra laps in training." They all laughed.

"I understand why you are feeling this way, sir," I said softly. They looked at me.

"You do," Nick asked.

"Yes, sir."

"How do you know how I am feeling?" He raised an eyebrow.

"Well, I have never had your particular feeling, but I know I wouldn't like getting my ass kicked by me twice, either, sir." I kept a straight face. He was dumbfounded by my words. The others laughed like there was no tomorrow.

"As I recall, I won that first fight," he said crossing his arms.

"I recall your face taking just as long as mine to heal…sir," I said smirking. The others were trying to contain their laughter.

"I wasn't the one who needed surgery," he grinned.

"This is true. However, I took something very valuable from you that fight."

"What did you take?"

"Your masculine card, sir." I winked, opened the gate, and walked out. All I could hear was laughter. I couldn't help but smile. Usually I wasn't very quick with my words, but that exchange came out of my mouth freely. Felt good to be amusing.

I walked down the street half a block ahead of them. I was smiling the entire time. I looked at the world around me. Everyone seemed to be happy in Lynx. There weren't any government troops patrolling the streets. They must've felt safe walking the streets. Lynx was a nice place.

There was a quaint café up ahead. People were outside drinking their beverages. A group of males were in front of the café laughing and having a good time. They stopped when they saw me and began whispering; typical men.

"Armistice," Commander Trials called out. I stopped walking and faced them. They continued walking towards me. "Going to let us walk with you? Or are you embarrassed?" I laughed, but they weren't laughing. They were all running towards me with the most serious look. They all drew their microwave beams. They were sore losers and this was going to seriously hurt. I braced for all their shots.

Chapter Eleven
Not a Word

"Get down, Kaitlyn," Commander Trials screamed. I didn't hesitate at all. I fell to the ground as shots flew over me. I looked to my right and watched as the group of males, now a few feet from me, laid on the pavement in pain. I was quickly pulled off the ground. It wasn't Nick, it was Commander Trials. He looked down at me and began examining me. "You alright?"

"I'm fine."

"Good, let's get you back to the academy." We all took off in a dead sprint to the academy. We took the elevator down in silence. The doors opened.

"So, nice to see all my commanders together," War Advisor Jennings said. I couldn't see him because I was behind everyone. "Anyone care to explain why you all smell like waste and why I was just notified of an incident that resulted in five civilians being shot with microwave beams multiple times?" I pushed past all of them and made it to the front.

"Armistice?"

"Sir," I said at attention. "I decided to leave the academy after all. I was unaccompanied and began walking through the streets looking for the other trainees. I was unsuccessful. I ran into those five males you spoke of. They began advancing on me so I opened fire. The commanders had just rounded the corner and saw me. They began reprimanding me for my rash decision and escorted me back to the academy, sir."

"Is that so?" He cocked his head to the side.

"Yes, sir." Commander Trials, who was next to me, began to open his mouth. "The commanders already discussed that they planned to tell you that they did it, sir," I said glaring at Commander Trials to keep his mouth shut. "However, I am solely responsible for this event and if I can suggest punishment, I suggest the water tank, sir."

"So be it. This way, Armistice," I didn't wait for anyone to say anything. I hit the 'close door' on the elevator and stepped off. The door quickly closed and I followed the War Advisor through the halls. I wasn't looking forward to the water tank, but I wasn't going to let the commanders take the fall since they had been protecting me.

The walk to the tank seemed to take forever. We, finally, stopped walking. I looked at the door and it read 'interrogation'. I think I'd have much rather preferred the water tank. He opened the door and gestured for me to walk in first. I stepped into the room and quickly looked at him. The room was an office. He grinned and walked around the desk. He took a seat.

"Have a seat, Armistice." I sat down and stared at him. "Do you know why I brought you here?"

"No, sir."

"I've noticed something about you."

"Yes, sir?"

"You are very loyal."

"Um... thank you, sir."

"You will protect information and people at all costs, even if it means inflicting pain to you." I nodded. "If it had been any other trainee, they would have just let the commander's take the fall for the incident and walked away. However, you don't operate on the same brain wave as everyone else." I frowned, which made him laugh. He held up his hand for me to allow him to continue, "You choose death before dishonor."

"I am responsible for the incident, sir." He laughed and turned his monitor so I could see. He pushed play. It was a video of the five males sneaking up behind me with weapons drawn, Commander Trials screaming for me to get down, and the commanders open firing. War Advisor Jennings stopped the video and turned the monitor back to him. "Someone must have edited the video, sir."

"Armistice," he laughed, "even though I have the evidence in front of me, you still say you are the one who shot them?"

"Yes, sir."

"You are quite stubborn. You know that right?"

"I've been called worse, sir." He laughed and opened a drawer. He pulled out a bottle and two glasses. He poured both glasses half way full. He put the lid back on the bottle and placed it back in the desk. Then he slid a glass over to me. "I like you, Armistice. You remind me of a female version of me."

"Thank you, sir. I think." He laughed again and picked up his glass.

"Pick up your glass. We shall drink to your loyalty."

"Are you sure, sir?" I raised an eyebrow. He nodded his head and I grabbed my glass.

"To Anguish loyalty."

"To Anguish loyalty," I repeated. We clanked our glasses together and downed the drink. It was the strongest thing I had ever tasted and burned like crazy. I tried to keep my composure.

"You alright, Armistice?"

"Yes, sir," I said trying to not cough.

"It's always rough the first time," I nodded my head and swallowed hard.

"So, I see, sir." He laughed.

"You are dismissed."

"I am, sir?"

"Yes. I know that even if I put you in the simulator or water tank you will continue stating that you shot the civilians and not the commanders. I could interrogate you for days and the result would be the same. I refuse to waste your time or mine, so we will just say that you did it out of self-defense and leave it at that." I nodded my head and stood.

"Thank you, sir." I headed for the door.

"Armistice," I turned around.

"He really cares for you." My whole world stopped. I'm sure my face went pale and eyes became big.

"Sir?"

"You may be good at withholding information, but it is obvious what's going on."

"I'm confused, sir."

"I figured you would say that. Just know that not all people are who they pretend to be. Sometimes it's someone else in front of us who is the better choice."

"Oh?"

"You are dismissed, Armistice."

"Um...Thank you, sir." I walked out the door and quickly walked down the hallway. How could he possibly know about Nick and me? Was he even referring to Nick? I wanted to ask War Advisor Jennings if he was referring to Nick, being the one who wasn't as he seemed, but just in case he wasn't I held my tongue. And who was the person who was the better choice?

Chapter Twelve
Truth Unfolds

The sleeping bay was full but no one was speaking. I walked in and all the trainees looked terrified. My eyes caught Kurtz's eyes and he shrugged his shoulders. He didn't know what was going on either.

"Armistice," Commander Orion shouted. It seemed like no one knew any other name, but mine. I refrained from rolling my eyes and looked in the direction of his voice. All the commanders were standing in the corner of the room with their arms crossed. I grinned and made my way over to them. They gathered around me.

"You are a stubborn female," Commander Mason whispered pointing at me. I shrugged my shoulders.

"Do you know how much trouble you could have gotten in to," Commander Kit asked.

"Yes, sir."

"And yet you took the blame, instead of us explaining what had happened," Commander Bruce said. They really were in a tizzy.

"If you had explained what happened, then War Advisor Jennings would have known that you all had taken me out of the academy and not the trainees. How would you explain that, sir?" None of them spoke. "It was easier for me to take the blame, because I am usually in trouble anyway, sir." I smirked. They all laughed and agreed.

"What was your punishment? We weren't expecting you back so soon," Dimitri asked.

"I was talked to, shown a video, and..." my words trailed off. "That's about it, sir."

"Then why do you smell like spirits," Commander Franklin asked sniffing me. Soon they all smelled me.

"This is awkward, gentlemen," I said laughing and stepping back from them.

"He offered you a drink," Nick asked seeming the most surprised.

"No. I was walking back and found a glass, sir." I held back a laugh. They all folded their arms. "Oh, come on. Certain things you just shouldn't ask me."

"She is quite stubborn," Commander Trials pointed out.

"Seems to be the general consensus on me, sir," I said grinning.

"So, let me get this straight," Nick began, "You claim to have shot five civilians, get talked to and offered a drink?" I shrugged my shoulders.

"At this rate, she will have all our jobs by next week," Commander Mason said grinning.

"Just means you should work harder so I don't, sir," I said. They all looked at me and busted out laughing.

"The next time we all play, we pick teams and she is on my team," Commander Burch announced with a grin. They began discussing whose team I would be on. Commander Orion and I just stared at the rest.

"Either way, you have gained a lot of respect from me for your actions during the game and your loyalty," Commander Orion said offering me his hand. The others stopped talking. Commander Orion and I shook hands.

"Awe, you guys really do have a heart, sir," I said sweetly.

"If you tell a soul, I will be forced to drag you to the water tank myself," Commander Trials said winking. I grinned.

"Not a soul, sir."

"Coming from you, I believe that," Commander Trials said. Commander Franklin faced the trainees.

"Carry on," he yelled and then turned to me. The room began to fill with noises and movements. He held out his hand and I raised an eyebrow. He laughed. "Weapon, Armistice."

"Oh," I laughed and handed him the holster and microwave beam. Each commander patted me on the back, as they walked by. Nick was the last one to walk by me. He leaned over to my ear.

"Take a shower and meet me in the training area in an hour," he whispered and walked off. I really didn't want to meet him anywhere. It hadn't been him to warn me or him to check on me. I walked to my room with the other trainees staring at me. Once inside, I gathered my bathing items and made my way to the bathing quarters.

The shower was refreshing, although it took me scrubbing twice to get the filth out of my hair and off my skin. When the water finally ran clean and the smell of death was off me, I turned off the water. Soon, I was dressed and back in my room. I limited my contact to the others so I didn't have to explain what had happened with the commanders and me. When an hour was up, I quietly left my room and very stealthily made my way to the training area. Nick was outside the doors and smiled as I approached. We walked into the room and like usual he shut and locked it. He pulled me into his arms and held me.

"You smell so much better now," he laughed against my head.

"Like you smelled like flowers earlier?"

"No. We both smelled rancid." I rested my head against his chest and laughed. He pulled me against his chest more and held me.

"What happens when I graduate?" I didn't mean to even ask him that. It just slipped freely through my lips. He instantly froze in place. I had just complicated everything. "Nick?" I looked up at him.

"I hadn't thought about that."

"Oh," I chuckled to play off my frustration with his answer. He hadn't considered anything past the academy. I was foolish to think otherwise.

"I didn't mean to upset you."

"Oh, you didn't," I said forcing a smile. "Oh, no, what time is it?" I looked at my watch. "I told Kurtz and Matthews that I would study with them for Commander Trial's exam tomorrow. Sorry." I unlocked the door and ran out without looking back.

Chapter Thirteen
All a Bad Dream

I was an absolute fool to think that someone like him would even consider someone like me. After all I was just a test subject, a female, and a Nevan. I was the pathetic female caught in the travesty of male lust. He had planned this all along and I was too stupid to know it.

Once I was in my room, I threw myself on my bed, covered my face with my pillow and screamed into it. I wanted to punch a wall, kick someone in the face, anything to get my pain out. I screamed again into my pillow. Why had I been so naïve? Was it his good looks, his godlike body, his intelligence? Twenty years of life and I still hadn't learned to identify a ruse when I saw one.

There was a soft knock at my door. I removed the pillow and looked at the door. Of course, it was Nick. I put the pillow over my face and growled. Then I stood up and walked over to the door. The door opened.

"May I help you, sir," I snapped.

"We need to talk," he whispered.

"Nothing to talk about. Besides, it's lights out, sir." His face darkened.

"We are going to talk."

"About what, sir? I think you have made it all very clear," I growled. He ran his fingers through his hair and took a deep breath.

"Let me inside."

"Not a good idea. I have an early morning and besides someone might see you, sir."

"I don't care," he grabbed me by hips, lifted me inside the room and stepped in. The door closed behind him. I crossed my arms.

"I think you should leave."

"Well, I think you should hear me out. We had a great day and now you are mad at me."

"I'm not mad," I said laughing. I refused to give him the satisfaction of knowing how I felt.

"Kaitlyn, it is written all over your face."

"No, what's written all over my face is sleep deprivation, now if you excuse me, I need to be getting some sleep." I walked towards the door to let him out, but he blocked the door.

"Move."

"Or what?"

"Or I will move you." he re-crossed his arms.

"I'd like to see you try." He didn't budge, just continued glaring at me. "Well?"

"Get out."

"Not until you hear me out."

"Speak, but hurry the hell up," I walked over to my bed.

"Not here. Let's go talk elsewhere." I turned towards him and laughed.

"Thought you didn't care if someone saw you in here?" I smirked.

"Kaitlyn," he warned.

"Talk or get out," I sat on my bed and took my boots off, while he stood in silence. "One more minute and I'm throwing you out on your ass."

"For someone who isn't mad, you sure are violent," he laughed. I looked up at him.

"You haven't seen violent, yet."

"Kaitlyn, what did I do," he asked softly.

"You didn't do anything."

"Then why are you so angry?"

"I'm not angry. I'm just finally realizing what things really are."

"And what's that," he walked over to the bed and sat next to me. I continued staring at the wall in front of me.

"That everything in this place is a simulation."

"Why would you say that," he growled.

"I was brought here to be a test subject. I have been tested time and time again. I now know the outcome of all of this. I was naïve to think otherwise; just like I was naïve to think that there was anything more than hidden kisses between the two of us."

"Kaitlyn," he said softly and I held up my hand to stop him.

"I am just a Nevan female test subject, who has forgotten her place in this world. I have been humbly reminded today, thanks to you." I faced him. "I thank you for reminding me of who I truly am."

"It isn't like that. I see…" His words were cut off by the sound of an alarm going off and red lights began to flash. Everyone began pouring out of their rooms and running out into the corridors.

"Let's go," Taylor said grabbing my hand. The door opened and we ran with everyone else. We ran into the assembly room and he slowly dropped my hand. In front of us was a giant screen and on it was a news broadcast of Emperor Brock Gable of Neva- my father.

"Oh, no," I covered my mouth with my hand. Taylor looked down at me and back to the screen.

"I am Emperor Brock of Neva," my father said, "and a war is upon our cantons." The room filled with uproar.

"Silence," someone shouted and the room fell silent.

"…the war was inevitable. For years, the tension has grown between our two cantons. After you took the life of something that was of great value to me, the treaty ended. As you have already discovered, all of your train employees have been killed and sent back to your city." An image popped up in the corner of the screen and pictures of train employees lying in pools of blood on the train was shown. I felt my heart drop in my stomach and my heart broke for those families affected. "I assure you, there will be more Lynxan deaths. You have by the next full moon to surrender." The broadcast ended and the room was again in an uproar.

"This has got to be a joke. Neva will never survive a battle between our cantons," Taylor said. I thought he was talking to someone next to him, but his eyes were on me.

"Armistice," someone shouted from the front of the room. The crowd fell quiet and heads turned to me. "Front and center." I knew what was about to happen. I made my way to the front and before me stood the Academy's Warfare Council. They were all staring at me.

"Come with me," War Advisor Jennings said right before he turned and began walking out of the room. "Carry on," he shouted before he stepped out of the room. I followed behind him a few steps as he led me out of the assembly room and into an office. His council took their seat and I remained standing. Jennings took his seat and all eyes were on me.

"Seems we have a problem, Armistice."

"So, it would seem, sir."

"And what do you plan on doing about this problem?"

"What would you like me to do about it, sir?" He grinned and sat back in his chair.

"I cannot speak for the government of Lynx Canton only for Anguish."

"I see, sir."

"Your father," Apparently, Commander Trials didn't need to keep my secret, because War Advisor Jennings already knew, "plans on bringing a war to our people. Are they equipped for a war?"

"Yes, sir."

"What will stop your father?"

"The only way to stop him is for him to be incarcerated or killed, sir." He considered my words for a moment, and then nodded.

"And are you capable of doing either of these?" I didn't even hesitate, I nodded my head. "Then you will lead the mission."

"Mission, sir?"

"Yes, the mission to handle your father. After all, you are one of us," he tossed something at me and I caught it. I looked down at my hand and I was holding an Anguish ring with my name on it. There was a ruby at the center and the Anguish crest on the side. "Try it on."

"I haven't completed my tests or graduated, sir."

"You've completed the tests three weeks ago," he said laughing. I raised an eyebrow. "You didn't think we honestly made Anguishes do that many exams, did you? Every time you maxed one, we gave you the next two. Then doubled it the next time, until eventually, we ran out of tests." He shrugged his shoulders.

"My final exam was what exactly, sir?"

"We were brainstorming what test to give you since you had passed all of them with flying colors, but couldn't come up with anything. And then the situation with the commanders this afternoon came up and how you were willing to sacrifice yourself for them. Then again, just now, when the problem with your father arose and your willingness to stop your father's madness is enough proof that you are Anguish."

"I see, sir."

"You may put it on now," he said grinning. I slipped the ring on to my finger and it was the perfect fit.

"Congratulations, Commander Armistice." I looked at him. To be Anguish was one thing, but to be in a position of leadership was astounding.

"Commander?"

"Yes, you have earned your place amongst our ranks. You may be a female, but you are one of the strongest Anguishes, both mentally and physically, we've had in a long while. We have placed you over Wolverine Regiment." The Wolverines were known for being rambunctious and wild. They didn't take well to leadership or orders. No wonder they wanted me as a commander. Fantastic.

"Are you sure you want me to take over such a position? After all, I am a Nevan, sir."

"The council and I have thought long and hard. We voted unanimously that you were the right person for the job."

"I am honored, sir." All heads in the room nodded.

"Now, back to the task at hand. We may be Anguish but we believe peace goes a lot farther."

"As do I, sir."

"Good. You have one day to come up with a plan, and 12 hours from then to execute your plan. That won't be a problem, will it?"

"Consider it done, sir."

Chapter Fourteen
Cold Shower

I was dismissed from the room with shaky legs. I made my way into the hallway and leaned against the wall. I had twenty-four hours to come up with a strategic plan to handle my father. Could I actually go through with my plan? He was, after all, my father.

"Armistice," I looked up to see Taylor walking towards me. "You okay?" I shrugged my shoulders. "Come with me." He offered me his hand and I slowly took it. I didn't want him to be the one to comfort me, but now, I needed someone. His hand was warm and gentle. He led me down the corridor and to a door. The door opened and the smell of him surrounded me. It was his room. My heart began to race. He led me into the room and the door closed behind us.

He led me over to the bed, which was twice the size of mine. We sat down and I looked around his room. He kept his room simple, clean, and organized. Three things I could appreciate. He rubbed the palm of my hand. I looked down and stared at our hands. My tan skin made his olive skin stand out more. He continued rubbing the palm of my hand. I could do nothing but stare at his fingers. I knew it was wrong to be in his room.

"I see that you are one of us, now," he was staring at my ring. "Apparently." He smiled and looked at me.

"You deserve it."

"I don't know about that," I said with a sigh.

"You have top marks in all of your classes. Excel at hand to hand combat. And, your team always wins the challenges thanks to your strategic battle plans. I'd say you deserve to be here, Kaitlyn." I looked at him. "What," he asked laughing. "You called me Kaitlyn, but I must remind you, I'm 'Armistice' to you."

"Well, that is what I would call you if you were still under my command; however, you are now my colleague."

"I see." He was still rubbing the palm of my hand. He slowly brought it up to his lips and kissed the top of my hand gently. "There's something about you."

"Nick, don't."

"I mean it." I rolled my eyes.

"Okay, then what about me?" I was becoming agitated.

"Everything." He released my hand. Next thing I knew, his lips were on mine. He placed a hand on the back of my neck to pull me closer to him and wrapped an arm around me. I needed to leave. I began to move away but he just held me in place. His hands began to roam the edge of my waistline. I slowly grabbed his hands and moved them back on to my sides.

"Kaitlyn," he moaned. "I need you." I was certain I knew what he was implying and definitely didn't want that to happen.

"I need to leave. Let me out." He just kept trying to touch me and move his hands lower. "Now, Nick!"

"Kaitlyn, come on," he began pushing me against the wall. I banged against his door.

"Let me out," I screamed. He wasn't moving. I was thankful when there was a knock at the door and he broke away from me.

Chapter Fifteen
And…it begins

"Who is it," Nick shouted.

"It's Eric." It was Commander Trials and he did not sound happy. "Please tell your visitor that Wolverine Regiment awaits."

"Stand guard for a moment, Eric."

"Hurry up," he snapped. Nick looked at me.

"Wolverine Regiment," he grinned.

"It would seem." I quickly moved away from him. I walked over to his mirror and began fixing myself so that I would be presentable. Nick watched me like I was his prey. "Do I look okay?"

"Look like an Anguish," he said, rolling his eyes.

"Thank you, I think." I walked over to the door.

"Eric," Nick called out.

"You are safe," he replied. Nick opened the door and Eric was standing across from the door. He didn't look happy. "Hello, Armistice."

"Commander Trials," I said nodding my head in acknowledgment. I looked over at Nick, who was grinning. "Give me a break," I growled. "You act like you were actually doing that."

"That? Are you referring to 'sex'?" He asked with a grin.

"When you put it like that, it seems vulgar, but yes. We weren't doing that, so stop looking like a youngling who has been caught with his pants down. I assure you, Commander Trials, we were not doing that." My blood was boiling. Nick was an absolute beast. He didn't know the meaning of 'gentleman'.

Commander Trials nodded his head and I began walking down the hallway towards the Regiment corridors. Both, Nick and Commander Trials followed me. I quickly stopped.

"What," Nick asked looking around.

"I need my boots," they both looked down. We ended up swinging by my room and grabbing my boots.

"This should be interesting," I heard Commander Trials whisper. Nick laughed but said nothing. We finally arrived at Wolverine Regiment and I threw open the doors. The room fell silent, as I walked into the center of the mat.

"Commander Armistice," Commander Trials shouted. Nick quickly looked at Commander Trials and then at me. He wasn't expecting that. I avoided looking at him, because I knew he would want answers.

"If you don't think you can follow orders from a female, you have two choices. One, you walk out those doors. Two, you man up and we take it to the mat. If I win, I stay as your commanding officer. If I lose, I walk away." They seemed surprised by my words. "You have to the count of three to make your decision. One!" No one moved. "Two!" Two males made their way to the door but were quickly turned around by Commander Trials. "Three!" One male of Asian descent stepped on to the mat.

"You have the nerve to challenge a superior officer?" Commander Trials began walking to the mat. I turned to him and grinned.

"It's okay." He stopped walking.

"It's your death wish," Commander Trials said pointing at the male who stood a few feet from me. "After Commander Armistice deals with you, you will have to deal with me." I chuckled to myself because I had never heard Commander Trials raise his voice. I turned and faced the male who clearly outweighed me by fifty plus pounds. He wore his black hair short. He was built very much like Matthews.

"Still wish to challenge me," I asked him. He smirked and nodded. "You will hold your end of the deal?"

"I am a man of my word."

"Ma'am," Commander Trials added. "You will add 'ma'am' to the end of your sentences when addressing a commanding officer."

"I am a man of my word… ma'am."

"Good then," I extended my hand and we shook. "You have one minute to take me down, when Commander Trials gives the word." He nodded his head. "What's your name?"

"Xi Chan, ma'am." I smiled and walked to the edge of the mat. I took off my boots and placed them next to the mat. Pulled my shirt over my head and catcalls filled the room.

"Silence," Commander Trials shouted. The room fell quiet. I turned and faced Chan. He didn't even bother a battle stance. Commander Trials was already on the mat.

"Ready," Commander Trials asked both of us and we both nodded. "Fight!" He quickly backed off the mat. Chan stood in place and the crowd laughed. I grinned.

"Scared?" He threw his head back and laughed. I took the opportunity to run at him full speed. The room filled with uproar. Some were cheering, others protesting. I jumped into the air, wrapped my legs around his neck, twisted around to his back and pulled us both down to the mat. I held his neck in place with my legs. This had become my fighting technique against almost every person I fought. I knew I would never win a fight against any of them by doing hand to hand combat. So, I learned I stuck with this technique and had it down to an art.

Just like all the others had done, Chan tried lifting me up. I arched my back and tightened my legs. He began frantically trying to rip my legs from him. I refused to let go. His movements began to slow down. I could tell he was at the point of passing out.

"Time!" Commander Trials shouted and I released Chan. He rolled on to his side and coughed. I stood up and looked down at him. He looked up at me and I offered my hand to him with a smile. He reluctantly took it and I pulled him to his feet. The room stood and cheered.

"I am humbled, ma'am," Chan said bowing his head. I bowed my head.

"There is no need to feel like that. We are all human." He looked at me and smiled. Chan took his seat where he had been sitting previously. "Anyone else?" I looked around the room and no one moved. The two males, who had attempted to leave the room, were sitting back in their seats. "I know that me being here has caused a lot of changes within the walls of Anguish. For that, I am sorry. It was never my intent. I hope that over time I can earn your trust as a leader and a comrade in arms. I will always be here to take your words and feelings into consideration, so do not hesitate to come to me. When we speak, we are speaking as equals. I will never ask any of you to do anything that I, myself, would not do. If there ever comes a time in which we must go to war, I will be the first one in and I will not leave until all of you are out."

Chan rose from his seat and stood at attention. Shortly, the room followed suit. He saluted me, as did the rest. At that moment, I was humbled. I saluted them and they dropped their arms down to their side.

"Wolverine Regiment's Commander! Commander Armistice!" Chan shouted. His words echoed throughout the room. The room filled with the Wolverine chant.

"Seems you made quite the impression," Commander Trials said standing next to me. I glanced at him and he was smiling. "Maybe the Wolverines can be tamed after all."

"Wild animals are not meant to be tamed, they are meant to run free," I whispered. I winked and turned my attention back to my new regiment. "You are dismissed, until after dinner. Once you finish dinner, meet me here. We have our first mission!" The room filled with the Wolverine battle cry. I had never seen males so excited in my entire life. "Dismissed!"

Chapter Sixteen
True Colors

They began filing out of the room. All of them discussing what could possibly be the mission. My task wasn't going to be an easy one, but it was an inevitable one. I had suspected when my father sent me to the academy that he did not plan on keeping the peace treaty. Over the years, he had turned into a man that I did not recognize. He executed those who did not agree with him on broadcast for all of Neva to see. And, he often resorted to physical violence towards my mother and me. I was too weak then to do anything, but not now. I wasn't going to stand by and let him kill more innocent people. These people did nothing to him and he murdered them in cold blood. He would have to answer for his crimes.

"Mission," Nick asked breaking me of the spell I was in.

"Yes," I began heading towards the door; Nick and Commander Trials both followed me.

"What mission?" I didn't answer just continued walking out the door and down the hallway. "What mission, Kaitlyn?" I stopped walking and faced them.

"A mission to stop my father." Nick's eyes were wide.

"Father," Nick asked.

"Yes, my father." I let out the breath that I had been holding. "I am not just a Nevan, I am the daughter of the Nevan emperor."

"Holy shit," Nick said. "A princess? What the hell are you doing here?"

"I was the bargaining chip for a peace treaty. Your canton needed a female volunteer and our canton needed a peace treaty."

"Some peace treaty," Nick said rolling his eyes.

"I know."

"Does your father wish for your return," Commander Trials asked in a whisper.

"I do not think he cares if I am on this side of the wall. If I die, then he can blame Lynx for my death."

"What is your plan?" Nick asked crossing his arms.

"I can handle myself."

"Doesn't mean you don't need some assistance."

"He is right. We can help you," Commander Trials added.

"I appreciate it, but this is something I need to do with my regiment. When we get back, we can go out and celebrate," I said laughing.

"This isn't funny, Kaitlyn. Your father will kill you," Commander Trials said. I hadn't thought about that option.

"That's been his game plan all along," I shrugged my shoulders. "He knew he planned on breaking the treaty long before he sent me. After all, why would he send the next in line to the throne?" I winked and went back to walking down the hallway towards the dining hall.

Nick complained the entire time about how it was a bad idea for me to go without him and his regiment. Once we were sitting at the table, he continued his argument as to why I needed them. The rest of the table listened in to his protest. It was going to be a long night.

"Wait," Conner said shaking his head, "Father? Armistice, your dad is Emperor Brock Gable?" I shrugged my shoulders and he laughed. "Holy shit!"

"Keep it down," Commander Trials said elbowing Conner in the stomach.

"That makes you the princess of Neva," Conner whispered. They were all staring at me. I rolled my eyes and went back to eating. Conner laughed again. "You have the hots for a princess, Nick!" Nick glared at him, but Conner just continued laughing.

"What's your plan," Matthews asked, "You know he won't let you capture him."

"I know," I took a sip of my water.

"Well, what is your plan?" Kurtz asked. I looked up to find all of them staring at me.

"I plan on killing him."

"Whoa, she didn't even bat an eyelash," Conner said pointing at me. "She's brutal." He threw his head back and laughed.

"I think I'm in love," Kurtz said laughing. The rest of the table laughed with him. I looked down at my watch.

"If you will excuse me, I have a meeting to get to." I quickly made my departure before any of them could protest.

I walked into the Wolverine Regiment and the room fell silent. I gestured for all of them to follow me. I led them out the door, through the academy and to the gathering hall. They filed in and took a seat. I closed the door and made my way to the front. I hopped up on stage and sat on the edge.

"The mission I am about to propose must be one carried out in stealth. We cannot let anyone know what the plan is, our timeline, or our objective. Understood?"

"Yes, ma'am," they said in unison.

"But before the mission takes place, I need you all to know a key factor before deciding whether you wish to accept this mission," I took a deep breath. "I am Kaitlyn Neva Armistice Gable. I am Emperor Gable's daughter." The room fell into shock, followed by roaring chaos.

"Silence," Chan shouted and the room fell silent. "You are the princess, ma'am." It sounded like a question, but somehow, I knew it was a statement. I smiled and nodded my head. "This mission is against your father, ma'am?"

"I am aware. My father has become more and more of a madman over the years. Killing innocent people goes against everything for which the Nevan existence stood for. He wanted a war, so now we're bringing the war to him." The room filled with cheers.

"What is your plan, ma'am," a guy with dark skin and short hair asked from the front row. I couldn't help but smile.

"Gather around," they quickly gathered around me and I shared my plan. They seemed shocked that I had come up with such an elaborate plan. I had every detail covered. Any question they asked, I had an answer.

"When do we leave, ma'am?" Someone asked from the back. "I was given 24 hours to come up with a plan and 12 hours from then to execute the plan," I looked around the room, "Anyone need a few hours of sleep?" They all shook their head no. "Good, then we leave in an hour."

"Wolverines!" The battle cry and cheers began. Wolverines were known for being rebels but they were rebels with heart. "Meet me at the Guardian Gate in an hour," I hopped off the stage and made my way out the room. Nick was leaned against the wall with his arms crossed. I frowned. "Checking up on me?"

"Concerned," he pushed away from the wall. "Can we talk?"

"You can have my attention for 45 minutes."

"Then what?" I grinned and he rolled his eyes. "You can't be serious. This has 'bad idea' written all over it."

"Why do you not have faith in me?" He just looked at me and said nothing. He followed me down the hallway and we walked in silence. I reached my destination and I knocked on the War Advisor's door.

"Who is it?"

"Armistice, sir."

"Enter." The door opened and I stepped through. "Oh, Taylor, just the man I wanted to see. Come in as well." Nick stepped in with me. The door closed behind us. "What can I do for you?"

"I have come up with a plan and plan on leaving to execute it in an hour, sir." Nick quickly looked at me.

"You can't be serious. You are a new commander and a new commander to that regiment. You guys have never even done a battle simulation! You would be crazy to go on a mission with no experience with them," he shouted. I rolled my eyes.

"Thanks for your faith in me," I looked back at War Advisor Jennings. "We need the Lynx train for the mission. Can you coordinate a train to go to Neva at 2100, sir?"

"Of course."

"And we will need weapons and supplies, sir."

"The Guardian Gate is at your disposal."

"This is a stupid ass idea! Why would you send a female in there?" I looked at Nick then back at War Advisor Jennings, who was laughing

"Always a hot head," War Advisor Jennings sat up in his chair. "I understand your frustrations. However, she is the one with the most knowledge on the Nevan Canton. Sending anyone else would be sending them in blind. I have my reasons."

"Send my regiment with her," Nick blurted.

"She isn't as weak as you may think she is," War Advisor Jennings laughed.

"I just feel that the mission would go more smoothly if I was there."

"I wouldn't," War Advisor Jennings said coolly. "I need you on this side of the wall in case there is an attack."

"You have other commanders," Nick pointed out.

"My answer is final." Nick threw a chair at the wall.

"This is bullshit!"

"Nick, you're acting like a child," I finally said. He stopped and looked at me.

"And you think running off to execute a plan against your own father is acting any better?" He had a valid point.

"I have seen a lot of death in my time," I whispered. Those words had gathered their attention. "Neva is not as peaceful as it may seem. My father's army runs wild following his orders. The Nevan are not safe. They need to be safe again. Once he is gone, my mother will step up to the throne and Neva will once again have peace. No one can get close enough to him to kill him. I am the only one he will allow to get that close."

"She is the perfect person for the mission," War Advisor Jennings said.

"I still don't like this and I refuse to be around when you decide to send a female in to do a male's job," Nick stormed out of the room. I looked at War Advisor Jennings.

"I need one more favor, sir."

"Anything," he said.

"I need clothes other than academy clothes, sir."

"Anything specific?"

"A dress, long, light, and light colored with shoes and undergarments. And, light colored makeup, sir."

"It will be delivered to your room within fifteen minutes. Anything else?"

"A garter to hold a knife." He nodded his head. "Thank you, sir," I turned to leave the room.

"Good luck." I looked over my shoulder.

"Thank you, sir." I left the room, expecting for Nick to be leaned against the wall, but he wasn't. I was glad he wasn't there, because I think I would have lost it on him. He had said some chauvinistic things, and didn't seemed phased by saying them in front of me.

Chapter Seventeen
A Train to Catch

I made my way to my room and began preparing for the
mission. As promised, the articles of clothing were delivered
on time. I quickly changed in to them and slipped the garter
up my leg. It was a snug fit, but I was still able to move. I fixed
my hair up eloquently. After I applied makeup, I stared at
myself in the mirror. I barely recognized myself. It seemed
like so long ago since I had seen this face in the mirror. I was
once a timid female living in a world of false hope. Now, I had
been born again into a strong willed being who would stop at
nothing to see justice to the Nevan people.

I opened the door and stepped out. The room fell silent as
everyone looked at me. I said nothing, only walked past them
and up the stairs to the Guardian Gate. The Guardian Gate
was where all weapons were kept. The Wolverines were
already there. They all turned and looked at me.

"Wow," Chan said and quickly cleared his throat. "Ma'am."

"Chan," I said and walked to the front. The Guardian Gate
Officer looked me over from head to toe. "Commander
Kaitlyn Armistice here to sign out weapons."

"Yes, ma'am." The Wolverines entered the gate and began
choosing weapons. I knew that the guards wouldn't search
me, but I couldn't just blatantly carry a weapon through the
front doors; so I selected a knife and lifted my dress up high
enough to secure it. I straightened my dress out and moved
around to see if it needed adjusting. It was awkward but not
unbearable.

I exited the Guardian Gate and most of the Wolverines were
already geared up. The final few came out and now they were
all ready.

"Looks like we have a train to catch."

Chapter Eighteen
Shadows in the Night

At the train depot, we discussed the mission one more time for clarification. Then I split them into four squads. They loaded on the back three cars of the train and I took my place in the first car. The train ride seemed much like the first time I rode it. It seemed like I'd never reach my destination.

When there was light at the end of the tunnel, I knew the mission was about to take place. I took a deep breath, said a prayer to the Armistice Angel, and stood at the doors.

"Remember, I'm the first one in and..."

"The last one out, ma'am," they said in unison. They were all grinning. I nodded my head in approval and made my way to the exit. The doors opened and the train employees were surprised.

"Princess," they said bowing.

"Hello," I said sweetly and stepped off the train.

"Shall we call a car for you," one of the females asked.

"No," I said laughing, "that won't be necessary. I prefer to walk." I looked up at the royal house and back at the employees. "Would you be so kind as to gather my things off the train?"

"Of course, princess," the same female said. They scurried onto the train. I knew they wouldn't be coming back out, because they were being tied up and stuffed in closets.

I walked a few steps towards the road and looked around. The patrol was walking up the hill towards the royal house. They had already patrolled the train depot. I signaled the squads to fall in to position. They flanked around me and scaled the depot's walls. Each building in Neva was a few feet from the ones next to it. It would be easy for them to make it through Neva unseen by jumping from roof top to roof top.

I walked down the center of the street. Those who noticed me bowed and said a greeting. I smiled and greeted them back. I continued walking the few blocks towards the royal house. I knew my father would be there.

I caught glimpses of the squads moving on top of the roof tops. They were like shadows. A few passersby thought they saw something, but quickly shook the notion from their minds and continued going about their evening.

I was two blocks from the royal house, when a patrol spotted me. They quickly made their way to me and bowed.

"Princess Kaitlyn," the captain of the patrol said, looking as though he had seen a ghost.

"Good evening," I said smiling.

"We did not know you were coming home. We would have sent a car and escorted you." I laughed and shook my head.

"It is unnecessary. I needed the fresh air."

"Then allow us the honor of walking with you." I nodded my head and they walked with me the remaining two blocks. I needed to get rid of them so the squads could get into their positions.

"Before we go inside, I need to compose myself." I sat down on a bench under a broken light. I hoped one of the squads would notice. I noticed movement on the adjacent building. "I am sorry."

"For what, princess," the captain asked smiling; a pair of muffled thumps sounded out and each guard collapsed to the ground, with a large tranquilizer dart sprouting from their chests. Before I could say anything, another squad was already next to me and pulling the guards into the nearby ally.

"Squad one and two, take the tunnel," I said so they could all hear me through the transmitter behind my ear. I pointed at the tunnel to the left of the entrance way. "Three and four, there are patrols every 15 minutes. Make sure none of them make it inside."

"Roger that," each squad leader said. Squad one and two moved into the tunnel. Hopefully, they would remember the details I had given them and be waiting for my mother.

I took a deep breath and made my way up the long set of steps to the gate. The gate was quickly opened and I walked through. Guards came out of the house and ran over to me. They began pulling security and led me inside the house.

"Kaitlyn," my mother said running down the hallway and pulling me into her arms. I embraced her, holding her tightly against me. She stepped back and held my face in her hands. She had tears in her eyes. "I thought you were dead." I laughed.

"Why would I be dead?"

"That is what your father said. That is why we are going to war with Lynx." I could tell by her tone that she believed I had been killed and that was, in fact, the reason the war was beginning.

"I was never hurt by the Lynxans." My mother was in shock. I pulled my mother against me, "Go to the dining room and stay there," I whispered in her ear. She tried to pull away, but I held her in place. "You will be empress," I whispered. She stepped back from me, looked my face over, smiled and nodded.

"This is something that has long been due," she turned to walk to the dining room, "Welcome home, Kaitlyn." She smiled and made her way down the hallway. My mother had endured my father's abuse for years and said nothing, because she didn't have the strength to face him. I would be her strength. I would be our people's strength.

Chapter Nineteen
Family Reunion

On my way up the stairs, I removed the knife and kept it flat against my side. I took a deep breath and reached the top of the stairs. The guards were surprised, and after a moment's hesitation opened the door. I walked into my father's office. The room was filled with advisors and my father. They all looked at me.

"She's alive," one of them whispered.

"I am very much alive," I growled and walked further into the room.

"It is a miracle," my father said coldly.

"A miracle indeed."

"You are just in time to hear my next broadcast. Please, have a seat, daughter," his eyes were piercing. I said nothing, just sat in the chair he offered beside him. I began fiddling with the hem of my dress. He took his seat and gestured for the camera to turn on. The red light turned on. "Attention Lynxans, I have decided to go forward with my plan of war. As you can see, my daughter has returned home. She has narrowly escaped her captors. I am quite pleased by this." He looked at me and grinned. He turned his attention back to the camera. "I am, however, extremely displeased at her treatment. As are my people. Neva will no longer be considered the weakest of the cantons."

"This is ridiculous," I spat. All eyes were on me. My father backhanded me. I grabbed my face as though he had pained me, but the truth was, after all the hand to hand training I'd endured, his strike was like a child's. I looked up at him.

"You will not speak unless you are given permission," he growled.

"You are no Nevan! Nevans are peaceful. They do not wish this," he struck me again. This time I didn't even pretend that it hurt, simply smirked. "You will turn yourself over to the Lynxan government."

"Silly child," my father said laughing. "I will never surrender!"

"Then you will die." He laughed more. "I beg of you, as your daughter, surrender so that you can live out your life in a prison, instead of facing a gruesome death."

"I will remain emperor. No one can touch me," he extended his arms out. "I am a god!"

"Even gods die." I spat.

"Not this one. I shall continue to purge those who should perish and there will be no one to stop me."

"End this madness."

"Or what?"

"Or I will have to end your life." he laughed at my words. "I dare you, pathetic daughter. I will end your life first," he drew a pistol from under his desk, pointed it at my chest and thumbed the hammer back. A smug grin covered his face. Every soul in the room was stunned to inaction, frozen in place.

"Is this how you want it?" I asked.

"Yes," he said grinning. He lifted the gun toward my head.

"So be it." In a silvery blur of motion, my blade opened his throat. The pistol fired, his hand jerking with the violence of my attack. My father gripped his throat trying desperately to staunch the bleeding, but it continued to spurt between his clutched fingers. Blood spray coated my dress and face in a fine mist. Soon, he fell back in his chair and his throat rattled its last breath. His life was gone.

"Put the camera on me," I growled and the camera turned toward my face. "I am Princess Kaitlyn. I can only offer my deepest condolences for the Nevan and Lynxan lives that have been lost to my father's madness. To the Lynxan government, you have the Nevans' condolences for the loss of your train employees who were massacred recently. We will do everything in our power to compensate those families who lost loved ones. To the Nevan people, you are once again safe and can now live your lives peacefully. For Empress Gazelle, my mother, will now take my father's place upon the throne. May peace be with us all." I signaled for the camera to be shut off. The camera's red light blinked off and the room stared at me.

"He was your father," one of them finally stammered. I looked at my father's dead body and turned back to the man. "He was a madman. And he needed to be stopped. If you wish to carry on his legacy, tell me now, so I can end your life." He shook his head.

"No, of course not princess," he lowered his head. "I want the Nevan way of life back."

"Then we will get along just fine. Now, if you would, please leave until my mother calls upon you." They bowed their heads and to their leave. I grabbed my father's body and carried it to the top of the stairs. I threw him over the edge and his body hit with a wet splat. The guards at the bottom looked up at me with horror on their faces. "Clean it up, please."

"Yes, princess." They said and began disposing of my father's body. I walked down the stairs and out into the hall way. I found my mother in the dining room surrounded by squads one and two. Guards' bodies lay on the floor. My mother turned and looked at me. Her face instantly turned pale.

"Oh my god, Kaitlyn," she screamed. She ran over to me and looked me over.

"I am fine, mother," I said laughing. "He is gone. He will never again hurt you." She looked at me and burst into tears. I held her against me and didn't let go until the last tear left her eyes.

"You are something special, Kaitlyn." I smiled and looked at my squads.

"Will you be safe here?" Concern had slowly been swelling inside me.

"Of course," she said laughing. "The Nevan Rebels are already at the gate waiting to come to my aid."

"Good. I do not trust the Nevan military or the guards, at the moment." She nodded her head. "I will come back often."

"You are not staying?"

"No. I found a place I fit in," she smiled and hugged me.

"I am so proud of you, Kaitlyn. You must come visit me at least once a week, you hear?" I laughed and nodded my head.

"Of course, mother."

"I am proud of the woman you have become," she moved my hair out of my face and smiled. "You will call me often." I laughed.

"Mother, I will talk and see you frequently."

"You had better or I will be on a train." We laughed and held each other once more. My mother now had the strength she needed to stand up for herself. I could already hear it in her voice. She was free of my father and the fear for her life had been lifted. She was ready to rule her people.

"I will talk with the rebel leader before I leave and ensure they know that they must protect you with their lives," she nodded her head. "If you feel that something isn't right, you are to hide in the tunnel and call me." She laughed and rolled her eyes. "What?"

"Now who sounds like the mother?" She asked. I laughed.

"I only want you safe. Our people need you." She smiled and pulled me against her. "Mother, I really must be going," I said laughing.

"Okay. Okay," she looked at me with tears in her eyes.

"Mother, you have to be strong. No more crying. I will be back in a few days to visit." She held back the tears and nodded her head. "I love you."

"I love you too." A tear slid down her face.

"Let's go," I said, walking out the door with the two squads in tow. We reached the gate and the rebels were waiting like my mother had said.

"Just say the word," Chan said over the radio. I could see the other two squads on the roof top with their weapons pointed at the crowd of rebels.

"Hold your fire for now." I opened the gate and much to my surprise the crowd bowed to me. They stood tall once more.

"Princess Kaitlyn, it is an honor to see you again." Maximus Trent said approaching me. Squad one and squad two pointed their weapons at him, which caused the rebels to point theirs at us. "It is okay," Maximus said to his people. They lowered their weapons, so I gestured for my squads to do the same. They slowly did.

Maximus Trent was once my father's war advisor, but when my father began ordering his men to massacre his own people, Maximus refused. My father tried to have him executed, but Maximus escaped. He hadn't been seen for almost a year.

"Maximus, I need your word that you'll protect my mother."

"I will give my last breath," he said placing his fist on his heart.

"Good, because you better be dead if something happens to her." Maximus laughed and I raised an eyebrow.

"You are all grown up, princess. You are no longer the timid youngling I knew. You are a warrior."

"She is Anguish," Grady said proudly from behind me.

"Ah. You were the female volunteer sent to Lynx," he nodded his head at the thought. "How ironic that your father sent you there to learn the Anguish ways and you would use the Anguish ways to end his life." The crowd laughed. "It appears you sit on the fence."

"I was born a Nevan and will always be Nevan. But I have found my calling as Anguish."

"And when it is time to rule our people?" I couldn't help but grin.

"Then I suggest you be ready to guard me." He laughed and offered his hand. I took it and he shook it firmly.

"I would be honored to guard you when you are empress. My men will escort you and your," he looked at my squad, and then back at me, "men to the train depot."

"Unnecessary," I pointed at the other two squads on the roof tops, who still had their weapons pointed. Maximus looked and laughed.

"I see you came with backup."

"Never leave home without it," I smiled and began walking through the crowd with the squads following behind me.

"You are a true Nevan, Kaitlyn. The Nevans and Anguish are lucky to have you on both sides," I looked over my shoulder and smiled.

"Until we meet again, take care of yourself, Neva, and my mother." He nodded his head and I approached one of my buildings.

"Need help, ma'am?" Julian asked standing next to me. I laughed and shook my head. I kicked off my shoes and tossed them into a nearby trash bin. Then I ran full speed at the building and scaled it. Soon squad one and two were on the roof.

"Shall we go home?" I asked looking around at them. They answered me with the Wolverine chant. I could only smile. We ran and jumped from roof top to roof top. The cool wind whipped across my face and through my hair as I ran. We didn't stop running until we reached the train. The train employees were already awake and waiting for us.

"Princess," the male employee said frowning.

"I apologize," I couldn't help but laugh, "however, if I had told you that I planned on killing my father, would you have let me by with my regiment?"

"Yes," the female said. I was thrown off by her words. "He was a tyrant."

"Maria," the male said.

"He is dead. You can speak freely once more," I smirked and stepped onto the train. The regiment followed behind me and we took our seats. The train doors closed and we all let out a breath. "Well, that was fun." The train filled with laughter and cheers.

Chapter Twenty
Walls Crumble

The train doors opened and I allowed for all my regiment to get off first. I stepped off expecting to see Nick, but he wasn't there. I looked around just to be sure that he wasn't.

"He's busy pouting in his room, Kaitlyn," Commander Trials said approaching me. I laughed. "I see you made it back in one piece."

"Mostly," I lifted my dress up exposing my bare toes and wiggled them. He laughed.

"If all you lost on a mission was shoes then I would say your mission was a success," he smiled.

"It was very much a success," I smiled, "and because of the Wolverines," I shouted. They stopped walking and looked at me. "I know it wasn't a war, but you guys followed every order and we all came back together." They thrust their weapons into the air and cheered.

After the cheering died down, we all began walking back to the academy. Commander Trials and I small talked about the building, its history. The doors opened and they began filing in. I stopped and looked at Commander Trials.

"May I ask a favor of you," I asked facing him.

"Of course," he said smiling. I lifted my arm and showed him where my father had shot me. Dismay covered his face. "We need to get you to the infirmary."

"No, that's not necessary."

"They can have you healed within the hour."

"I just need you to remove it and stitch me back up; the less people who know about this the better."

"Okay," he said without arguing with me any further. We walked inside and waited for the elevator. It arrived shortly after and we were on our way down into the compound. We reached the bottom. "Meet me in the conference room. I will run to my room and grab an aid kit."

"Thank you, Commander Trials." He nodded his head.
"I know you would do the same," he smiled and stepped off
the elevator. I stepped off and swiftly made my way down the
halls, cautious not to run into anyone. I made it to the
conference room and shut the door. My side was killing me,
but I knew I didn't have any internal damage. At least I hoped
not.

The door to the conference room opened and Commander
Trials walked in. He closed the door and locked it. He walked
over to me and spread the aid kit's contents on to the table. He
had even brought an ultrasound tablet. I wasn't even going to
ask where he got that from. I slipped my arms through the
arm holes of my dress and lowered it to my waist. I turned so
that he could reach my wound easily. I raised my arm and
placed it on top of my head.

"This is going to hurt," he took a deep breath. "I could go get
some medicine."

"No," I said shaking my head. "I will be fine." I smiled and
looked at the wall in front of me. Commander Trials leaned
closer to me and the smell of him filled my nose. He had a
pleasant smell. Suddenly, he poured something cold on me. I
bit back a scream. Next, he began digging around inside the
hole for the lodged bullet. After a few minutes, he withdrew
the tool and I heard a clank. I looked down at the table and the
bullet was in the tin cup.

"Now the fun part," he said grabbing the sutures. "But first,"
he put them back down, "we need to make sure you are okay
on the inside." He picked up the ultrasound tablet and began
scanning me. "All appears to be normal." He set it down and
grabbed the sutures once more. He worked his magic and I
did my best not to cry like a child. You would think after
everything I had gone through at the academy that my body
would be tougher. "All done."

"Thank you." I looked down and examined his work. It
looked like a doctor had done it.

"I have studied medicine," he said. He must have noticed the look on my face.

"You do nice work, doc." He smiled, began cleaning up. I slipped my arms back through the dress and put it back in place.

"Did you want to keep the bullet?" I looked down at the bullet.

"Yes," I picked it up and placed it in the palm of my hand. The reality hit that my father would have killed me, if I had not killed him first. Emotions tore through me. I wasn't sure if I was sad or angry.

"Everything happens for a reason," I looked up and Commander Trials was looking at me with compassion.

"That it does." I smiled and helped him finish cleaning up the rest. We walked through the hallway and stopped at the trash bins. Once we were done there, Commander Trials walked me to the sleeping bay to ensure that I made it there without passing out along the way. We entered the sleeping bay. All eyes were on us as we entered. It was lights out, but due to all the news and excitement I'm sure they were given leeway. Nick was in the back of the room. His facial expression was hard to read. It was a cross between anger and disgust.

"Armistice, are you alright?" Kurtz said running over to me.

"I am fine," I said laughing as he examined me. "The blood isn't mine." I looked up in time to see Nick storm out of the room.

"Good. Good."

"She needs to get cleaned up," Commander Trials said reminding Kurtz that he was standing there.

"Of course," Kurtz faced the room. "Make room for Commander Armistice!" He looked over his shoulder and winked. Apparently, everyone knew of my new position.

"Make room for our Commander," Chan shouted. I hadn't even noticed the Wolverine Regiment in the room. This was not common to see Regiments in a trainees' area.

The Wolverine Regiment was once again doing their battle cry. I was beginning to get used to it. I didn't bother hiding my smile as I walked next to Commander Trials. He walked me to my room.

"Your decision was not an easy one, but you did well," he whispered. Then he turned and walked off.

I entered my room. I placed the bullet on my desk and grabbed my clothes. As I made my way to the bathing quarters, many stopped me to congratulate me on my promotion and on my success in killing my father. I thanked them and continued walking.

Once I was in the bathing quarters, I locked the door and undressed. I looked at myself in the mirror. And I looked like a train wreck. My face was covered in my father's blood and my hair was matted and ragged. I released my hair from the bobby pins and it hung down to my shoulders.

I started the water and stepped inside. I began washing up and my feet were soon submerged in a pool of blood. I stared at my feet and soon the tears began to fall. I knew no one could see me, but it didn't matter. I placed the water on my face and cried. For the first time in years, I cried without the walls of strength holding them back.

I don't know how long I cried for, but when the water began to turn cold I snapped out of it and began to wash myself again. I scrubbed and scrubbed making sure there was no trace of blood on me. I stepped out and checked the full-length mirror to ensure the blood was all gone. When it finally was I turned off the water and exited.

I felt refreshed, but still the pain of killing my father tore at me. I quickly dressed and made my way back to my room. I was exhausted from the day's events and just wanted to rest; however, cheering kept me awake. After tossing and turning for a few minutes, I decided to investigate the excitement. I threw on my pants and boots, and then made my way through the halls following the sounds of celebration.

I finally found everyone in the gathering hall. On the screen was me slitting my father's throat. The video clip kept rewinding and playing again. I watch the terror in my father's eyes as I took his life. I felt my stomach churning.

"Commander Armistice," someone shouted and everyone turned in my direction. I smiled politely and showed no emotion of how the video was affecting me. Deep down, I wanted to run from the room and puke. I was a murderer. My father's murderer.

"Commander Armistice, front and center," I heard the War Advisor call out from the front of the room. The crowd parted, as I made my way to the front. Most congratulated me and patted me on the back. The war council were all standing in the front and smiling. "You did well, Commander Armistice."

"Thank you, sir."

"We never got to pin you properly," he said holding out his hand to Councilman Mill. Councilman Mill placed a commander rank in War Advisor Jennings hand. War Advisor Jennings faced me and pinned me with the rank of commander. "Today, you earned this."

"Thank you, sir," he smiled and removed his hand from the rank. The rank was now pinned to my collar for all to see. It should have been an honor, but it was a blood token. I had killed my own father to earn it.

I looked up and the video was still playing over and over. I couldn't take my eyes off the screen. It was a nightmare; yet, reality. I felt my emotions ready to erupt so I tore my gaze from the screen and looked at War Advisor Jennings.

"Anything else, sir?"

"No," he smiled, "that will be all." I nodded my head and made my way back through the crowd. I received more 'congratulations' and pats as I made my way out the door. Once in the hallway, I didn't bother walking, I ran. I ran through the halls.

"Kaitlyn," Commander Trials called out as I blazed passed him. I didn't bother to stop, I just ran. I didn't stop until I made it to the restroom, through the door, and into the stall. Everything I had eaten in the past 24 hours came back up. The video was now playing over and over in my mind. I shouldn't be so emotional. After all, he had intended to kill me first. I began questioning everything. Would I feel just as horrible if I had killed someone else? Could I do it again, or would this moment forever haunt me?

I sat on the floor with my back against the wall of the stall. I closed my eyes and attempted to drift myself into a state of Nevan peace, a quality ingrained in our people. I needed to find peace within myself, even if it was only for a little while. I was a Nevan. I wasn't born to be a killer. I was born to live in harmony and one day watch over all of Neva. No, my fate was written. I was meant to be here. I was meant to kill my father. Now, I just needed to wait for the next page of my book to be written.

PART TWO
War to Anguish

Anguish Transformations

The next morning, I woke up feeling like a train had run me over and then backed up over me. I slowly made my way to the mirror. My hair looked like a flock of birds had taken up residence in it. My eyes were bloodshot. I looked like death. Not even warmed over. Just death.

Last night had been bot, physically and mentally draining. It seemed like all the tears I had held in my whole life had come pouring out last night. No matter how hard I tried to think of how my decision had been justified, I couldn't help but feel guilty for ending a life. The fact it was my father's life just made it seem even more immoral. I just wanted to stay in bed all day and swim in self-pity. However, I knew I had a duty and responsibilities to my new regiment, the Wolverines. No matter how large a toll last night took on me, I'd have to suck it up and move on. After all, death was inevitable for us all.

The sound of everyone stirring brought me back to the world around me. They were all preparing for receiving their graduation orders and their duty orders. If last night's events hadn't taken place, then I would be waiting to hear my fate; however, my fate had already been decided.

Chapter One
New Boots to Fill

Anguish was even louder than usual. I opened the dining hall doors and the sound of cheering filled my ears. Everyone within was cheering amongst themselves. Most them were holding their orders, laughing, and having the time of their lives. I closed the doors and began heading back to my room. I was in no mood for celebration or social festivities.

Chan, Grady, and Commander Trials were all outside my door. They were all holding boxes. Chan noticed me first and brought everyone else's attention towards me. Commander Trials smiled, as I approached.

"Kaitlyn," he said smoothly.

"Commander Trials," I said acknowledging him.

"Eric," he said correcting me. I nodded my head.

"Good morning, Eric. To what do I owe the pleasure?" He laughed.

"We are here to help you move your belongings to the Commander Corridor." I nodded my head.

"I see. I don't have much, so I won't require assistance," I turned to Chan and Grady. "Tell the Wolverines that I'd like them standing outside their rooms at 0900 hours."

"Yes, ma'am," Grady said.

"You may go," I said. They stood at attention, and then took their leave.

"You alright," Eric asked. I smiled and opened my door.

"I am fine. How are you?" He laughed.

"I'm fine, but then again, I'm not the one who had a rough night." I froze in place. "Kaitlyn?" I turned and looked at him. "Are you okay? I didn't mean to upset you. Sometimes I forget that there are social lines that aren't to be crossed." I laughed to play off the emotional whirlpool within me.

"Relax," I smiled and grabbed a box from him. I began placing my belongings into it.

"Anything I can help with?" I shook my head and continued. As I had told them, I didn't have much so I was done in less than five minutes. "All done?"

"So, it would appear," I said looking around the room one last time. I spotted the distorted bullet that Eric had retrieved from my side. I walked over to the desk and placed the bullet into my pocket.

"How's the wound?"

"Healing nicely, thanks to you." I grabbed the box and gestured for Eric to leave the room. We stepped out and I looked back one last time. This insignificant, plain room had turned into a home.

"You ready to go?" I turned away from the room and nodded. There wasn't any choice in the matter, so there was no need to reminisce about my time within those walls.

Eric tried to help me unpack, but thankfully his watch went off, so he had to leave. The door closed behind him and I was finally alone. My new room was three times bigger than my other room. It had both a bathing quarter and a laundry quarter. It was decorated in black and white. Wasn't anything like my room back home, but it would suffice, as my previous room had. I took off the charm Nick had given me and threw it in the trash, along with his shirt. I took the trash bin to the disposal and got rid of both, and then returned to my room. I unpacked faster than I had packed, and was soon sitting on my new bed rolling the bullet between my fingers. My father had every intention of killing me. I was his flesh and blood, but that didn't matter. Either way, one of us was leaving that room as a murderer. I made the right decision. A new mantra was forming in my mind. I made the right decision.

My watch beeped at fifteen 'til 0900 hours. I looked myself over in the mirror, grabbed a script tech pad, and made my way to the Wolverines Regiment. Several new trainees spotted me and quickly moved out of my way. Some whispered 'she's the only female here' when I was a few feet from them, which just made me laugh to myself.

The Wolverines were already in the corridor and standing next to their rooms. The hallway was filled with laughter and talking.

"Attention," someone shouted. The hall instantly fell silent and they all stood at attention.

"You can relax," I said walking towards them. They all relaxed. "I plan on going through each one of your rooms. I am not looking for contraband so I will not report any that I see unless it is life threatening; however, I highly suggest you dispose of it as soon as I am gone. Do you understand?"

"Yes, ma'am!"

"I understand that you are used to certain," I thought long and hard before going on with my words, "ways of doing things. I will do my best to transition you slowly to my ways. Today will not be one of those slow days. Once the day is over, we will have a meeting and speak freely on what we'd like to see differently. "Any questions?"

"No, ma'am!"

"Good. I will go through all your rooms. I will make notes on all your rooms and keep track of the progress of all your rooms. I expect all your rooms to be clean, organized, and kept in a professional manner. This does not mean you can't have personal touches to your rooms. I just ask that they are kept somewhere discrete like your closet, behind a door, in a drawer, and anywhere else that might be out of view when we have a regiment inspection. Understood?"

"Yes, ma'am!"

"Good, let's get this over with so we can get to the real fun," I said laughing. They of course began the Wolverine battle cry. Before long, I would know it by heart.

An hour and a thousand notes later, we were all gathered in the Wolverine training area. I was exhausted from all the room inspections, but I wasn't going to show them that, so I made them hit the mats. They were precise and swift in their movements. I was very impressed.

After the mats, we all went for a run around Lynx. I kept the pace, since they were all much faster than me and proved it by passing me every chance they got. I'd remind them of who was setting the pace, they'd laugh and fall back behind me. After the lap around Lynx perimeter, we headed to the dining hall.

There were still congratulations for me killing my father. I steadied my breathing, smiled and kept walking. I was not ready for any of this. The Wolverines sat in their respective section and I began to head that way.

"Armistice," someone shouted from across the room. I turned my head and saw Matthews standing on top of his chair waving. I could only laugh, because he looked like an absolute fool. I walked over to his table, which happened to be the commander's table. "Saved you a seat," he said smiling.

"Thanks." I sat in the empty seat. The table was awkwardly quiet and they were all staring at me.

"So, how's everything," Conner asked. I looked at him and smiled.

"Well thank you," I ended the conversation at that and began eating; none of them even moved, they just watched me. I took a few more bites and stopped. "What?"

"We are just wondering how your day is going," Eric said.

"It is going well. How are your days going?"

"Fine, but we aren't the one who killed our father," Nick snapped. I froze in place and my fork fell from my hand.

"Kaitlyn," Eric asked. I stood up and grabbed my tray.

"He didn't mean to upset you, Armistice," Bruce said. I looked at him and smiled.

"He didn't. I just remembered I have somewhere to be." I walked over to the Wolverine section and they all began to stand. I laughed and gestured for them to sit back down.

"Have room for one more?"

"Of course, ma'am," Evans said, sliding over. I took my seat and we all began to eat. I didn't speak the entire time. I just listened to all of them talk amongst themselves, tell jokes, and laugh. Despite every negative thing I had ever heard about them, they were the complete opposite. Very much like the rumors about me when I first arrived at Anguish.

We all remained seated until the last person finished eating, which was Hess. Once he finished his meal, they all turned and looked at me. I grinned and grabbed my tray.

"You are all off until 1600 hours. At 1600 hours, meet me on the mats."

"Yes, ma'am," they roared causing the dining hall to look at us. We stood and made our way towards the trash bins. The commander's table was all staring at me, but I didn't bother stopping. There wasn't anything to say to them.

I found shelter in my room and lay on my bed. I didn't bother taking off my boots or jacket. I set my watch and drifted off to sleep. I wasn't asleep very long before there was a knock at my door. I sat up with a groan and opened the door. Nick was standing there. I rolled my eyes.

"Yes?"

"Commander's meeting, in the Gathering Hall, in fifteen minutes," he said, but didn't budge.

"Okay." He still didn't move.

"I'm sorry, Kaitlyn."

"What exactly are you sorry for, Taylor?" I crossed my arms.

"I'm sorry for everything I said, last night."

"I'm a big girl." He rolled his eyes.

"We finally speak alone and that is all you have to say to me," he growled.

"What else is there to say? You had the audacity to insult me, and women in general." I poked him in his chest. "Didn't seem too damn concerned about my well-being when you were storming out of the sleeping bay. What is there to say?" He didn't say anything just stared at me. "Thanks for the information." I stepped back and let the door shut in his face.

Once I knew he was gone, I grabbed my script tech pad and made my way to the Gathering Hall. I was the last one to show. War Advisor Jennings gestured for me to come closer. I walked over to him and he pointed to an empty chair between Eric and Orion. I quickly took my seat and turned on my tech script pad.

War Advisor Jennings began speaking over regulations, training schedules, weekly goals, perimeter duties, and other Anguish matters. The new aquatic training center was opening, tomorrow. I took detailed notes and kept my eyes down. He spoke of the new treaty between Lynx and Neva. All eyes turned to me, but I kept my eyes on my pad and continued writing. War Advisor Jennings cleared his throat and all eyes were back on him. He continued to speak for over an hour.

"Any questions," he asked. No one spoke. "Good, you are dismissed," we all stood, fell to attention, and began making our exit. "Armistice?" I somehow knew this was coming. I don't know why I thought I could go a whole day without a senior officer calling my name.

"Yes, sir?"

"Let's walk and talk." The other commanders were looking at me. I couldn't quite read their faces, but I didn't look too hard either.

"Yes, sir." I walked over to War Advisor Jennings, who was looking at the other commanders.

"I said you were dismissed."

"Yes, sir," they said and made haste of leaving. War Advisor Jennings shook his head and laughed.

"I have arranged for you to speak to the Psych Doctor regarding recent events," I looked at him. "There will be no arguments. What you did was incredibly brave. If I had been in your shoes, I am not sure if I could have gone through with it, but you did." An image of my father's throat squirting blood flashed through my mind. I took a deep breath.

"I understand, sir."

"How did you sleep last night?"

"Like a rock, sir." He stared at me.

"I imagine so. I always sleep like a rock when emotionally drained," he nodded his head. "Well, your first appointment with the doctor will be tomorrow at 0700 hours, in my office. Understood?"

"Yes, sir."

"You are dismissed."

I walked out of the room with a plain face, but on the inside, I was outraged. I didn't need to talk to anyone about killing my father. I had done it, he died, and it was over. There was nothing to discuss. No one would understand what I was going through, so there was no point to speak about it. Everyone always thought that talking was the solution to everything. Talking did not solve everything and the sooner people realized this about me, the better.

Chapter Two
Babysitter

I spent a good portion of my afternoon in my room, at my desk. I was coming up with a training plan. War Advisor Jennings expected all commanders to have their training plan turned in by the end of the week. I had every intention of getting mine turned in by the end of the day.

I read over my training plan one more time and sent it via correspondence to War Advisor Jennings. I had half an hour to kill before the next training session with the Wolverines. And after the training session, I had an hour to eat and be prepared for the training session with the other commanders, which I was dreading.

I decided to head to the training area early and walked through the halls. I could hear commotion coming out of a male restroom. There was banging of lockers and yelling. I barged in the door, and there was a fight in progress. The spectators spotted me and came to attention, while the two barbarians continued beating each other to a pulp. One of the barbarians was Robinson from my regiment and the other male wore a Vipers patch. Robinson was now winning the fight and showing no mercy to the other male.

"Enough," I screamed stepping in between them. Robinson instantly stopped and stood at attention. The Vipers' male was already in mid-swing and hit me right in the face. The fight instantly ended. My eyes were on him and he turned pale. "Ma'am, I am so sorry. Are you okay," he asked stuttering.

"Outside! All of you, now," I screamed and they all scurried outside. I stepped out of the room, right as Orion, Franklin, Dimitri, and Eric came around the corner. They had the worse timing ever. They all looked at me and I closed the door. I brought my attention back to the rowdy bunch.

"I'm sorry, ma'am," the Vipers' male said. I read his name tag 'Staggs'. The commanders were now standing behind me.

"What was the fight over," I asked, crossing my arms. No one spoke. "What was the fight over," I yelled, causing all of them to stand taller at attention.

"You, ma'am," Robinson whispered.

"Oh. What about me?" Robinson looked embarrassed.

"Well?"

"Staggs made a comment on how you were just a female, who was not suitable for command, but suitable for taking to bed, ma'am." I wasn't expecting that. I turned to Staggs, who kept his eyes forward. I stepped to where I was standing in front of Staggs, my arms no longer crossed. He tried to divert his eyes from me.

"Is this so?" He didn't speak.

"She asked you a question," Eric shouted now standing next to me. "You will answer her!" The vein on the side of his neck was pulsating and he had death in his eyes.

"Yes, ma'am," Staggs shouted. I stared at Staggs for a while debating on what I was going to do. Finally, I grinned and faced Eric.

"Since he's part of your regiment, he's all yours, Commander Trials," I said sweetly and turned to Robinson. "Let's go killer." Robinson relaxed and grinned. I turned to Staggs. "Consider this a warning, next time I won't pull one of my Wolverines off you."

"Understood, ma'am," Staggs said. Eric looked at me.

"Are you sure you don't want the honors," he asked me.

"No, but I suggest he doesn't walk the corridors unescorted," I glared at Staggs and began walking down the hall with Robinson next to me. I could hear Eric yelling at the top of his lungs. Nothing that came out his mouth was pretty. He was vicious with his words, which surprised me, because he was usually passive.

"I am sorry, ma'am. I shouldn't have lost my cool," Robinson said softly.

"I'm not mad at you, Robinson," I said laughing. "I'm just wishing now that I hadn't broken up the fight." He looked at me and grinned.

"I would be facing execution for murder, ma'am, if you hadn't."

"No body, no crime," I said grinning. He laughed.

"This is true, ma'am."

Training went smoothly, until I announced to them that tomorrow at 0900 hours we would be having academics instead of the mats. I received a lot of grumbles. I crossed my arms and they all stopped complaining.

"What is so bad about academics," I said laughing.

"We suck at academics, ma'am," Scott announced and they all agreed. I hadn't thought about that. They were a regiment known for their muscles, not their brains.

"Okay, that is a fair answer. How about we start off from the beginning and work our way up?" None of them commented, which made me laugh again. "Come on you guys! You all graduated, so obviously you have a brain."

"We graduated because of our fighting and weapon skills, not because of our intelligence, ma'am," Chan said. I groaned, because I had a feeling they were telling the truth.

"We will figure this out together," I said letting a sigh escape me. "Until then, let's go hit the weapons module." They were happy about that.

They were brutal in the weapons module. They were precise and deadly. All their shots were grouped together and dead center. None of them missed a shot. Once all the rounds were expelled, they turned and faced me with a grin.

"See, weapon skills, ma'am," Chan said making all of us laugh.

"So, I see," I hopped off the platform. I picked up a magazine of rounds and Chan's weapon. "I have an academic score of 400 out of 400."

"Impressive, ma'am," Grady said. I aimed the weapon at the target and emptied the entire magazine of rounds. The target moved up towards us displaying my grouping of shots that were dead center. They looked back at me.

"My point is that you can have brains and still have skills." I cleared the weapon and handed it back to Chan. "We will have academics at 0900 hours tomorrow and if you don't like it, then you are more than welcome to request to go to another regiment. Understood?"

"Yes, ma'am," they said without protest.

Once all the weapons were cleared and turned back in, we made our way back to the regiment hallway. They talked amongst themselves while I walked, thinking about life. I needed a good outlet to escape thinking, but here at Anguish I had none. Things were different between Nick and me. I no longer felt the butterflies within me when I saw him. Perhaps, it was lust all along. He had taught me a lot, though. Taught me what I wanted in life and what I didn't.

Eric, Dimitri and Nick were in the corridor talking, but instantly stopped when they saw us. Eric and Dimitri smiled, while Nick shook his head and walked off. That earned him a frown from Eric and Dimitri. The Wolverines began walking past me saying, "good night, ma'am" or "have a good evening, ma'am." I acknowledged them until the last one was out of sight.

"About ready for commander's training," Dimitri asked me, smiling.

"I suppose," I said grinning and walking over to them.

"We aren't going to go easy on you," Eric said laughing.

"The last time you did, the lot of you were doing an awful lot of screaming, I recall." I smirked and they both laughed. Dimitri's watch went off and he groaned. Eric laughed and patted him on the back.

"Training calls," Eric continued laughing. Dimitri shook his head and looked at me.

"I shall see you at commanders' training." I nodded my head and he walked off. Eric turned to me.

"Oh, good, just the two I was looking for," War Advisor Jennings said walking up behind us. We quickly stood at attention and he laughed. "Relax. This will be slightly informal." Eric and I both relaxed and looked at him.

"Sir," Eric asked.

"Commander Armistice is new to commanding a regiment and although she did very well on her first mission, she could use a mentor." A pain struck me in my gut at his words regarding the mission. I kept a solid face, but I wanted to run down the hallway and out of Anguish.

"Mentor, sir," Eric asked crossing his arms and raising an eyebrow. War Advisor Jennings nodded his head.

"Yes."

"And, you want me to be that mentor?"

"Yes, will that be a problem, Commander Trials?" Eric stared at War Advisor Jennings for some time. I saw the vein in Eric's neck pulsate.

"When will this mentorship end, sir," Eric asked. I quickly looked at Eric.

"If you don't want to be my mentor just say it. I'm sure there is another commander who wouldn't mind teaching me. Perhaps Commander Aiyetoro," I asked facing War Advisor Jennings, who was glaring at Eric.

"That won't be necessary, Armistice," Eric said. I didn't bother turning to him. "I would be honored to be your mentor." I rolled my eyes.

"Will this be a problem for you, Armistice," War Advisor Jennings asked. I clenched my jaw.

"No, sir," I said firmly.

"Good, then it is settled," he said nodding his head. "The mentoring starts today."

"Yes, sir," Eric and I said in unison.

"Carry on." War Advisor Jennings walked off and I glared at Eric.

"Look, I will make this easy for you. I will meet wherever you would like, show up, sit quietly, listen, take notes, and be on my way. You won't have to even worry about me opening my damn mouth." I stormed off without giving him a chance to even open his mouth.

Chapter Three
Well, that went well

Commanders' training was not what I expected. We formed into a squad and each took a turn making commands to the squad. Our task was to get through the module without anyone dying. Nick failed miserably when it was my turn to lead. He refused to do anything I said.

"What the hell, Nick," Dimitri snapped in the middle of the module. I had never seen Dimitri angry before. "How hard is it to follow a simple command?" The others pointed their weapons to the ground and the module ended.

"What seems to be the problem," War Advisor Jennings said over the loud speaker. All the commanders pointed at Nick. "Taylor, what's the problem?"

"I just don't think a female should be in command, sir," he shouted up to the watching room.

"Is that so?" War Advisor Jennings asked.

"Yes, sir," Nick shouted.

"Armistice, how do you feel on the matter?"

"I believe that Commander Taylor needs his diaper changed, sir," I shouted as loud as I could. The room filled with laughter to include War Advisor Jennings. Nick was glaring and stepping up towards me. Dimitri stepped between us.

"Not today, my friend," Dimitri said.

"Taking her side over mine?"

"I do not agree with how you are acting. Keep your personal problems out of here."

"You can have her," Nick said to Eric. "She doesn't put out anyway." Eric began to grab Nick but Bruce pulled him back. Nick stormed out of the room. I was mortified. I wanted to run out the other door and hide my face. I never expected Nick to be so childish and say something like that about me.

I took a deep breath. This was not the place to cry. The past few days had been a nightmare and Nick had just added insult to injury. Why had I been so stupid to fall for his lies? Now I had to turn around and face my peers after his outburst.

"Don't feel bad, Kaitlyn, I didn't put out to him either," Jordan finally said. I turned around and he was grinning. They all broke out into laughter.

"Thanks," I said and he winked.

"We'll call it a day," War Advisor Jennings announced. We all went and put up our weapons. Nick was sitting in front of the Guardian Gate. I didn't even look in his direction. No one spoke to him. We all handed in our weapons and began walking off.

"Kaitlyn," Nick said. I stopped and looked at him. "Can we talk for a minute?"

"Nothing to talk about, Nick." He stood up and walked over to me. Eric stopped talking to Jordan and walked over to me.

"Relax, Eric, I'm not going to say anything rude to your sloppy seconds." Orion pulled me back, right as Eric punched Nick in the face. All hell broke loose. The other commanders didn't even attempt to break up the fight.

"You guys," I said asking the other commanders to step in.

"They've been feuding for years, Kaitlyn," Bruce said standing next to me. Eric and Nick were still going at it. Eric had Nick pinned on the ground and was beating the crap out of him. I didn't realize how strong Eric was, but then again, I had never actually watched him fight before. I had watched enough.

"Eric," I shouted. He looked over his shoulder at me. "Enough already." To my surprise, Eric stood up and walked over to us. His nose was bleeding and lip was busted up, but not nearly as bad as Nick's face.

"Sorry," he said. He had just stood up for me and he was apologizing. I shook my head and laughed. Orion finally released me.

"Someone going to help him up," I asked. They all looked at Nick and shook their head.

"Always running his mouth," Walter said and began walking off. I walked over to Nick and offered my hand. He growled, stood up on his own and stormed off.

"You're a bigger person than I am," Mason said laughing. "I wouldn't have offered my hand to him and he didn't even run his mouth about me."

"He will continue running his mouth," Covington said. I quickly looked at him and he laughed. "What?"

"I don't think I've ever heard you speak other than during training," I said. Everyone was now laughing.

"Occasionally, I speak," he grinned. "Now let's go get your face cleaned up, Eric. You are bleeding all over the floor." He laughed and patted Eric on the back.

"Let's get Kaitlyn to her room first," Eric said.

"I'll be okay."

"No, he has a point," Dimitri said. "I will escort you to your room." Eric nodded his head.

"No, I will," War Advisor Jennings said behind us. We all turned around and stood at attention. "Relax." We all complied. "I just passed Taylor in the corridor and judging by your face, Eric, I would guess you won the fight."

"You would be correct… sir," Eric said. War Advisor Jennings laughed.

"He has been requesting to be released from the academy for a year now," the other commanders were surprised by this news. "I have decided to grant him his wish."

"Just like that," Eric asked.

"He isn't focused on the mission anymore. He is only focused on himself," everyone nodded their head in agreement. "I have already given him his release paperwork and he will be leaving Anguish within the hour."

"I didn't mean to cause any problems, sir," I whispered.

"Nonsense, he was requesting to leave long before you showed up at our doors."

"Oh."

"Let's take a walk, Armistice."

"Yes, sir," I said. I was beginning to feel that War Advisor Jennings was my personal body guard.

"Mentoring in the commanders' library at 1800 hours, Armistice," Eric said. I nodded my head and began following War Advisor Jennings. We were finally out of sight of the others.

"Do you like it here?" I stopped walking and faced him. "Sir?"

"Do you like being at Anguish?"

"I do, sir." He nodded his head. "Why do you ask?"

"I just know that you have responsibilities to Neva."

"My mother has the responsibilities, for now, sir."

"And you don't want to be there to help her?" I shrugged my shoulders.

"She will be a great leader. I would understand, if you do not want me here anymore, sir."

"Nonsense, I just wanted to make sure that you didn't feel obligated to stay here." I shook my head.

"I don't, sir."

"Good, because I wouldn't want to lose a commander like yourself."

"Thank you, sir." We continued walking, again. We walked in silence the rest of the way. We arrived at my door in short order.

"Enjoy your mentor training, Armistice." He grinned and walked off. I looked at my watch and I had twenty minutes until my mentoring with Eric. I retrieved my tech pad from inside my room and headed to the commanders' library.

I found a table off in the corner and began scrolling through archives. Nothing in the archives was appealing, but I wanted to know more about Lynx and Anguish. Lynx was the supreme government of the canton, yet, Anguish had free reign.

"Reading anything good," Eric asked startling me. I looked up and his face was healing nicely.

"Not particularly," I said closing the tech windows and setting the tech pad on the table. Eric gestured to the seat and I nodded. He sat down and placed his tech pad on the table.

"I didn't mean to offend you earlier," he said. I shrugged my shoulders.

"It doesn't matter. Can we please just get this session over with?" I was feeling testy. He looked down at the table and growled. Then he returned his gaze to me.

"First, we need to get everything out on the table." I leaned back in my chair and crossed my arms. "Your body posture tells me that you are in a defensive state of mind."

"Your observation would be correct, Commander Trials," he rolled his eyes and laughed.

"Earlier, with War Advisor Jennings, was not what you thought."

"Can we just get on with the mentoring?"

"No," he said firmly. "You misunderstood me and I'd like to fix the hostility between us… well, the hostility you have towards me."

"I don't have any hostility towards you. I am beginning to learn my place in Anguish, so it is just time that I accept it." He raised an eyebrow, leaned back in his chair, and crossed his arms.

"And what is your 'place'?" I leaned forward and placed my elbows on the table.

"Let's cut the crap, Eric. I'm just the token for Anguish to parade around in front of your government. If I hadn't killed my father, I'd be back in Neva on the first train out of Lynx." He just stared at me. I could see the vein in his neck begin to pulse. My words were upsetting him. He took a deep breath.

"This is how you truly feel?" My inner demons were rattling their cage within me. I had nowhere to go and no one to turn to. Nick had been my only semi-outlet in Anguish and now I was completely on my own.

"Yes," I said.

"Then you are misinformed. Perhaps, we will try this again tomorrow." He began to stand and I placed my hand on his. He looked at me and then at my hand. I slowly removed it. "I'm sorry," I whispered. "I would appreciate it, if you would stay and mentor me." He didn't say anything right away. He just stared at me, as though he was searching for something. "Why should I stay," he finally asked. I let out a sigh. "Look, Commander…"

"Eric," he corrected me. I nodded my head.

"Look, Eric, I'm going through a lot right now. You have always been kind to me and I don't mean to snap at you," I said softly, swallowing my pride. He nodded his head and placed his arms on the table. He leaned towards me.

"Kaitlyn, you don't need to apologize. I completely understand that your emotions are a little… off balance," he whispered. I didn't trust my words, so I simply nodded my head. Even though I had been defensive towards him, Eric was still kind to me. He had always been kind to me. He had made a few teasing jokes when I was in his class, but other than that, he had always been kind. "Let's skip this mentoring session and go hit the mats."

"What?" He laughed and stood up.

"I think it will do you some good to let some… emotions out," he grinned and grabbed his tech pad. I stood and grabbed mine as well. I followed him out of the Commanders' library and silently down the corridors. We finally reached the Viper training area. He opened the door and held it open for me. I nodded, walked in and he followed behind me. The lights turned on and Eric was already removing his jacket. I had never seen him with his jacket off. He was more muscular than Nick. Eric's muscles were bulkier and more defined. He had warrior tattoos down his arms, telling a tale.

I removed my jacket, placed it on the bench and began unlacing my boots.

"You always fight with your boots off," he asked laughing. I looked at him and nodded. "Very well." I removed my boots, placed them next to my jacket, and then I slipped my shirt over my head. I dropped it to the floor and turned to Eric, who looked shocked.

"And, yes, I always fight like this, as well. Won't be a problem, will it?" I smirked and walked on to the mat. I could hear him walking behind me. We stood in the middle of the mat and he was still staring at me and in shock. I crossed my arms and laughed. "You going to be able to fight or do I need to throw a shirt on?"

"Your fighting attire is… unique, but I shall manage," he slipped his shirt off and tossed it to the side. Then he bent down and removed his boots. They were the next things to be tossed off the mat. He was now standing in front of me like a deity.

His torso was chiseled like it was crafted by a master sculptor. He had more warrior tattoos running up his arms and across his torso. I couldn't help but stare at his body. His body was more masculine than Nick's. Eric's body was built like a warrior's, perfect in a sense but marked with scars. I felt myself wanting to reach out and touch his scars to learn their tales.

"Kaitlyn," Eric asked. I shook my head and laughed.

"I am ready," I said taking a battle stance. He laughed and walked closer to me. My breath became ragged.

"You need to work on your techniques."

"I thought you were just going to let me blow off some steam?"

"We can, but let's take it to the mat." He kneeled and took up a floor stance. I reluctantly did the same. He shook his head and laughed. "You really hate floor techniques, don't you?"

"I only have one move perfected and eventually someone is going to catch on," I said grinning. He laughed.

"Then I will teach you something different. Sound good?" I nodded my head. With the speed of his regiment's namesake, he grabbed me by waist and slammed me to the mat. "Never let your guard down," he said looking down at me.

"I see this," he laughed and I flipped him over me. Now I was on top of him. "Never let your guard down." I smirked and he laughed. This began our session. We started off slow and eventually the session became intense.

Soon, we were both covered in sweat. My heart was racing and emotions running high. He slammed me on the mat and straddled my waist. Sweat was glistening from his skin and the light was hitting him just right. He was very attractive, and I was surprised I hadn't truly noticed it before. I shook the thought, bucked my hips and rolled him over.

"Is that all you got," he growled. I placed my hands on his throat and proceeded to choke him. In return, he did the same. With another twist, he rolled me over. He was now on top of me and our hands still on each other's throats. Neither one of us was backing down.

The feeling of his hands around my throat was exciting. I had never had an opponent do this move on me before and have this reaction on my body. The fact was Eric made it even more exciting. He had always been passive and kind. Now he was grunting, sweating, and had me pinned on the mat. His facial expression was that of a predator.

My hands relaxed from his throat and fell to my sides. He leaned down closer to me, his hands still on my throat but he wasn't squeezing. We were both staring at each other and panting.

"I guess this can conclude our session unless you feel you need to go longer," he said huskily.

"Why'd you hit Nick," I asked and his hands fell to the sides of my head. He shrugged his shoulders.

"He had it coming."

"Was it because he insulted you by assuming we had something going on? Or because he spoke ill of me?"

"Kaitlyn," he warned. My cheeks burned from embarrassment.

"Sorry," I rolled him off me and quickly stood up. I walked off the mat and began redressing. I don't even know what possessed me to ask him that. He was just helping me release some emotions and I had to make things complicated. He walked over to me, running a hand through his hair.

"You really have to stop misunderstanding my words and actions," he whispered. I shrugged my shoulders and finished lacing up my boots. I threw my shirt over my head. "Kaitlyn?"

"I understand, Eric. No big deal," I smiled and grabbed my jacket.

"It is a big deal," he grabbed my wrist and spun me towards him. I was thrown off by his forwardness.

"Yes," I asked looking down at his hand and back at his face.

"I fought him because he disrespected you. I don't care what he assumes, but I won't let him talk about you like that. I won't let anyone talk about you like that." I searched his eyes for sarcasm, but found none. He was holding my wrist and staring down at me.

"Well, thank you. That was nice of you, but unnecessary."

"Why would you say that?" He let go of my wrist and crossed his arms.

"Males will always talk about a female who no longer has interest in him."

"And you no longer have interest in him?"

"I don't think I ever truly had interest in him. We had nothing in common, and he wasn't a gentleman."

"I am glad you finally realized this."

"And I suppose you knew this all along?" I crossed my arms and glared at him.

"Sometimes people have to learn others' true colors on their own. Things that are good for us are often right in front of us." My mouth fell open.

"It's you," I said softly. He raised an eyebrow.

"Me," he asked laughing.

"How often do you talk to War Advisor Jennings?" He was no longer laughing.

"Why," he asked in a whisper. "What has he said?"

"He said the same thing to me about true colors and the right person being in front of us."

"Oh. Perhaps, great minds just think alike," he said shrugging. His cheeks were beginning to redden and he was running his hand through his hair.

"Perhaps you are right." I threw my jacket on. "I appreciate the session. I do feel much better." He nodded his head and began dressing. I stood in silence and waited for him to finish. When he was done, we headed out of the room and he shut the door.

"I talk to War Advisor Jennings quite often." I stopped and looked at him. "You weren't the only one with a family secret, Kaitlyn, and since you trusted me with yours, I will confide in you with mine." I held up a hand.

"You don't have to do that, Eric."

"I feel like it will make things clearer, besides I know I can trust you." It was the first time anyone had said that they trusted me. I had been told many things throughout my life, but never those words.

"That means a lot to me." He nodded his head.

"Take a walk with me?" I nodded my head and followed him. We walked throughout Anguish and finally to the commanders' corridors. We stopped in front of a door with his name written on it. I raised an eyebrow. "We can leave the door open, if you would find it more appropriate."

"I shall live." He opened the door and we walked in. He closed it behind us and I looked around. His room was like mine, apart from the aroma of him throughout the room. I took in a deep breath and basked in the smell.

He gestured at the bed and the chair. I took a seat in his chair and he sat across from me on his bed. We both placed our tech pads on the desk. He was nervous about telling me the secret. I could tell because he ran his hand through his hair once more.

"You do not have to tell me," I said. "Sometimes secrets are meant to be kept."

"Eventually, you will put two and two together. I'd much rather you hear it from me."

"Okay?" He opened his desk drawer and pulled out a photo tablet. He turned it on and handed it to me.

"You may scroll through them." I began sliding my finger across the screen. There were pictures of Eric as a child doing different things. He was a happy child. There was a picture of him with what appeared to be a younger brother, his mother, and his father. My fingers froze and I stared down at the picture. My eyes slowly came up and met his eyes.

"Your father is War Advisor Jennings?" He nodded his head. I looked back down at the picture. I could now see the family resemblance. Eric favored his mother, but he had his father's features as well. I began scrolling through the pictures once more. There were pictures of Eric with War Advisor Jennings on the day Eric was pinned to commander. Finally, I reached the end of the photos and handed the tablet back to him. He slipped it back into his desk drawer and looked at me.

"Say something, please."

"What's there to say? We both have fathers of authority." Pain struck me. "Well, I had a father of authority. Now I have a mother of authority."

"I'm sorry for your loss, Kaitlyn."

"Nonsense, he deserved to die." He frowned and leaned towards me. He grabbed my hands in his and looked at me. "That did not mean you had to be the one to do it. I am sorry my father put you in that position." I shrugged my shoulders. "You don't always have to be strong. I have two shoulders and you can cry on either one of them."

"I appreciate it, but I don't need to cry."

"Kaitlyn," he whispered. "I can see it in your eyes."

"Maybe the eyes are deceiving." He shook his head.

"No, not your eyes; you speak with your eyes. Always have since day one." I hadn't realized he had paid that much attention to me. I always sat in the back of his room, quiet. Well, at least the first few weeks I did.

"My eyes are liars then," I snapped. He simply laughed.

"Kaitlyn, give me a break. I am trying to help you."

"Maybe I don't need help." Everyone thought that they could be my hero. I didn't need a hero. I just needed to be left alone.

"Okay. Let me do one thing to prove I'm right?" I raised an eyebrow as he stood. "Come on, just one thing. Even you can handle one thing, right?"

"Fine." I stood up, reluctantly. What he did next blew my mind. He wrapped his arms around me and pulled me against his chest. He rubbed my back and held me. Without thought, my arms wrapped around him and I laid my head against his chest.

I don't know when the first tear slid down my face, but soon a flood of tears left my eyes. Eric said nothing. He just held me and rubbed my back. As much as I didn't want to admit it, it felt good to be held by someone and cry. I hadn't cried in someone's arms since I was a child. My father had always frowned upon me crying.

Now here I was in Eric's room, in his arms, crying. Deep down I knew he wouldn't tell anyone, not even his father. I cried for what seemed like forever. Eric lifted me up gently and carried me to his bed. My heart began to race as he laid me down. He removed his jacket and climbed in next to me. He wrapped his arms around me and held me once more. I instantly began to cry into his shirt.

I cried for eternity, at least it seemed like eternity. When I finally stopped, Eric kissed the top of my head and rubbed my back.

"Feel a little better," he asked softly. I nodded my head and placed it in the crook of his arm. "Good. Get some sleep," he kissed my head and shut off the lights. I knew I needed to leave his room, but I didn't want to.

"Are you sure," I asked in a hoarse voice.

"Yes," he kissed the side of my head. "I will wake you in a few hours. Okay?"

"Okay." I closed my eyes and relaxed in his arms.

"We will get you through this," he whispered.

Chapter Four
Sleeping Beauty

I woke up feeling refreshed, and startled. I had forgotten where I was until Eric pulled me against his chest. I could hear him breathing softly. He was still asleep. I smiled to myself and stayed in his arms for a little while longer. Finally, after several minutes passed, I sat up on my arm.

"Eric," I said softly. He didn't move. I laughed and shook his arm gently. "Eric." He began to stir, but didn't wake. I found myself running my fingers down his arm. His skin was smooth and his muscles firm. Even with me touching him he still didn't move. Finally, I bent down and found his lips. I gently placed a kiss on them.

"Hey," he said softly, startling me. My cheeks instantly burned and I quickly sat up.

"Hey," I said embarrassed. He pulled me back down into his arms and kissed the top of my head.

"That was a nice surprise," he said chuckling.

"Sorry. I don't know what got into me."

"Well, I'm not complaining."

"No?" He shook his head and laughed.

"Definitely not." He rubbed my arm and yawned. "How'd you sleep?"

"I slept surprisingly well. How about you?" He rolled on to his side and was now facing me.

"Like a youngling." We both laughed and he placed his forehead on mine. He ran fingers gently down my face and I trembled. I thought he'd move his fingers from my face, but he did the gesture again and I trembled. "What are you thinking about?"

"I'm not really thinking of anything besides this moment."

"Good." He ran his fingers down my neck and a moan escaped me. "I meant what I said earlier."

"Which part?" He laughed.

"All of it, but I was talking about the 'getting you through this' part." I flipped the light on and looked into his eyes. Why was he being so kind? Was he being honest, or just spinning a web for me to be trapped in?

"Thank you." I whispered. He smiled.

"You're welcome." He looked at the time and sighed. "I guess I should allow you to escape so you can go get some food." I laughed and rolled my eyes.

"That is not food." I quipped. He laughed.

"You never have liked our food." I shook my head.

"Hopefully you don't starve to death."

"I won't. I plan on bringing back lots of Nevan food after my visit with my mother."

"Oh," he sat up on his arm. "When do you plan on going?"

"I hadn't really talked to War... your father about it, but I am hoping to go sometime soon." He nodded his head.

"I've never been to Neva." Eric said, sounding mischievous. I grinned.

"You could come with me," I began. He looked at me and laughed, "to ensure that I do not get into any trouble."

"I wouldn't be intruding," he asked and I shook my head.

"I must warn you Neva is not much different from Lynx."

"Really?" He ran a finger down my arm. "Tell me more."

"Thought you wanted to kick me out of your room so I could go eat," I said smirking. He laughed and shook his head.

"My intention was never to kick you out. I enjoy your company, especially now that you aren't one of my trainees." I laughed.

"What does that mean?"

"I can talk freely now," was his response. I rolled my eyes.

"Like you had any problem speaking freely." I retorted. He laughed.

"If you were still a trainee, you would not be anywhere near my room." He had a valid point. He didn't appear to be one to cross that line. "Even if it's what I really wanted." I looked at him.

"Is that what you wanted?" He didn't say anything right away. Finally, he nodded his head and smiled.

"Every time Nick would comment about you, I wanted to punch him in the face." I couldn't help but laugh. The look on Eric's face was quite serious.

"Why?"

"I could tell his intentions weren't any good. He only had one goal." I frowned.

"I began to see his true intentions." I groaned and laid my head back on the pillow. "I found myself not wanting to be alone in a room with him. He tried to treat me like some common whore."

"I wanted to tell you, but I knew it would only be a matter of time before he crossed a line and you handled him."

"I was glad you knocked on the door," I said bashfully.

"I could hear you knocking at the door and asking to be let out. I was going to break the door down, if he hadn't opened it."

"I was debating on doing the same," I rolled my eyes.

"Well, now he is gone and shouldn't be a problem."

"I hope so." He ran his finger down my arms. I closed my eyes and took in his touch. I slowly opened my eyes.

"I want you to know that you are free to leave anytime you'd like." I nodded my head.

"You can kick me out anytime, as well," I teased. He smiled and leaned towards me. My heart began to race and I waited for his lips to touch mine, but he sat back up on his arm. He closed his eyes and shook his head. "You okay?" He opened his eyes and stared at me.

"Yes."

"Why the sudden inner battle then," I asked laughing.

"I don't want to cross any lines with you, Kaitlyn. You have been through enough and don't need me adding to your plate." I nodded my head. He had gained even more respect from me. He wasn't trying to force himself on me or fill my head with lies.

"The past few weeks have been…challenging, I will admit. And I thank you for letting me set the boundaries." He nodded his head.

"Every part of me is saying to kiss you," he whispered. I bit my lip and smiled. "But I know that I want to spend time with you again and I think kissing you would ruin that chance."

"Why do you think that?"

"I don't want you thinking I only want one thing from you, Kaitlyn."

"Oh." He leaned his forehead against mine.

"I want to spend one-on-one time with you again."

"What if I said that I want to spend time with you, again, too?" He kissed my forehead.

"I'd love that."

"What if I wanted to kiss you?" His breath became ragged.

"If you initiated the kiss, I wouldn't stop you." I grabbed the sides of his face and leaned towards him. I expected him to meet me half way, but he didn't. He was serious about me initiating the kiss. I leaned closer to him and finally our lips met.

His arm pulled me closer to him and we were now kissing; a passionate, warm, enticing kiss. He was gentle with me. I felt a beast stirring within me and I wanted the kiss to intensify. I wanted his hands all over me and mine all over him. I thought the kisses between Nick and me were heated, but they were nothing compared to Eric's. Eric's kisses were intoxicating and made me crave more. I felt the shameless beast inside me rattling at its cage.

One of his hands gently stroked my face. My back arched as our kiss deepened. My hands began roaming down his neck and down his back. My nails gently scraped down his back and he arched. He moaned against my mouth and the kiss became more passionate. It was like someone had ignited a fire between us.

Finally, I rolled on top of him. It was like my body was possessed and my mind no longer in my control. We kept kissing and his hands were now moving along my sides. I scooted my legs down to become more comfortable. I could feel how aroused he was underneath me. I had never felt any man's arousal. I found myself aroused, and was intrigued by the whole situation.

"You okay," he asked. I didn't realize I had broken our kiss. "Uh huh. I just wasn't expecting to feel…um…" I moved against him so I wouldn't have to say the words.

"Oh. Sorry." He began to move but I kept him pinned down with my legs. "Kaitlyn," he whispered. "I'm sorry." I laughed and kissed his neck.

"I'm not. I find it… exciting."

"Is that the first one you have ever felt," he asked trying to not laugh. I bit his neck and laughed. "Ouch."

"For your information, yes, yours would be the first."

"And what thoughts do you have?"

"I wasn't expecting it to be quite so big. Are they all this size," I asked in a whisper. He laid his head on the pillow and laughed.

"No. They aren't."

"Oh." I was blushing, since now I knew he was one of the anomalies that I had heard females speak of.

"Does that bother you?"

"No. Surprises me, but doesn't bother me." I leaned down and kissed him. "You must think I am a rookie." He laughed. "You would be correct," I said laughing.

"I assumed as much. Just another reason why I wanted to take things slow with you and not rush you into anything you might regret later." I nodded my head.

"I appreciate that." I slipped my shirt over my head and tossed it to the side. Then I moved my hips and he moaned. I couldn't help but grin. I wanted to reach my hand inside his shirt and explore him. The beast inside me was half out of its cage and I wanted to open the cage wide-. Eric was driving me past the point of rational thought.

"Kaitlyn," Eric warned.

"Eric," I said teasingly and he laughed. He grabbed my hips and moved me against him. My head fell back and I moaned. He continued grinding me against him. I couldn't help but moan at the touch. I found myself aroused, hot, and becoming wet in hidden areas. He began moving me faster and harder against him. "Eric," I moaned.

"Kaitlyn," he moaned in return. I began moving my hips at the same pace he had been moving me. He moaned more, which only excited me more. He placed his hands on my thighs and squeezed. A lustful moan escaped me.

"Eric, please," I begged before I even thought. He squeezed my thighs again and I grinded harder against him. We were both moaning. He moved his hands up my sides and removed my sports undergarment. My breasts were now free and even though he couldn't see me, I felt like covering up.

"Relax, Kaitlyn. You're beautiful." His words eased my mind. He began roaming his hands across my breasts. Soon he was squeezing and pulling at my nipples. A loud moan escaped me and I flooded in my hidden areas. "You're so wet, Kaitlyn."

"You made me this way," I said with my eyes closed. He sat up and I thought he was going to get off the bed, but instead he removed his shirt. Then his mouth found my nipples. His mouth was warm. He grazed his teeth against my nipples and I grinded hard down on him. He continued touching my nipples with his mouth and I found my hands on his back. My nails lightly scratched his back, but when he sucked harder and bit, my nails dug deeper in to his back. I thought I had hurt him, but he moaned against me.

"We should probably stop. Our day begins soon," he groaned against me. I was still panting from his touch.

"Okay."

"If we continue, I might not stop until I have you."

"In what way," I asked playfully. He laughed and bit my nipples.

"In a way that you won't want to leave this room, ever again, as long as I'm in it." Without thought, I grinded against him and pushed him down on to the bed. I pressed my chest against him and took his mouth with mine. He didn't object. His hands roamed down my back and found their way to my ass. He squeezed and I moaned in his mouth. I nipped at his lip and he nipped at mine. His hands were at the edge of my underclothes and I desperately needed him inside them.

"Eric," I panted, "please."

"Kaitlyn, you need to be sure." His voice was serious.

"Make me forget everything," I begged. With his arm still around me, he rolled over on top of me. He leaned down and kissed me softly.

"I want to ease all of your pain," he whispered. My lust was dying and my weak emotions running high. "Give me all of it, sweetheart." My heart melted at his endearing words. He laid on his back and pulled me against him. I had expected him to take it to the next sexual level, but a softer side of him appeared.

"I'm sorry." I stammered. "I didn't mean to ruin the moment." He laughed and kissed my forehead.

"Nonsense." He rubbed my arm. "I just want to see you happy and right now your heart is heavy. Besides, if we take it to the next level, I want it to be because you want me and not because you're hurting on the inside." I nodded my head.

"I do want you, but you are right. There is a lot on my mind." He kissed my forehead, again.

"Whenever you are ready to talk, I'm here to listen."

"Thank you." I wrapped my arm against him and snuggled against his chest. I soon drifted asleep. I hadn't slept that well in weeks.

Chapter Five
Let's Talk

I woke up to a light. Eric was walking out of the bathing quarter. He walked back into the room and smiled.

"Morning," he said cheerfully. I looked at the clock and it was 0530.

"Morning," I said smiling. He began putting his clothes on. "I like you better undressed." He looked at me and grinned.

"I could just take them back off, climb back into bed, and hold you all day."

"That would be divine." He grinned and buttoned his pants.

"It would be, but then," he stepped towards me, "neither one of us would get anything done. And our regiments would be running amok." I laughed at the thought of the Wolverines running wild through Anguish.

"I suppose you are right," I laid my head back on the pillow and laughed. He sat on the edge of the bed and looked down at me.

"How'd you sleep?"

"Like a baby," he smiled. "You?"

"The same. I usually wake up throughout the night, but surprisingly I slept the whole time." I smiled.

"That's good." He nodded his head.

"Guess I need to make my great escape," I said sitting up and grinning. He frowned and I laughed.

"Could just hold you hostage?"

"Can't hold the willing hostage, Eric," I teased. I looked around the bed and found my clothing. I threw them on and stood up. I glanced at the clock and groaned. I quickly straightened my uniform and grabbed my tech pad.

"Still want me to mentor you," he asked. I looked at him and grinned. "I'm serious, Kaitlyn," he said laughing.

"I can keep professional and personal separate, so yes, I would like it if you would mentor me." He nodded his head and walked over to the door. He looked out the peep hole and then signaled for the door to open. He gave me a swift kiss. "I will see you later," he grinned and I quickly made my way to my room.

I wanted to lie in bed and think about him all day, but I had responsibilities. I jumped in the shower and began my routine. Soon, I was ready and heading to the dining hall. The food reminded me of the restaurant and how Anguish food was better than what I had picked. I looked at the Wolverines table and it was half empty. I walked over to the table and they began to stand. I gestured for them to stay seated.

"Where is everyone," I asked.

"Most are still sleeping, ma'am," Chan said. I laughed and shook my head.

"What time do they get up?"

"About ten minutes 'til 0900 hours, ma'am," I nodded my head and laughed. I wish I could have that mentality.

"Well, academics is still at 0900 hours." A few groaned. "Oh, come on, it won't be that bad." I walked off laughing. I strode over to the commander's table. They stopped talking and said their greetings. I took my seat next to Dimitri. Eric was across the table from me and to my left. He smiled and continued eating.

"We were just discussing the new aqua facility and what we thought it might entail," Orion said. I nodded my head and took a bite of food. It was awful. They all looked at me and laughed.

"After being here for months, you still can't stomach our food," Walter asked laughing. I shook my head and swallowed.

"I don't know how you tolerate this."

"I'm sure if we were in Neva we would not care for the food either," Dimitri said. The others nodded their head and began eating. I choked down as much food as I could. I looked at my watch and it was ten minutes 'til 0700 hours. I groaned and gathered my stuff.

"Commander Armistice," I heard War Advisor Jennings shout. I groaned again.

"Oh, come on. It is too early to be in trouble already," I said standing. The others laughed. Eric looked at me and smiled.

"Good luck," he said laughing.

"Gee, thanks," I said rolling my eyes and making my way over to War Advisor Jennings. I disposed of my breakfast and followed him out the doors.

"Good morning," he said.

"Good morning, sir." We walked silently through the hallways and to his office. I wasn't in the mood to talk to anyone about my problems, but given the situation I don't think I had a choice. I'm sure it was therapy or the simulator to work out my problems.

"I know you are resistant to this idea, Armistice."

"I am, sir."

"It will do you a lot of good to get it off your chest."

"I understand, sir." I walked into his office. Councilman Shaffer was in the office sitting in a chair. He turned his head to me and I closed the door.

"Armistice," he said pointing at an empty chair across from him.

"Sir," I said taking my seat.

"This morning I am just someone to talk to. I am not your superior officer. Understand?" I nodded my head. "How are you?"

"I'm well."

"Good," he took notes in his tech pad. "How have you been handling the situation?"

"You mean the situation of having slit my father's throat open on live broadcast," I asked smirking. This wasn't going to go well at all.

"Yes. That would be the situation that I am referring to," he said calmly. I shrugged my shoulders.

"He was insane. He killed people for no reason and needed to be stopped."

"But how do you feel about having done it?"

"How would you feel if you killed your father in cold blood," I snapped. He took more notes. I growled and leaned back in the chair.

"I see. I have never had to face my father in that way. Do you feel your decision was rational?" I growled again.

"How about we just get to the point?" He looked up at me.

"You want to know if I am still capable of functioning. Yes. I am perfectly capable of carrying out my duties and doing whatever is necessary to keep the peace; even if that means killing another family member who has lost their damn mind!" He nodded his head and went back to taking notes.

"How do you feel leadership should handle you?"

"Handle me?"

"Yes. Handle your emotional state of mind."

"I think my 'leadership' should stop babying me and realize that I can handle myself. They gave me the mission and I succeeded. Now you want to punish me and play mind games with me, because I did what you asked of me?" He didn't say anything, just take notes. "And what exactly are you writing down?" He looked up at me.

"Just taking notes, Armistice."

"Would these notes include my resistance to talking to someone? Or how I am perfectly capable of handling myself? Or how I have survived every type of torture that Anguish has thrown at me? You can't expect me to endure hell, kill my father, and walk away without some questioning thoughts! I wouldn't be human if I didn't question my actions! However, I contained my emotions, stuck to the task at hand, killed my father and returned. Hell, I was even shot!" He looked at me. "Shot?"

"Yes, shot! My own father shot me," I lifted my jacket and shirt so he could see my wound. "If I hadn't killed him, he would've killed me! My actions have been justified, sir. Repeatedly." I put my shirt and jacket back down.

"Why are you so angry then?"

"Because I feel that no matter what I do in Anguish, it just isn't good enough." The words slipped past my lips and there was no retrieving them. He didn't take notes.

"Why would you think that?"

"Look around you. Everyone is waiting for me to fail. I was given two simulators in one day and no one has ever gone through that before. I was put in the water tank shortly after the simulators. My mind was in no condition to handle the water tank, yet I was subjected to it. And, I know that is why I was given the Wolverine Regiment. No one thought they'd accept me. I have been expected to fail."

"What if that was all to prove how strong you are?" I stopped and looked at him. I had never considered that.

"Why would they need to do all that?"

"To prove that you deserved to be here, would be my guess." He was gazing rather pointedly at me over his tech pad. I nodded my head.

"And is this the case?"

"Perhaps. However, we are here to discuss the recent event of killing your father." I froze in place. It sounded even more horrible coming from the mouth of someone else.

"Armistice?" I nodded my head and looked at him.

"Yes?"

"We do understand that killing a family member, or anyone for that matter, can take a toll on emotions. We are not questioning your ability to do your duties. We are just offering an ear for you to talk to without judgment." I nodded my head again. "My notes aren't notes they are monitoring your vitals to ensure your heart rate doesn't get too high." He showed me his tech pad which had vitals running across them.

"Oh."

"Despite what you think of Anguish not all of us are risen from the underworld to spread misery and suffering." He chuckled and turned the tech pad back to himself.

"I apologize for blowing up at you, sir." I sat up in my chair.

"We aren't in here under formalities. I am just here to allow you to let some burdens off your chest that way you don't devour anyone." I looked at him and he grinned. I bit my lip to keep from laughing. There was one person I wished to devour.

The rest of the session went more smoothly. Despite my resistance to talking to anyone, it was easier to talk to Councilman Shaffer once everything was placed on the table. We didn't just talk about me killing my father. We talked about my time at Anguish, my plans on staying at Anguish, and what I would do when my time came to take on the role of Empress. I didn't realize how much I had on my chest until I opened my mouth and let it fly out.

Chapter Six
All is Fair in Love and War

When it was 0800 hours, I thanked Councilman Shaffer and took my leave, heading towards my room. The halls were filled with trainees, who were scurrying to their next classes. I couldn't help but laugh, because a few months ago that was me. A group of trainees were rushing through the hallway and one of them ran smack dab into me. The group instantly froze and went to attention. The one who ran into me looked scared to death. I grabbed my forehead where he had collided and rubbed it, and then I looked at him.

"Ma'am, I am so sorry," he said with fear in his voice.

"You make it a habit to run into commanders, Bates," Kurtz asked walking over to us.

"No, I didn't mean it, sir."

"Commander Armistice, Bates is in my class. How would you like him handled, ma'am?" Kurtz was now facing me and trying not to smile. I removed my hand from my forehead and laughed.

"He could come to physical warfare training with the Wolverines and me," I said looking at Bates. He looked like he was about to pee himself. I laughed. "Relax. I am only kidding. I am sure Training Officer Kurtz will be able to persuade you to watch where you are walking," I looked at Kurtz, "Right?"

"Yes, ma'am," he said smiling. "Alright, off to class you go."

"Yes, sir," they said and walked quickly down the hall. Kurtz laughed.

"Your forehead is so red," he said laughing. I frowned and rubbed my forehead.

"Well, it was your bigheaded trainee who decided to collide head on with me." I grinned.

"Perhaps we should get you a helmet?" He busted out laughing and I whacked his arm.

"Perhaps, you should get to teaching your hardheaded trainees."

"Fine. Fine. See you later… ma'am." He walked off laughing and I continued down the hallway careful not to run into any more trainees. I walked down the regiment corridor and the Vipers were lined up against the wall receiving mass punishment. I bit my lip and began walking down the hallway. Eric spotted me and smiled. He faced his regiment.

"Attention," he shouted and they all went to attention. "Say good morning to Commander Armistice," he said gesturing to me. I wanted to run down the hallway to avoid public embarrassment.

"Good morning, ma'am." I laughed and looked at them.

"Good morning, Vipers. I see you are all… together." Eric laughed.

"Apparently, they think it is funny to harass other regiments."

"Oh?"

"Sad but true."

"Which regiment?" I crossed my arms because I had a feeling I already knew. Eric grinned and I rolled my eyes. He laughed.

"Let's just say, there will soon be a feud between our regiments. In fact, I would even go so far as to call it a 'war'." He threw his head back and laughed. He quickly looked at me. I heard hollering down the hallway towards the Wolverine corridor.

"Oh, no," I whispered. "What'd they do?"

"Filled the entire corridor with bubbles," Eric couldn't stop laughing. The Vipers were smirking. "Down!" The smirks were quickly wiped off their faces as they squatted down with their backs against the wall.

"Of all pranks, they did bubbles?" I could hear the Wolverines going crazy over the bubbles. "You didn't have them clean it up?" He was still laughing and shaking his head. I laughed and shook my head.

"Up!" The Vipers stood back up. "After their punishment, they will clean it. I promise." He laughed.

"Yeah, yeah." I began walking off.

"Have a great day, Commander Armistice." I looked over my shoulder and grinned.

"You too, Commander Trials." I walked around the corner to the Wolverines, who were battling bubbles.

"Attention," someone shouted. They all went to attention. Bubbles surrounded them. I bit my tongue and turned my head for a moment. I faced them once more.

"Is there a reason you are all covered in bubbles?"

"It would seem someone has pulled a prank, ma'am," Reed said. I could barely see him with all the bubbles.

"This side," I pointed to my left, "gather as much water as you can from your room; this side," I pointed to my right, "gather all the foot powder you can find." They looked at me like I had lost my mind. "Hurry." They all ran into their rooms and shortly came out with the items.

"Ma'am, not to question you, but why these items," Harlan asked.

"Well, perhaps a certain regiment is one corridor over being punished for placing bubbles in another regiment's corridors. It would be a shame if they were to be attacked while unsuspecting and vulnerable." They all grinned. "However, you are to avoid Commander Trials. Understood?"

"Yes, ma'am," they screamed.

"See you at 0900 hours." I began walking the other way and they took off running. The water group ran first, and then the powder group. I heard splashes and shouts coming down the hallway. Then I heard more shouts.

"Armistice," I heard Eric shout. I laughed and quickly made my way to the training area. Around 0845 hours, they began filing in. Once they were all in the room, we headed to the academic room with grumbling following behind me.

Academics went horribly. They weren't lying when they said they'd only graduated because of their fighting and weapon skills. They didn't have any idea about anything else. I felt bad for even subjecting them to academics. All I had done was upset them.

"Don't hate me," I said. Their faces were full of disappointment. "This will benefit all of us in the long run. Just give me a chance." They just stared at me. "Oh, come on," I said laughing. "I let you have your revenge on the Vipers." They all busted out laughing.

"That was funny," Hewitt announced. They laughed more. "Commander Trials didn't look very happy though, ma'am."

"I can only imagine." I laughed and stood up. "Let's go hit the mats." That got a cheer out of them. We walked down the corridors and all the trainees quickly moved out of our way. Once again, the Wolverines began their battle chant trying to intimidate the trainees. I kept from laughing and just followed behind them. Eric poked his head out his classroom and watched. I began passing him.

"Not so fast, Commander Armistice," he said. I stopped and looked at him innocently.

"Yes, Commander Trials," I said sweetly. He laughed.

"You aren't slick. Water and powder, really," he asked in a whisper. I shrugged my shoulders.

"I don't know what you are referring to." He opened the door to his classroom a little wider and I peered in. Some of his Vipers still had powder on them. I stepped away from the doorway, covered my mouth and laughed. Eric grinned.

"All is fair in love and war," he winked. "See you later, Commander Armistice."

"Commander Trials," I said and hurried down the corridor to catch up with my regiment. They were already walking through the training area doors. Training began and they hit the mats hard. I must have really pissed them off, because they were taking it out on each other. Finally, I called time and they stopped. They were all sweaty and panting.

"Feel better," I asked laughing.

"Yes, ma'am," they shouted.

"Good. Go hit the showers and I will see all of you at 1600 hours for more physical training." They gave each other high fives and ran out the doors. I could only shake my head at the youngsters I called 'Wolverines'.

Chapter Seven
Aqua Training

I didn't even make it halfway back to my room, when the announcement came over the speakers.

"The following commanders need to gather their regiments and head to the aqua training facility: Trials, O'Conner, Orion, Aiyetoro, Bruce, and Armistice. You have fifteen minutes."

I took off in a dead sprint down the corridors towards the regiment corridors. I finally arrived and they were already out in front of their rooms waiting. I smiled.

"Well, let's go get this over with." We walked down the hallway and towards the aqua training facility. It seemed like it was miles away.

"How far is this, ma'am," Chan asked. I could only laugh and shrug my shoulders. I had never actually been on this side of the academy. There was so much more to Anguish than I had discovered. I could hear commotion up ahead.

"I'm guessing we are almost there." We soon reached the aqua training facility and it was massive. We filed in and took a seat on the bleachers. The other regiments continued filing in. The last to file in was O'Conner's recently assumed Diablos. They took their seat.

The pool in front of us was filled with dark water and you couldn't see the bottom. The War Council entered. We were all on our feet.

"As you were," War Advisor Jennings shouted. We took our seats once more. "Welcome to the new aqua training facility. This is where we will work on water tactics. As you can see, you can't see the bottom. There may come a time when you are forced to advance by water. Empty your pockets." We all began emptying our pockets. "Looking for a volunteer regiment to go first," he shouted. I stood up without thought.

"The Wolverines will go first, sir," I shouted. The Wolverines were on their feet and once again doing their battle cry. War Advisor Jennings grinned.

"Somehow it doesn't surprise me that you all would volunteer. Front and Center." We made our way down to the edge of the water. I looked down in the water hoping to see the bottom but it was pointless. Suddenly, the water began splashing, turning, and crashing against itself. The entire room was staring at War Advisor Jennings, who just laughed.

"Welcome to the water pit, Abyss," Councilman Hyde said grinning.

"Commander Armistice, order your regiment in to the water," War Advisor Jennings shouted.

"Negative, sir," I said shouting at him. All eyes were on me.

"Negative, Commander Armistice?"

"Yes, sir!" I faced down the line and looked at my regiment. They were all looking at me. "First in!"

"Last out, ma'am!" I jumped into the water and they followed seconds behind me. The water was no joke. Some of the Wolverines were having trouble keeping their head above water. My mind began to race with techniques to get us through this training exercise.

"Battle up," I shouted over the water's noise. They were soon partnered up and keeping each other afloat. "Form up on me!" They made their way over to me. "We got this," I shouted over the water. The lights went out but the water continued. I growled. This was just what we needed, I thought.

"Get them across the water, Commander Armistice," War Advisor Jennings shouted to me.

"Yes, sir!" I knew that I had been facing towards the opposite side of the pool when the lights went out. "You're going to follow my voice. When I call out something, you repeat it. Understood?"

"Yes, ma'am," they screamed over the water. I began making my way through the water.

"One," I said.

"One," they shouted back.

"Two," I said continuing to battle the water towards the opposite side. I was getting tired but refused to let the Wolverines look weak.

"Two!" They were keeping up with me.

"Three!"

"Three!" The water seemed to get stronger or I was getting tired.

"Four," I shouted trying to keep my head above water.

"Four," they shouted back. They were just as tired.

"We're almost there. Keep going. Five!"

"Five!" I could tell we were nearing the other side, because I could hear our words echoing off the walls.

"Almost there! Six!"

"Six!" I hit the side of the pool and latched on to it.

"Seven!"

"Seven," they screamed. I waited a few seconds to catch my breath.

"Head count. Sound off from the right to left!" They began counting down the line- thirty-two. The lights came back on and they were all staring at me. "Wolverines!" They were chanting, cheering, and acting crazy. I laughed and wiped the water and hair from my eyes. They began hopping out of the water. Chan and Scott bent down and with ease pulled me out of the water.

"Last out, ma'am," those in formation shouted. I laughed and took my place in front of them I turned and face War Advisor Jennings.

"Well done, Wolverines," War Advisor Jennings shouted. "Fine display of leadership and teamwork. You all should take notes," he said looking around the room. "Commander Armistice, you all may take a seat."

"Thank you, sir," I shouted. We took our seats and the rest of the regiments took their turns. I didn't bother critiquing any of them; because I was sure our regiment had some issues as well. When all the regiments had gone through the training, we were all worn out. The water was turned off and went back to a resting state.

"This is the beginning of many new training exercises. I will be posting a patrol roster by the end of the day." I had a feeling that there was more going on then what War Advisor Jennings was telling us. Everything added up to a war and since Neva was now controlled by my mother, I knew that it had to be the canton to the North of Anguish, Fritz. "Dismissed!"

We were on our feet. I signaled for my regiment to wait. There was no need to try to fit six regiments through one door. Eric had the same idea and kept the Vipers seated. When everyone had filed out, I looked at him. He smiled and gestured for us to go first. I nodded my head and gestured for the Wolverines to follow me. We began walking passed the Vipers. I stopped and faced the Wolverines.

"Does anyone else smell powder," I asked. My regiment was howling with laughter as they exited the chamber. I looked at Eric, winked and kept walking.

Chapter Eight
The Replacement

We were not even an hour into our 1600 hour training, when the doors flew open and Councilman Hyde came storming in. The Wolverines were already on their feet. I walked over to Councilman Hyde, who was searching the room, and holding an electric lash in his hand.

"Councilman Hyde," I said nodding. He began walking to the center of the mats with me following him. He stopped walking and glared at me.

"I want Faber, Goss, and Ingram front and center," he snapped at me.

"Very well," I turned to the Wolverines. "Faber! Goss! Ingram!" They quickly made their way over to us. All three of them were young, no older than me.

"All three of you are being reprimanded for trespassing in a senior officer's office! My office!" I looked at the three who were being accused. None of them showed a hint of emotion. They just continued staring ahead.

"Then we shall take this to War Advisor Jennings. Thank you for bringing it to my attention," I said gesturing for him to leave.

"Oh, it doesn't work like that Commander Armistice," he spat. "If you recall regulation 13-2 section 6 clearly states 'any Anguish caught trespassing in a secure area will be punished by one electric lash before his peers'." That earned a jaw tightening from all three of the accused.

"That regulation is ancient," I said crossing my arms.

"That regulation is Anguish law." He was right and there was no argument there. I could see it in the three accused that they were scared. Electric lash was extremely painful. I knew this because my first two weeks into training a group of males thought they'd make their point, that I had no place being at Anguish, by striking me with one.

"The regulation also states, 'the guilty, if not deemed physically fit to withstand such punishment, may be replaced'. CHAN!" Chan quickly ran over to me.

"Yes, ma'am," he asked standing at attention.

"Take Faber, Goss, and Ingram to the infirmary."

"Yes, ma'am."

"Not so fast, Commander Armistice," Councilman Hyde spat. "They have to be replaced!"

"Would you do your actions again," I asked Goss.

"Yes, ma'am," he said.

"What about you, Faber? Ingram?"

"Yes, ma'am," they said in unison. I nodded my head.

"I will be their replacement," Chan, Faber, Goss, and Ingram quickly looked at me. They were horrified by my words.

"Ma'am," Faber began, but I cut him off by holding up my hand. Councilman Hyde looked at me like I had lost my mind. Perhaps I had, but I refused to stand by and let anyone be brutally punished. Besides I had some pent-up emotions to release, and what a better way than physical pain?

"I stand by my Regiment. Now, if we may proceed with this punishment because we have training to continue, sir," I snapped. I removed my jacket and threw it on the mat.

"You think that I will not strike a commander before his... her regiment," Councilman Hyde asked.

"If you were a councilman of the regulations then no, you would not." He grinned.

"Good thing I'm not, then. Turn around, Commander Armistice." I turned my back to him and he stepped away. I gestured for the others to move. I heard a door slam shut and the regiment began to whisper. "Silence!" The room fell silent.

"Commander Armistice has decided to replace the guilty! She will receive an electric lash for each guilty party." The room was filled with uproar.

"At ease," I yelled and they silenced. "Councilman Hyde wishes to prove a point. The regulations are meant to be followed. Therefore, I will be the puppet!" The Wolverines war cry began. It was a few seconds later when the first lashing struck me. My body tensed up and I bit my lip to keep from screaming. The room fell quiet. The second lashing followed shortly after and I felt my knees buckle beneath me. The Wolverines were staring at me in horror. A few began walking over to me, but I held up my hand and they stood in place.

"And, finally," Councilman Hyde said right before he whipped me with all his strength. I steadied my breathing as best as I could. The tears were on the verge of spilling from my eyes and the screams were still lodged in my throat. I took a few more breaths. I heard a door open and close. I hoped he was gone.

"What in the hell is going on in here," I heard War Advisor Jennings say behind me. I quickly turned and stood at attention. Next to War Advisor Jennings was Chan.

"Regulation reprimand, sir," Councilman Hyde stuttered.

"Is it true that you are preparing to reprimand one of my commanders," War Advisor Jennings asked.

"Commander Armistice volunteered to be the replacement for the guilty, sir."

"Is this true, Armistice?" I didn't trust myself to speak so I nodded. "What is the punishment?"

"One lashing for each guilty party," Councilman Hyde said. War Advisor Jennings nodded his head.

"And how many guilty were there?"

"Three, sir."

"When were you planning on getting my authorization to reprimand these three, let alone one of my commanders," War Advisor Jennings asked crossing his arms in front of his chest.

"Authorization, sir?"

"Yes, regulation 109-21 section 34 states that all reprimands must first be approved by the War Advisor, which last time I checked was me. Correct?"

"Yes, sir," Councilman Hyde was starting to fidget and sweat. I, on the other hand, was about to pass out from the pain.

"When is Commander Armistice schedule to be reprimanded?" Councilman Hyde didn't speak. "Well," War Advisor Jennings shouted.

"She's already been reprimanded, sir!" Someone shouted. War Advisor Jennings eyes grew large and he rushed over to me. He spun me around.

"Hyde," I had never heard War Advisor Jennings use such a demonic voice. War Advisor Jennings turned me back around and looked at me. "Are you okay," he whispered. I nodded my head. "Armistice, talk to me." I held back the tears as best as I could, but I felt one roll down my cheek. His face softened. "Hyde, in my office now!"

"Yes, sir," Councilman Hyde made haste out the door.

"Wolverines, dismissed," War Advisor Jennings yelled. They all began moving, but not out the door. They gathered around us. War Advisor Jennings looked around at all of them. "I hope you understand how honored you are to have her as your commander."

"Yes, sir!"

"Good," he looked at me. "Let's get you to the infirmary, Armistice." He bent down as though he was going to pick me up and I shook my head. He laughed and stood up.

"Stubborn, as always, Armistice. You are all dismissed until further notice."

Chan grabbed my jacket and handed it to War Advisor Jennings, who folded it over his arm. He then proceeded to escort me out the training area and into the hall.

"You don't have to hide it, Armistice," he whispered. I said nothing, only continued walking. Each step grew more and more painful. My breathing became sharper with each step, as well. I could feel the blood dripping down my back.

"Armistice, you aren't doing your body any justice. We could have already been there, if you had let me carry you." I shook my head and we continued walking.

Classes had just let out, so they were filled with trainees and regiments. They all quickly moved out of our way. We rounded the corner. Eric was standing with Dimitri and Walter. They were joking about something.

"Attention," someone yelled. The hall fell silent and they all went to attention.

"Carry on. Just get the hell out of the way," War Advisor Jennings snapped. He was growing irritated with my stubbornness, but I refused to have my commanding officer carry me. We began walking by Eric. His smile instantly faded when he saw my face.

"Kait...," he began to say.

"Not now, Eric," War Advisor Jennings snapped. "Everyone, get back to your schedule." With that we continued walking, until finally we reached the infirmary. "I need a doctor over here immediately!"

"Yes, sir," someone yelled from the corner of the room. I didn't get a good look at them, because I could barely see War Advisor Jennings who was two feet from me. The team rushed over to me and I held up my hand. They allowed me to walk into the room.

Once inside the room I gestured for them to give me a minute. I closed the door and turned my back to them. The medical team was confused, but I didn't care, I opened my mouth and let the screams escape. The tears flooded down my face and I fell to the ground in pain. The door quickly opened and I was swarmed by people. The first thing they did was gave me a shot of something powerful which knocked me out.

I woke up feeling lightheaded and my back a little sore. I opened my eyes and War Advisor Jennings was standing over me with his arms crossed.

"Oh, hell, am I dead," I asked. He smiled and shook his head. "No, but by the end of the day Hyde may be." I grinned.

"You can't seem to stay out of trouble for one day." He shook his head and laughed.

"Seems to be a habit, sir."

"Am I going to have to assign someone to be your voice of rationalization?" He was now staring at me. I shrugged my shoulders.

"What fun would that be, sir?" He laughed wholeheartedly. I had never actually heard him truly laugh. His laugh was very like Eric's.

"The doctors say you had fresh stitches on your side and that it appeared to have been a bullet wound." I raised my eyebrow.

"Oh?"

"Yes. Know anything about this?" He grinned and I just shook my head. He laughed and ran his hand through his hair like Eric does when he isn't sure what to say.

"Was Eric…. Commander Trials the one you were referring to that day, in your office, sir?" He looked at me and shrugged.

"I'm unaware of what you are talking about, Armistice." I rolled my eyes and laughed.

"I understand, sir."

"Just know that Commander Trials is an outstanding commander and an even better man." I nodded my head in agreement and did my best not to smile. "I understand you want to go to Neva to visit your mother?" I should have known Eric would address it with his father. I could only laugh and nod my head.

"Yes, sir. I would like to, with your permission, of course."

"Eric… Commander Trials will escort you," he said grinning. I laughed and nodded.

"I assumed as much, sir."

"You are also to bring two squads made up of Wolverines and Vipers." I looked at him. "No arguments."

"Yes, sir." I sat up and began to move my legs off the bed.

"Don't you think you should rest, Armistice?"

"Negative. I have a regiment to lead, sir." He grinned and helped me out of bed. There were clothes folded in a nearby chair. I looked at him.

"I had them bring you new uniforms. You were overdue for some new ones anyway," he shrugged his shoulders and headed for the door. "You are a hell of a commander, Armistice."

"Thank you, sir."

Chapter Nine
Never-ending…

After an hour of arguing with Doctor Thomas, as usual, about releasing me, I was finally changed and walking out the door. The hallway was filled with the Wolverines, who were sleeping like newborns. I was half tempted to tiptoe pass them. I cleared my throat and a few woke up. They quickly elbowed the person next to them. They were soon up on their feet.

"Ma'am," Chan said wiping the sleep from his eyes.

"Chan," I looked around at all of them. "Is there a reason why you are all sleeping in the hallway at," I looked at my watch, "2200 hours?"

"We were waiting to see you, ma'am," Oden said. I nodded my head.

"And for what reason were you waiting to see me for?"

"We just wanted to make sure you were okay, ma'am," Adams said.

"I am well."

"You didn't have to stick up for us, ma'am," Ingram said stepping forward. "We did the crime, we were willing to accept the punishment, ma'am."

"You do understand why I took your place don't you?" I crossed my arms and they all stared at me.

"Not really, ma'am," Faber said.

"If you are willing to do something even though the consequences are severe, then your cause must be justified. I will always stick up for what is right and I will always stand up for your decisions if they are justified. I could see it in all three of your eyes that you were all willing to sacrifice everything for your actions. So, I took your place." They just stared at me.

"You could have been killed, ma'am," Goss said. I shrugged my shoulders. I hadn't thought about that. I just knew those three couldn't withstand the punishment and opened my mouth. My mouth usually sent me in through the gates of hell without thought.

"Did you tell War Advisor Jennings?"

"Ma'am," Ingram asked.

"Did you tell War Advisor Jennings what Councilman Hyde was up to?"

"Yes, ma'am, we did," Goss said. I nodded my head. "But how did you know?"

"There was no other reason for one of you to be in his office, let alone all three of you. I have been known to do some digging when I feel there is evidence to be found," I grinned and so did they. "Now let's get some sleep. Sunlight will be upon us soon and we have the 0900-hour perimeter shift."

We walked through the halls quietly. The only lights on were the ones marking each corridor junction. We finally arrived at the Wolverine Regiment.

"Would you like a few of us to escort you to your room, ma'am," Freeman asked. I laughed and shook my head.

"That won't be necessary, but thank you. I will see all of you at 0830 hours at the Guardian Gate," they nodded their heads. "Goodnight."

"Goodnight, ma'am," they said in unison and made their way to their respective rooms.

The walk-through Anguish in the dark was quite peaceful. I don't know why I never noticed it before, but then again, I was never by myself to notice the tranquility. I slowly made my way through the hallways to the commander corridor. A shadow moved when I rounded the corner. I stopped in place.

"Kaitlyn," Eric said walking towards me. "I came to check on you at the infirmary once my father told me you were awake. You were talking to your regiment so I decided to meet you here." I nodded my head and opened my door. I stepped part way in and looked over my shoulder.

"You may come in, if you'd like." He stepped inside with me. The light flashed on and the door closed behind us. As soon as the door closed, he had me wrapped in his arms.

"You scared me to death," he whispered against my hair. "I waited in the infirmary for hours. Finally, he made me leave."

"Well, yeah, that's called stalking," he looked down at me and I grinned. He laughed and kissed my forehead.

"I've never been so scared in my life."

"And here I didn't think you cared," I said teasingly. He laughed and took a step away from me.

"Can I take a look?" I nodded and turned my back to him. I lifted my shirt up and over my head. I placed my shirt on my bed. "Holy hell, Kaitlyn."

"It's not that bad and it barely hurts."

"I'm going to kill him." I laughed. "No, seriously." I turned and faced him.

"Relax. It's over." He pulled me back into his arms and kissed the top of my head.

"I couldn't concentrate on anything with you being in the infirmary. I dismissed my regiment and gave them free training until tomorrow."

"Awe, big bad bear getting emotional," I said teasingly and he laughed.

"You say that like it's a bad thing." I looked up at him and shook my head.

"Different, but not a bad thing."

"Good, get used to it." He leaned down and kissed me. He slowly pulled away and rested his forehead on mine. "You're a hell of a woman, and commander."

"Thank you," I whispered.

"But, you almost caused a man to lose his life, today," he chuckled and I looked up at him.

"How's that?"

"Well, between my father and me, Hyde was almost murdered." I laughed and shook my head.

"I figured he would just be reprimanded and that'd be the end of it." I shrugged my shoulders and Eric shook his head. "What happened?"

"I asked Chan from your regiment who had done that to you. He explained everything. I went searching for Hyde and found him in my father's office and handled my anger with my fists."

"Eric," I said frowning.

"He had it coming, Kaitlyn. He had no right to punish anyone with an electric whip, especially a commander. And the fact that it was you just set me off more."

"So, what happened?"

"My father came into his office with the other councilmen. They were quick to pull me off Hyde."

"Well, that sounds like fun," I said laughing.

"Then my father asked me to leave the room, which I reluctantly did, and I heard all hell break loose. I didn't stick around to see them carry him out. I went straight to the infirmary and waited by your side, until my father found me again and sent me away."

"Awe, you kept getting kicked out of rooms, poor thing." He looked down at me and frowned. I laughed and stood on my tippy toes to kiss him. He smiled.

"What can I do for you?"

"What are my options," I said sweetly. He laughed and shrugged his shoulders.

"For you?" He asked and I nodded my head. "Anything!" I smiled like a youngling. My cheeks were burning from blushing. "What can I do for you?"

"Well, I could use some of your sweet kisses," I said grinning.

"Temptress," he said smiling.

"I could have said 'you can join me in the shower'." He grinned.

"Like I said, you can have anything," his voice was husky. My back arched and I closed my eyes. I slowly opened my eyes. "But, tonight, you rest." I frowned and he laughed. He bent down and picked me up. I laughed, as he carried me to the bed.

He set me on the bed and undressed me until I was only wearing my underclothes. Then he stripped down to his underclothes. I just sat back and admired his body. He caught me looking and grinned.

"What," he asked looking over himself. I laughed and shook my head.

"I was just admiring." He looked at me and smiled.

"Oh. Like what you see?" He made his pecs bounce and I melted. He grinned and walked over to me.

"Now, who is the temptress," I asked smiling. He grinned and sat next to me on the bed.

"We can take turns," he whispered. He leaned over and kissed my cheek. I released my hair from the band and placed the band on my desk. I shook my hair free of the bun. Eric was staring at me. I laughed.

"What?" He smiled and ran his fingers through my hair. "Your hair looks nice down."

"Thank you. Keep feeding me compliments and I may keep you around for a bit," I grinned and laid down in the bed against the wall. He laid next to me and pulled the covers over me. "You are staying the night, right?" I asked laughing.

"I kind of just assumed I would," he said looking down at his attire. I grinned and shut off the light. "Besides, I'd feel better being here so I could take care of you." I smiled and leaned my head against his chest. He wrapped an arm around me and scooted closer to me. "Let me know if I hurt you."

"I will."

"I mean, ever." My heart stopped and I sat up slowly. I turned on the light and looked down at him. "Did I cross the line?" I shook my head and smiled.

"Why are you so sweet?" I asked him. He laughed.

"I'm usually not."

"Then why now?"

"I'm not too blind to see a good thing in front of me." I couldn't help but smile. I leaned my head on his chest to keep from him seeing my smile. His words were breathtaking. The look in his eyes was genuine.

"Well, I like the sweetness." I purred.

"But?" I laughed and sat up.

"But, I'm afraid that someone is going to shake me awake and this will all be a dream," I whispered. He sat up on his elbow and rubbed my arm.

"I don't expect you to believe my words, but with time I will show you with my actions." He proclaimed quietly. I smiled. He cocked an eyebrow. "How do I know you aren't a dream?" I laughed and raised an eyebrow as well.

"How could I be a dream?"

"You're perfect in every way." I frowned and he laughed. "You are."

"I have a tendency of running my mouth and getting into trouble." He nodded his head in agreement, so I whacked him with my hand. He laughed.

"Well, it's true. You are quite feisty."

"Apparently, you like that," I teased. He grinned and kissed me gently.

"I do, but you are going to cause a lot of men untimely deaths." I rolled my eyes and laughed.

"Easy, big bad bear." I laid back down and turned off the light. I felt him lay back down. He put his arm back under me and I laid my head down on his chest.

"Can you try to not get yourself hurt tomorrow?" I could tell he was grinning. I nodded my head and he kissed the top it again. "You're going to be the death of me." I laughed against his chest.

I don't know if it was the medication or being in Eric's arms but I fell asleep soon after. I woke up to him rolling out of bed and beginning to get dressed. I looked at the clock and it was 0530. I laughed.

"You always wake up this early," I asked, startling him? He turned and grinned.

"If I didn't think anyone would spread rumors about me leaving your room, I'd stay until you were leaving."

"That would be nice," I sat up on my arm and my back was sore.

"You okay?"

"Yeah, just a little sore," he frowned and walked over to me. "Have anything for it?" I nodded my head.

"In my pants pocket." He grabbed my pants, dug through the pockets and pulled out the cream.

"Lay on your stomach." He ordered. I laughed.

"I can put it on." He frowned and gestured for me to roll on to my stomach. I rolled my eyes and then laid on my stomach. He began rubbing the cream on me gently. I instantly felt relief on my back.

"Am I hurting you?" I shook my head and he continued spreading it across my back. "It's healing nicely."

"That's good," I said relaxing from his touch.

"Are you falling back asleep?" He asked laughing. I grinned and nodded.

"Maybe."

"Then I will leave you be. Going to sit at the commanders' table for breakfast?"

"If I get up by then," I said laughing. He moved my hair to the side and kissed the back of my neck. Then he bit my neck and my back arched. "Eric," I warned.

"What, sweetheart?" He bit the side of my neck. "Come to breakfast with me and there will be more of this later." I laughed.

"Tempter." He laughed and stood up. I rolled over and looked at him. He began getting dressed again. "I like you better undressed."

"Kaitlyn," he warned. I stood up and stretched. He looked me over from head to toe. "Beautiful."

"Thank you," I stood on my tippy toes and bit his neck. He moaned and wrapped an arm around me.

"Now who is the temptress?"

"I don't know what you are talking about," I said laughing. I stood flat footed and he continued holding me.

"You make me not want to be noble, Kaitlyn," I grinned against his jacket.

"I'm sorry."

"No, you aren't," he said laughing. I grabbed the sides of his face and kissed him. He was gentle with my back, but kissed me like it would be our last kiss. We slowly pulled apart. "My little temptress."

"My big bad bear," he grinned.

"Let me go before we stay in here all day."

"Would that be such a bad thing?" I questioned. He shook his head and laughed.

"Let me out, temptress, before you seduce me with your feminine ways." I laughed and walked over to the door. I leaned over and looked out the peephole. Eric grabbed my ass and I quickly turned and faced him. He just grinned.

"Yet, I'm the temptress?" He shrugged his shoulders. I rolled my eyes and looked back through the peep hole. "You are clear to leave me."

"Don't say it like that," he said walking towards the door. "I'll never leave if you make me feel bad." I laughed and opened the door.

"See you later, Commander Trials." He rolled his eyes.

"Ma'am," he winked and walked out the door.

Eric was starting to grow on me. He wasn't a typical male. I didn't think he would take my whippings that hard. I figured he would be upset, but I didn't think he would hunt down Hyde and physically hurt him.

I couldn't help but smile thinking about him. He had been in front of me this entire time. He had been there for me after the water tank. He had kept my family secret to himself. He was always asking if I was okay. He was always there and I was too blind to see the evidence. Nick had just been a lesson to be learned. He was put in my life to show me more about myself. I had him to thank for the new path I was on.

Chapter Ten
Your Mother

With my tray, I walked over to the commanders' table and they all looked at me with grins. I shook my head and took my seat.

"To what do I owe the grins," I asked.

"We were just discussing how resilient you are," Dimitri said taking a bite of his bread. I laughed and picked up my cup.

"I wouldn't say that," I said before taking a drink. They all looked at me with eyebrows raised. I almost spit my water out. "What?"

"You do know that none of us have gone through two simulators in a row, right," Jordan admitted.

"Wait, what," it came out a shriek, which made them laugh.

"We thought you knew," Orion said grinning.

"And none of us at this table have taken three electric lashings. Hell, we've never taken one," Bruce said continuing to eat his food.

"I really hate you guys right now," I said crossing my arms and pouting. They all laughed. "What else haven't you guys done?"

"The water tank," Walter said grinning.

"And you call yourselves commanders." I admonished them, frowning. Once again, they found this funny.

"We've also never kicked Taylor's ass… well, besides Eric here," Jordan said patting Eric on the back. Eric was grinning and staring at me.

"Well, I personally think everyone of you should hit the simulators, followed by the water tank, and then get a little taste of electric lashings." They were all staring at me in horror. I couldn't help laughing. "I understand if you can't keep up with me." I winked and began eating my food. They laughed and began eating.

"Nervous about your first patrol," Covington asked, looking at me from across the table.

"No. Should I be," I asked setting down my fork.

"You are going out with the Vipers," Milton said making the whole table laugh and Eric frown.

"What's wrong with the Vipers," he asked.

"Who pulls a bubble prank," Kit asked pointing at Eric.

"He has a valid point, Eric," Dimitri said patting Eric on the back.

"However, the Wolverines attacking your Vipers with water and foot powder was entertaining," Bruce said grinning.

"Yeah, I wonder where that idea came from," Eric groaned. They all looked at me.

"What," I asked laughing.

"I know it was you," Eric said pointing his fork at me. I just grinned and crossed my arms.

"The Wolverines came up with that idea on their own and they were punished as I deemed fit," I continued to grin. Eric just shook his and laughed.

"Yeah, she came up with the idea," Rival said grinning.

"You can tell by the grin," Dimitri said taking a bite of food.

"And I'm sure the punishment was promotions to all of them," Mason announced. They all laughed and I rolled my eyes.

"They avoided hitting you, didn't they," I asked looking at Eric, who rolled his eyes and laugh.

"Even more evidence. I know it was your idea," he laughed and began eating.

"Armistice," War Advisor Jennings called out from across the room.

"Jeez, I can't even eat in peace," I grumbled and stood up.

"Stay seated, Armistice," he said walking over to the table. The rest of the table began to stand and he gestured for all of us to take a seat. I looked up at him. "How's your back?"

"Healing well, sir." He nodded his head.

"That is good. I just wanted to be the first to tell you that Councilman Hyde has been terminated from Anguish."

"What," I asked, almost choking on my words.

"He was given a choice. It was confinement or termination. He chose termination."

"Oh. I see, sir."

"Any Councilman or anyone who thinks that they outrank me and take matters into their own hands will be made an example of. I do not take lightly to insubordination."

"I understand, sir."

"Good. Be vigilant on today's patrol," he said looking at Eric, who was nodding his head. War Advisor Jennings looked at me again. "Nervous?" The table laughed and War Advisor Jennings raised an eyebrow and crossed his arms.

"We were just asking her the same thing, sir," Roy said.

"Ah, I see," War Advisor Jennings was now laughing. "So, are you?" All of them laughed at my expense.

"Why would I be nervous, sir," I asked.

"That is true. You have proven to be a strong Anguish," he said nodding. The other commanders laughed more. "What now?"

"We were just saying that as well, sir," Franklin said. War Advisor Jennings looked at me and grinned. Right then, chaos broke out behind us. I turned my head to see two of my Wolverines, Sabins and Kaelin, the two newest Wolverines, fighting each other. I groaned to myself, because it figured it would be two of mine. The other commanders were grinning, as well as War Advisor Jennings.

"I got this, sir," I said, standing up and sprinting over to the table. Without thought I jumped on top of the table. "At ease," I screamed and the entire dining hall froze in place. I looked around the table and at the two troublemakers. They were hanging their heads down.

"Sorry, ma'am," Kaelin said.

"Have a seat," I growled and they quickly sat down. I began walking down the tables, looking at all of them. "Do you want to be Anguish?"

"Yes, ma'am," they shouted.

"Then you better start acting like it!"

"Yes, ma'am!"

"You are to finish your food. Do not move from your seats until the last Wolverine is done eating! Understood," I snapped at them.

"Yes, ma'am!"

"Then you are to meet me at the Guardian Gate in full gear to retrieve your weapons; however, you are to move as a unit. If any of you are caught somewhere without the entire regiment, it will be mass punishment. Do you understand?"

"Yes, ma'am!"

"Finish eating and after patrol, we will be having academics." They all groaned. "Is there a problem?"

"No, ma'am!"

"Good. Later," I said, turning my attention to Sabins and Kaelin, "we will be having a little talk."

"Yes, ma'am," they said in unison. They both were pretty beat up.

"Now, excuse me while I go take a punishment for your behavior," I began walking towards the end of the table.

"Negative, ma'am," Kaelin shouted. I turned around and glared at him.

"Excuse me?"

"We accept responsibility, ma'am," Sabins said standing.

"We will accept it with them, ma'am," Chan said standing. Soon all the Wolverines were on their feet. I smiled despite the fact I was very angry with Kaelin and Sabins.

"You sure?"

"Yes, ma'am," they all shouted.

"Very well. Go get rid of your trays and meet me by War Advisor Jennings," I said hopping off the table.

"Yes, ma'am." They moved swiftly to dispose of their trays. I waited for them and then we walked over to the commanders' table where War Advisor Jennings. He was sitting in my seat looking at us. The Wolverines fell into formation. I stepped to the side and Kaelin stepped forward.

"We accept full responsibility, sir. We have embarrassed ourselves and Commander Armistice, sir," Kaelin said with his head high and eyes front.

"I see. What was the fight over," War Advisor asked grinning?

"Excuse me, sir," Kaelin asked.

"The reason for the fight. What was it?" Kaelin was nervous to speak. Sabins stepped next to Kaelin.

"I told Kaelin to tell his mother that I'd see her later, sir," Sabins said with a straight face. I had to turn my back to keep from laughing. The commanders' table erupted with laughter to include War Advisor Jennings. I took a deep breath and faced everyone. The Wolverines were doing their best not to laugh.

"You may all relax," War Advisor Jennings said wiping the tears from his eyes. The Wolverines relaxed, and all but Sabins and Kaelin laughed. War Advisor Jennings stood and looked at Sabins with no hint of emotion. "Sabins?"

"Sir," Sabins asked.

"I will make you a deal."

"Yes, sir."

"Kaelin will relay the message to his mother," Kaelin quickly looked at War Advisor Jennings with his mouth opened, "if you relay the same message to your mother for me." Everyone within earshot was dying laughing. War Advisor Jennings grinned and walked off.

Chapter Eleven
Patrol

Once the Vipers and Wolverines were geared up, including weapons, we exited Anguish walls and loaded up in trucks. We were driven to the north end of Lynx. Every few hundred feet one Viper and one Wolverine were dropped off at a lookout point and two Vipers would climb into the truck. Eric and I were the last ones out of the truck. The truck circled around and stopped at the command tower, which was at the midway point of the north wall and where Conner was. We did a quick briefing. Then he climbed into the truck and the truck returned to Anguish. We had to climb stone stairs to get to the command tower. The wall ran for miles across Lynx. Fritz couldn't be seen from here because of the trees between the wall and Fritz. I hadn't seen trees since I was a little girl. There were miles of trees in front of me. Their leaves colored like those in a painting. The fresh air was nice to breathe in and the wind blew gently across me. I couldn't help but smile. "You okay," Eric asked walking up behind me. I smiled and nodded my head.

"Yes, just taking in the moment."

"Good, but like War Advisor Jennings said, 'be vigilant'," I nodded my head and shook the pleasant thoughts of the scenery from my mind. We were here to do a job, not bask in the moment.

"With all the technology in your canton, why do you still do foot patrols," I asked staring at Eric.

"War Advisor Jennings feels that we do not know anything of Fritz Canton and that their technology may be more advanced; that our technology may not catch something that a human eye would find out of place." I nodded my head and looked back at the trees. War Advisor Jennings had a valid point. None of the cantons knew much about Fritz. None of the people of Fritz had been seen in years. I often wondered if they still existed behind their walls.

"Why is Lynx concerned with Fritz suddenly?"

"There are rumors that Fritz wants to expand their boundaries south. We refuse to give them even an inch." I nodded my head and continued looking out.

"Where do these rumors come from?"

"We have our sources." He wasn't giving me any information. I turned and faced him.

"Am I still considered the enemy," I asked. His eyes got wide, and then he frowned and shook his head.

"Why would you ask that?"

"You are withholding a lot of information." I returned my gaze back out the command tower.

"I do it for your own protection, Kaitlyn." I nodded my head and he stepped up beside me. He began looking out at the land. "Fritz has a mole among them, who shares information with us in exchange for safe haven when the war begins." I didn't say anything just nodded.

"And you think you can trust them," I asked softly.

"Yes," he said nodding his head. I pushed the button on the side of my ear piece to activate the communication hi-fi.

"Stay alert. If something seems off, then it probably is. Radio it in, immediately," I said and pressed the communication hi-fi button, once more.

"We haven't had to do a patrol in months, but now, with these rumors circulating it looks like we will be doing them twenty-four hours a day."

"Looks like my regiment was correct, when they said that academics wouldn't matter in war," I whispered.

"Academics are important." Eric stated, cocking his head to the side. "However, tactical skills will keep them alive in war." I nodded my head.

War was something I hoped to never see. I had seen enough death in Neva to last a lifetime. A war would be tragic and countless lives would be lost in an unjust battle. In a war, there is no way to keep the innocent out of the middle of it. Each soldier fighting for what they feel is right. War was an ugly place to be.

Eric and I scanned the horizon for hours in silence. All was calm and nothing appeared out of the ordinary. A gleam began flashing in my eyes. I turned my head and it was the lookout tower to my left. They were trying to get my attention. I gently tapped Eric, but kept my eyes on the tower. I grabbed my lookout oculars and looked at them. Chan was pointing down, frantically, while the Viper, Bates, had his weapon pointed at something. Eric and I quickly looked over the edge of the wall.

Next to the wall was a giant black bear with her two cubs. I bit my arm to keep from laughing. Eric frowned at the lookout tower next to us and shook his head. I continued watching the bear sniff around the wall, and then she and her cubs slowly walked back into the trees.

Eric leaned over to me, "Later on, we are having academics on wildlife." I chuckled to myself and nodded.

The rest of the shift was uneventful and soon we were all replaced by Orion and his Falcons. The truck ride back was quiet. Eric turned to Bates from the lookout tower.

"Have you never seen a bear before," he asked and I couldn't help but laugh. I covered my mouth, because everyone was looking at me.

"No, sir, only in books," Eric shook his head and laughed.

"I assume the same for you, Chan," Eric grinned.

"Yes, sir."

"Well, both regiments will be having wildlife academics in the morning," Eric announced and the truck was filled with groans. I looked at Eric and grinned. He smiled and leaned back against the wall of the truck.

Eric and the Vipers parted ways from us once we were back inside the walls and had dropped all our gear off. I had the Wolverines eat quickly and then meet me in the Wolverines' academic classroom. Once they were all in the room, I began lecturing them on wildlife. They weren't too happy, but I refused to have a heart attack thinking Fritz was attacking, when it was just an animal minding its own business. After I felt like it had been drilled into their heads, I released them. Franklin and Covington caught up with me in the hallways laughing.

"What happened now," I asked frowning.

"We heard about the bears," Covington said laughing. I shook my head and laughed.

"Bears are scary beasts. They could have shot us at any given time, I will have you know," I said sarcastically.

"Well, we are glad that you are all safe and sound," Franklin said. "You know that the Wolverines are going back out in a few hours, right?" I stopped walking.

"What," I asked. I hadn't heard anything about another patrol duty.

"Yeah, the patrol schedule says 2200 hours," Franklin said pulling out his tech pad and showing me. I had been too busy lecturing on wildlife, and I had forgotten to check my tech pad. I nodded my head and sighed.

"Looks like I need to grab some food and then a nap. Thanks," I said to both of them.

"Hey, Kaitlyn," Franklin said. I turned and faced him. "We're glad Taylor is out of your life." Covington nodded his head in agreement. I raised an eyebrow.

"Oh, yeah?"

"Yeah, he was bad news," Covington said.

"It seems like everyone knew this, but no one thought it would be a good idea to tell me," I said placing my hands on my hips.

"We were commanders and you were a trainee. That's something we don't tangle with," Franklin said. He had a point. Saying anything would have meant they knew what was going on.

"I know," I said sighing. "Thanks." I began to walk off.

"Eric is a much better pick," Franklin announced. Covington and he both laughed. I didn't even bother turning around because I knew my cheeks were bright red.

I found the Wolverines and told them about our next patrol shift. They grumbled and made their ways into their rooms. I soon found myself curled up on my bed. I was exhausted mentally and physically. I couldn't wait to get away from Anguish for a little bit and go see my mother. It would be a nice respite.

Chapter Twelve
Night Patrol

It seemed like as soon as my head hit my pillow my alarm went off. I groaned and sat up. It was 2130 hours and I felt like the living dead. I freshened up and made my way to the Guardian Gate to sign out weapons. I looked for Eric, as I walked down the corridors, but didn't see him. Shortly after my arrival, the Wolverines, fully geared, began filing in to the Guardian Gate to retrieve their weapons and night optics. They looked exactly how I felt.

We were soon on our way to the north wall. Bruce briefed me and took his leave with the Reapers. We took up our posts and the shift began. I scanned the section to keep from falling asleep and used the communication hi-fi frequently to keep everyone awake. I often had them check in by lookout towers.

"Ma'am, movement. Sector 2.32," Robinson called over the radio. I pressed the communication hi-fi button for open mic and quickly located 2.32, which was two towers over, in my night oculars. I was thankful it was nearby. I didn't see movement, but I kept my eyes peeled.

"Still see it," I asked quietly.

"Yes, ma'am."

"I see it, too, ma'am," Edwards said.

"Keep observing and make sure it's not wildlife," I said continuing to scan the section.

"Movement in sector 3.53, ma'am," Chan called out. That sector was one lookout tower over from me. I began scanning that sector looking for any movement. Finally, I saw what looked like a silhouette. I raised my weapon in that direction.

"Ready your weapons," I said in a whisper. I continued scanning. My heart was racing and my nerves were running wild. It was our first night patrol and if we were to open fire, we needed a damn good reason. We would never hear the end of it, if it ended up being wildlife or our minds playing tricks on us.

"Ma'am, movement sector 3.53 and moving fast," Chan called out. I brought my attention back to that sector.

"Fire a warning shot," I shouted and I heard a shot ring out in the air. I pressed the button to call back to Anguish.

"Wolverines to Command Base."

"This is Command Base," a voice I didn't recognize said.

"Movement in sector 3.53 one warning shot fired."

"Roger, Wolverine."

"Any friendlies outside the wall?"

"Negative." I kept the Command Base frequency open and went back to Wolverine frequency.

"Moving fast. What are you orders, ma'am," Chan asked in a rush? I could finally see the movement he was talking about and it clearly wasn't wildlife, it was people and they were carrying weapons.

"Open fire," I said without thinking. Chan fired five shots. Silence fell and I didn't see any more movement. I heard a whistle then saw a flame soaring through the air. "Chan, run!" I don't know if I was too late, but a few seconds later his lookout tower exploded in a shower of fire and debris. "Open fire! Shoot to kill," I yelled over the comms. I began sending rounds of my own down at the silhouettes.

"Wolverines," War Advisor Jennings said right as bullets flew past my head.

"We need backup, now, sir," I said, continuing to fire. Adrenaline was flooding through my body and I could barely breathe. This was just supposed to be a simple night patrol and we would be back in our beds in no time. It seemed like my bad luck had poured on to the Wolverines.

"Backup is on their way, Armistice," War Advisor Jennings announced.

"Ma'am, do you need us," Faber asked from the far side of the wall.

"Negative, hold your positions," I said. I stopped firing and scanned for any movement. "Chan?" There was no response. "Chan," I asked against frantically.

"I'm here, ma'am," he said softly but I could tell in his voice that was something was wrong.

"You keep talking to us. Faber, scan your sector but keep talking to Chan."

"Roger," Faber said and began talking about random stuff to Chan.

"Towers ten, thirteen and fourteen. I want grenades in Sector 3.52. Light the whole damn thing up!" Whistles could be heard, but this time from our side of the wall. A few seconds later, the artillery rounds hit the trees and exploded. We could hear screams filtering through the thick trees and saw four flickering shapes moving through the trees.

"Kaitlyn, we're five minutes out," Eric said over the communication hi-fi.

"I need a medic, immediately, to lookout tower eleven," I said. I could barely breathe, thinking of what happened to Chan, and the extent of his injuries. I went silent and continued scanning. I thought I saw movement farther down the wall in the tree line. "All towers, fire heat seekers at the tree line. Ten rounds right after that."

They didn't bother replying, just did as I said. I did the same. The trees ignited and bullets zipped through the air. Silence fell over the night, other than crackling of the trees burning.

"Movement in sector, 5.2, ma'am. Group of ten people moving fast towards the wall. What do I do ma'am," Adams shouted?

"Light em' up. All towers permission to fire at will. Expend all rounds if need be. Back up is on its way," I said knowing that all deaths would be on my head.

The wars I saw on broadcast were nothing compared to this; explosions enveloping the scene in front of me, bullets flying in all directions. I heard screams of pain on both sides of the wall.

"I need an update, Armistice," War Advisor Jennings said calmly.

"We need immediate backup and medics."

"Understood. Are you injured, Armistice?"

"I don't know, sir. I will look later," I open fired on a moving target. I fired two more rounds of grenades in that direction. A ball of flames came back in my direction and missed the tower by a few feet. A fresh wave of adrenaline poured down my spine and into my limbs. My pulse pounded in my ears and my skin tingled.

"Ma'am, what do we do," Hewitt asked.

"Sound off from tower one and over. If there is even a second pause, go to the next tower." They quickly began sounding off and only 27 sounded off. A pain in my heart struck me.

"We hit a snag. We will be there in four minutes," Eric said. Four minutes wasn't going to do us any good. I kept thinking about never seeing Eric again and never being in his arms again. I wished he was there so I could tell him how I felt. Now, I would never get the chance to tell him. Back up was minutes out and I knew we would eventually run out of ammo.

"Light up the sky. Fire flares," I said firing the first flare. The sky illuminated and clusters of troops could be seen. "Kill all of them," I said in a growl and the war officially began. I don't know how long it lasted or how many of them were killed, but I didn't stop shooting. I could see someone walk up next to me and begin firing, but I didn't stop to look who it was. I just kept firing. Bullets whizzed by our heads and we didn't stop shooting.

I heard 'retreat' off in the distance and the sounds of bullets ceased at the tree line.

"They called 'retreat' ma'am," Adams said.

"Do not put your weapons down. If you even think you see movement, you shoot," I growled. My anger was hot and red, radiating from my neck and face. I wanted to jump over the wall and hunt down every one of them for what they had done. "Sound off from tower one just like we did before." They did and the count was even less, now the count was twenty-four.

I held in the tears and bit my lip to keep from crying. Eight from my regiment were unaccounted for. I could hear trucks behind me. Doors opened, and a few minutes later closed. The trucks drove away quickly, their rumbling exhaust fading into the background. They were taking the casualties, or fatalities, back to Anguish. I kept my eyes front and remained vigilant. I don't know how much time passed, but the sun was coming up on the horizon and I removed my night oculars, and then I went back to scanning.

"Armistice," War Advisor Jennings said.

"Sir," I said in a whisper.

"The Guardians are coming to relieve the Wolverines." All I could do was nod my head and hold back the tears.

"She understands, sir," Eric said coming into my view. He didn't say anything, just looked at me. I didn't bother looking at him, because I knew I would break down and cry. I just kept staring at the tree line. He finally returned his gaze to the tree line. Several minutes went by.

"We're here, Armistice," Roy said over the communication hi-fi.

"Get them all first. And then come get me," I said in a raspy voice.

"Understood," he said without argument. There seemed to be endless silence. Finally, I felt someone walk up behind me. They moved to the left of me and it was Roy. "Go get some rest, Kaitlyn." I didn't say anything or look at him, just turned and began walking towards the stairs.

"You guys did a great job, Kaitlyn," Eric said softly. I didn't bother looking over my shoulder. I just walked down the stairs and got in the truck. The truck was filled with eighteen Wolverines, who were banged up bad. All of us were covered in explosion residue, blood, and dirt. The doors to the truck closed. I took a deep breath as the truck began to move. None of us spoke, just hung our heads and waited for the truck to reach Anguish.

We, finally, reached Anguish and the doors opened. War Advisor Jennings, Covington, Bruce and Rival were waiting for us, along with a team full of doctors and medical aides. The Wolverines slowly offloaded from the truck, their movements stiff and blundering from the fatigue. Doctors quickly began looking all of them over and taking them off to the infirmary. Once they were all taken off, I climbed out of the truck. War Advisor Jennings and the commanders were all staring at me. None of them spoke, which was good because I didn't have any words to speak back.

"Kaitlyn," Covington said walking towards me. He took my weapon from me. Then he pulled me into his arms and I did everything in my power not to cry. "Proud of you." I nodded my head and he looked down at me. "Anything I can do for you?"

"Take me to them," I whispered and he released me. They all looked at me in horror.

"I object to that, Armistice," War Advisor Jennings said. I quickly glared at him.

"I prefer to have your permission, but either way I am going to see their bodies, sir," I said in a slight growl. He nodded his head and gestured for me to follow him. I don't know how I had the strength to walk, because I was terrified to see them, but I owed it to them.

We walked through the corridors in silence. I tried to prepare myself for what I was about to see, but I knew there was nothing to prepare me for the horror. We arrived at the infirmary overflow room. I could hear screams coming from the infirmary that made me shudder. I took a deep breath and faced the infirmary overflow room.

"You sure you want to do this," Rival asked softly. I nodded my head and stepped towards the door. The doors opened.

"By myself," I said stepping inside and the door shutting behind me. The lights came on and there were eight bodies displayed. I felt my lunch coming up and I covered my mouth with my hands. My heart was racing and the tears were waiting to explode. I took a deep breath and made my way to each body. They were all covered with sheets. I pulled back the sheet, said a prayer, and put the sheet back over each of the Wolverine bodies: Kaelin, Champion, Scott, Gentner, Vale, Carter, Reed, and Harper.

I felt my stomach rising into my throat, as I said my last prayer to Harper. I made my way to the door and looked over my shoulder, "May the archangels look over you now." I stepped towards the door again and it opened. War Advisor Jennings and the commanders were standing in front of it. I said nothing, only walked by them and into the infirmary. It was pure chaos and blood was everywhere.

I stood at the door and looked around at all the injured Wolverines, Vipers, and Warriors. I made my way over to the ones who were injured the most and talked with them regardless of which regiment they were part of. I tried to settle their minds, even though my mind was nowhere near peace. Ingram was the last severe Anguish I visited. The doctors told me that he most likely wouldn't survive the hour.

"You made me proud, Ingram," I said looking down at him. Smiling and holding his hand. He had lost an arm and his face was tattered on one side. He looked up at me, appeared to smile, and took his last breath. I placed his arms over his chest and closed his eyes. I said a prayer over his body and quickly left his room. I didn't know how much more I could handle before I broke. It felt like my soul was screaming in my chest, fighting to get out.

"Ma'am," I heard a soft voice say. I turned and peered into a room behind me. It was Chan. I moved swiftly into his room and over to his side.

"I'm here, Chan," I said smiling, holding back the tears, yet again.

"You saved me, ma'am," he said. "You saved me," he repeated. All I could do was nod. "Doctors did what they could." He moved to the blanket to the side and revealed his lower half. He was missing a leg. I steadied my breathing and looked up into his face.

"They did a fine job," I said smiling. "Just like you did." He nodded his head.

"How many, ma'am," he asked with his eyes piercing through me. I debated on whether I wanted to tell him. "Ma'am, please." His eyes were filling with tears.

"Eight. We lost eight Wolverines." He closed his eyes and the tears began to flow out of his eyes. I held his hand and he cried more. "They were warriors, Chan. They made us all proud." He nodded his head and opened his eyes.

"They were warriors, ma'am." He squeezed my hand.

"I will be back to check on you, soon. If you need me, tell the doctors and I'll come rushing back."

"Okay, ma'am."

"Kaitlyn." He looked up at me. "Just Kaitlyn." He nodded his head and smiled.

"I like that name, ma…Kaitlyn." I smiled, squeezed his hand one last time and walked out of the room. I finished seeing the remainder of Anguish. I walked out of the infirmary. War Advisor Jennings and the commanders were waiting for me. The rest of the commanders, excluding Eric, Dimitri, and Roy, were standing there.

"Hey," Orion said. I nodded my head.

"Have you been looked over by the doctors, yet," War Advisor Jennings asked. I shook my head because I could barely breathe. Walter and Franklin walked over to me and began removing my gear. Franklin removed my jacket and began looking me over. Franklin began pointing things out and all their eyes got huge.

"What," I asked trying to find what they were looking at.

"You've been shot, Kaitlyn," Walter said lifting me into his arms. I tried to get out of his arms. "Not, today, Kaitlyn."

"You're shot at least four times that I can see and you're bleeding everywhere," War Advisor Jennings said following Walter, who was carrying me in to the infirmary. I seemed to be a frequent patient.

A medical aide pointed to an open room and Heat carried me in there. He laid me on the bed and a doctor came in. It was Doctor Thomas. He saw me and laughed.

"You came to visit me, again, Armistice," he said walking over to me.

"So, it seems, sir," I said laying my head back. He began cutting my clothes off me, and War Advisor Jennings and Walter removed my boots. Doctor Thomas frowned and pushed the communication button.

"I need a surgeon in room three," he said and pushed the button again. Walter and War Advisor Jennings moved out of the way, as the surgery team came into the room. They shut the door and walked over to me. The surgeon approached me with a syringe and I shook my head.

"You need pain medication," War Advisor Jennings said.

"No. I will be okay. Save it for someone else," I said pushing the words out. The surgeon nodded and placed it back on the tray. They began poking and prodding around in me. I turned my head away from Walter and War Advisor Heat to hide the tears pouring down my face. The pain was excruciating but the mental pain was unbearable. Someone walked around the bed and held my hand. I looked up and it was War Advisor Jennings. He sat in the chair next to the bed. He didn't say anything, just held my hand. The surgeons continued with the task at hand.

"Last one, Armistice," Doctor Thomas said as the surgeon moved to the side of my head. He reached down towards my chest.

"This is going to hurt, but it will help your breathing," the surgeon said. I nodded my head and kept my eyes focused on the corner of the room. War Advisor Jennings squeezed my hand gently. I felt something probe into my chest. My scream caused the War Advisor to jump hard. It was the most agonizing pain I had ever experienced. "Almost done."

"You're doing great, Armistice. Look at me," War Advisor Jennings said. I looked at him. "Focus on me." I nodded my head and the surgeon continued again. The deeper he got the louder my screams were. Jennings' face turned white, but his grip remained strong around my hand.

"We can give you pain medication," Doctor Thomas said and I shook my head. I needed to suck it up and not let the rest of the infirmary hear me. They were going through enough without hearing me. The surgeon went back to digging around. I held back the screams but the tears slid down my face.

"All done," the surgeon said stepping back and looking me over.

"One more," Doctor Thomas said softly, and I felt his hand touch the side of my neck. War Advisor Jennings stood up and looked over me.

"Holy hell, Kaitlyn," he said. It was the first time he used my first name. "You really got yourself banged up."

"You're going to have to scan to see where the bullet is before I even attempt to retrieve that," the surgeon whispered to Doctor Thomas.

"Understood," Doctor Thomas whispered back.

"Just leave it," I said turning to face them.

"They can't just leave it, Kaitlyn," Walter said, walking over to the edge of the bed. I shrugged my head and turned my attention back to the corner of the room.

"Just do whatever. It doesn't matter at this point anyway." A tear slipped down my face.

"Come on, Kaitlyn. This isn't like you. You're a fighter. Don't give up, now," Walter said.

"Let's scan first and go from there," the surgeon said. Doctor Thomas began scanning me. He let out a breath and set the scanner down. "Let's get her medicated."

"I don't want any," I growled.

"Armistice, enough!" War Advisor Jennings snapped at me, "Let them give you medicine or…," He continued to say. I quickly sat up and glared at him.

"Or what, sir," I growled. His face softened. "You can't do anything to me that hasn't already been done." The true tears that I was trying to hold back escaped my eyes. I laid my head back on the pillow and sobbed. I didn't bother hiding the tears. "Just knock me out," I said and that was the last thing I remembered.

Chapter Thirteen
Archangels

I woke up screaming, sweat pouring down my body, and shaking. I quickly sat up and laid back down. The door opened and the lights came on. Dimitri was over by my side and stroking my face.

"It's okay. Relax. You're in the infirmary. You've been out of surgery for five hours. It's just the pain medication wearing off," he said softly. I nodded my head and wiped my eyes. The infirmary was quiet and I could only hear monitor machines steadily beeping.

"How many did you lose," I finally asked. He looked at me and shook his head.

"None." I nodded my head.

"Good," I whispered. I sat up and he tried to lay me back down. "I need to get out of this bed." He nodded and helped me stand up. My legs were wobbly and I began to fall. He caught me and held me in place.

"You sure you want to get up so soon?"

"Yes, I can't stay here, Dimitri." He nodded and helped me over to the door. He grabbed the robe in the chair and draped it over my shoulders. We walked out of the room. Doctor Thomas was already getting up out of his chair and storming over to me.

"She needs to be in bed," Doctor Thomas said.

"You tell her that," Dimitri growled. It was the first time I heard his voice in an unpleasant tone.

"Armistice, get back in that bed," Doctor Thomas said pointing behind me.

"We both," I took a deep breath, "know that isn't going to happen." I was more winded than I thought, but refused to lay back down.

"I will release you under one condition," Doctor Thomas said, flustered. I looked up at him. "You have to have someone with you for the next 24 hours." I nodded my head and waited for him to sign the discharge papers. Before I left the infirmary, I went by all the rooms and talked to everyone. Dimitri waited outside of the rooms for me. Finally, after I talked to the last one, which was Chan, we left the infirmary. Orion, Bruce, Franklin, Mason, and Milton were all leaned up against the wall. They frowned when they saw me.

"I thought you were just going in to check on her," Mason said looking at Dimitri.

"As did I," Dimitri chuckled to himself.

"I knew I should have gone in with you," Franklin said pointing at Dimitri, "but they said only one person at a time."

"She isn't allowed to be by herself for 24 hours," Dimitri announced. I saw the infirmary overflow room and began walking towards it. Dimitri held me back from it.

"I need to," I whispered. They all shook their heads.

"They have been laid to rest," Orion said, placing a hand on my shoulder. A tear slid down my face and I nodded my head. I wiped away the tear.

"Let's get you out of here," Milton said, bending down to pick me up. I shook my head and stepped back.

"I can walk," he stood back up and laughed.

"You have got to be the most stubborn female in the world," he said continuing to laugh.

Dimitri supported me on my left side and we all walked down the corridors. Trainees and Anguish were quick to move out of our way. They stood at attention and didn't move until we were out of the corridor. This was something new. The same thing happened down the other corridors we walked down.

"Hungry," Milton asked. I looked at him. "Whoa, easy," he said holding up his hands and laughing.

"The food here is awful," I said.

"True, but you need to eat. I could talk to one of the cooks and have them make you some soup," Orion said. I was now looking at him. "What?"

"You mean this entire time I could've had soup?" They all laughed and helped get me to the dining hall. We walked in and everyone stood at attention. "What in the hell," I whispered.

"Anguish respect," Milton whispered. I stopped walking and felt wobbly. "Kaitlyn?"

"I'm fine," I whispered.

"You sure? We can leave," Dimitri whispered.

"I will be fine." We walked further into the dining hall. The Wolverines who weren't injured or released from the infirmary were standing at attention facing me at the commanders' table, which now had an extra table attached to it. A tear slid down my face and I froze in place.

"Kaitlyn, we can leave," Bruce whispered. I shook my head, wiped the tear from my face and walked over to the commanders' table. Dimitri helped me into a chair and everyone in the dining hall took their seat. The other commanders, excluding Dimitri who went to get me some soup, sat down. The Wolverines looked at me, but no one said anything.

"I am proud of every one of you," I said looking at each of them and smiling. They nodded their heads.

"We are honored to have you as our commander, ma'am," Goss said. I nodded my head.

"One on one I am just Kaitlyn to you. You have all earned it." They seemed surprised but nodded. They were now staring behind me. A hand reached around me and placed a bowl of soup in front of me and a glass of water.

"Thank you," I said turning around and looking up. I froze, and felt the tears building up once more. Eric was standing in full gear with Dimitri by his side. Dimitri grinned and took a seat. Eric just stood there. "Hi," I whispered.

"Hey," he replied. He ran his hand through his hair. "I just got back from patrol and came as soon as I heard you were awake." I nodded my head. Milton, who was sitting next to me, got up.

"Here, you can have my seat, Eric," Milton said. Eric nodded and sat down. Milton sat a few seats further away.

"You need to eat," Eric whispered. I nodded and picked up the spoon, but my hands were shaking. Bruce reached over and steadied my hand. I looked at him and nodded. He smiled and nodded. I took a deep breath and he let go of my hand. I brought the soup to my lips and sipped. After a few attempts, my hands were steadier. Eric said nothing; he just watched me.

"They are talking about disbanding the Wolverines and sending us to other regiments, ma'am," Ulloa said. My spoon fell to the table and I looked at him.

"I won't serve under another commander," Oden said. The rest agreed.

"Perhaps going to another regiment is in your best interest," I whispered.

"Negative. You have our best interest in your heart, ma'am," Edwards said. A tear slid down my face and I quickly wiped it away. I didn't speak just nodded my head.

"I was scared to death, ma'am," Adams admitted. "I froze but then you came over the communication hi-fi and gave us orders. If you hadn't said anything, I wouldn't be here right now, ma'am. And you held you word." I looked at him. "You told us you'd be the last one out… and you were." I nodded my head and another tear slipped down my face. I wiped it away and Eric handed me a napkin. I dabbed my eyes and bit my lip.

"If it was to happen all over again, ma'am, I'd want you as my commander," Ulloa said.

"That," my voice was cracking. I took a deep breath and started over. "That means a lot to me."

"I hope you stay our commander, ma'am," Ulloa said. They were all looking behind me.

"I don't see why she wouldn't be allowed to be the Wolverines' commander," War Advisor Jennings said coming around the table and facing me. The table began to stand and he gestured for them to stay in place.

"There were rumors that the Wolverines were being disbanded," I whispered. He nodded his head.

"They would be disbanded, if you chose to give up your command, Armistice." I nodded my head. The Wolverines at the table were smiling. Despite being banged up and almost killed, having lost so many comrades, their spirits were high.

"Do you wish to remain the Wolverines' commander?" They were all staring at me.

My emotions were high. I had eight of my Wolverines killed in one firefight, had taken electric lashings to protect my Wolverines, and killed my father a few days prior to all of that. I wasn't sure if I could even command myself any more, much less my people. So much had happened. I wasn't the same person I was before, when I walked in through the Academy's doors, and I wasn't the same person who went into the command tower.

"Kaitlyn," Eric asked me. I just stared at War Advisor Jennings.

"The decision is solely yours," War Advisor Jennings said. I nodded my head and swallowed hard. I looked around the table at the Wolverines, who were anxiously waiting my decision. We had been through hell together, and yet, they were willing to do it again, if I was their commander. They were true warriors. I looked back at War Advisor Jennings.

"I'd be honored to continue being their commander, sir," I said firmly. Smiles broke out on all the Wolverines' faces and they were soon chanting the Wolverines' battle chant. The whole dining hall joined in on the chant. I looked around at those standing with me at the table and then around the room.

I was overwhelmed, my chest swelling with pride. I felt like the room was spinning and my stomach was spinning with it. I needed air and soon. I faced War Advisor Jennings, who had one eyebrow raised.

"Are you okay," he asked. I smiled and nodded my head. "Of course, sir, I just think my medicine has kicked in," I whispered. He laughed and nodded his head. Dimitri looked at me and frowned because he knew I was lying. "I think I need to go lay down for a few." War Advisor Jennings nodded his head. I stood up and the entire room did as well. I sighed and went to grab my bowl and glass. Bruce grabbed my hand. I looked down at him.

"I'll take care of it," he said softly. I nodded my head and began to walk towards the door. My legs were once again wobbly and I felt like the floor was disappearing beneath me. An arm wrapped around me. I looked next to me and it was Eric.

"Thanks," I whispered and he nodded his head.

"She has to have someone with her at all times for the next 24 hours," Dimitri said walking over to us. Eric looked at Dimitri and nodded his head.

"I have patrol in," Eric looked at his watch and groaned, "ten hours. Can one of you come by her room in nine hours?"

"I will be there," Milton said. Eric nodded and proceeded to help me out of the room. No one sat down until the doors closed.

Chapter Fourteen
Where to now?

I let out a sigh and Eric picked me up in his arms.

"I can walk," I whispered.

"I know you can, sweetheart," he whispered and then planted a kiss on my head. He began carrying me down the corridor. He didn't stop until we reached my room. The room scanned me and the door opened. He walked in and the door shut behind us. He walked over to the bed and set me down.

"Thanks," I whispered. He kneeled and held my hand. The color in his face was drained. He held my hand against his face.

"I have never been so terrified in all my life," he said. I looked at him and he kissed my hand. "When I heard the announcement that your regiment was under attack, my heart stopped. I couldn't gather the Vipers fast enough. My father wanted to send the Reapers and Cobras, but I refused. I wasn't leaving you out there." He shook his head at the thought.

"I'm fine," I whispered and he held my hand to his face again.

"Kaitlyn, I can't explain how much I care about you." My heart stopped. "It's been only a short amount of time, but you're all I seem to care about. I didn't care if anything happened to me. I just cared if something happened to you. When I received word that you had been shot several times, it took everything within me not to leave my post and go running to you."

"You have obligations to the Vipers," I said. He nodded his head.

"I know, but I couldn't think about anything but you." He kissed my hand again. He was lost in thought and just kept staring at me.

"You can hang your gear up, if you'd like." He looked down at his gear and shrugged his shoulders. "You aren't climbing in to bed like that." He looked up at me and our eyes met.

"I'm filthy though," he whispered.

"I don't care, but if it's that big a deal use my shower."

"I will be quick," he leaned down and kissed my forehead. He began taking off his gear and then his clothes. It was the first time I saw him completely naked. He was covered in dirt, smudged with black residue from nearby explosions. He was dirty, bruised and scraped, but still looked incredible.

He walked into the bathing quarter and I heard the water turn on. I stood up slowly, and then took off my robe and clothes. I climbed back into bed and pulled the covers over me. A few minutes later, he walked back into the room wearing a towel. I slowly scooted over and he climbed in to bed. His skin was dry and warm. He set his watch and placed his arms around me. He ran his fingers down my arm.

"So smooth," he said and kissed the top of my head. He held me close to his body. He leaned his head against mine. "I don't know what I would have done if something would have happened to you."

"I'm fine," I whispered.

"I don't think you understand. You've become my entire world," I looked up at him and he was looking down at me. "I don't mean to scare you off."

"You aren't," I said shaking my head. "I thought about you, while I was out there. Kept thinking how I'd never see you again. When I kept doing headcounts and learned that I was losing more and more Wolverines as the bullets flew, I knew it was the end. I knew I'd never see you again." My eyes were swelling up with tears. He kissed my forehead and ran a finger down my cheek.

"You're safe, now, sweetheart."

"I'm glad you're here," I whispered. He gently squeezed me.

"Me too," he turned on his side and looked at me. "Kaitlyn, what if I asked you to walk away from Anguish?"

"What," it came out a shriek.

"It's not what you think. You are an excellent commander and Anguish. I just want you safe."

"So, you want me to leave? And go where, back to Neva?" Tears began to fill my eyes. He lifted my chin and looked at me.

"Sweetheart, I want you to move upstairs with me," he said smiling. I raised an eyebrow raised.

"What?"

"That's where all the other commanders live with their families." My heart skipped a beat. I hadn't realized the other commanders had families or that they lived upstairs in the academy. I never realized what was in the Academy. I just knew what was in the compound under the Academy.

"There are families up in the Academy," I asked. He rolled his eyes and laughed.

"Out of what I just said, that's the only question you have?" He was still laughing.

"What's wrong with," I stopped dead in my sentence. "Wait, what?" He grinned. "What do you mean move upstairs with you?" He kissed me gently.

"I want you in my life, Kaitlyn." A tear slipped down my face. He frowned and wiped the tear off. "I don't mean to upset you." I shook my head.

"You didn't," I said leaning my head against him.

"I understand, if you want some time to think about it before you decide."

"I can't give up being a commander, Eric," I whispered. He rolled over his back and sighed. "Don't be mad."

"I'm not mad, sweetheart." He rolled back on his side and looked at me. "I had a feeling you would say that and I respect that." I could tell he wasn't happy with my decision.

"Does that mean you don't want me," I tried to say it without shrieking, but it happened anyway. I became an emotional bomb waiting to explode. He kissed me gently.

"That's not what I'm saying at all. I still want you." The emotions settled down somewhat, but were still running high. "Get some sleep." I nodded my head and wondered if I could even fall asleep with everything on my mind. I felt calmer being in Eric's arms knowing that he was here with me. I didn't know how long he'd be in my life, but as long as he'd there when I woke up, I'd worry about the rest later.

PART THREE
Anguish Reborn

Anguish Reborn

Several weeks had passed and I was still battling my demons. I saw Councilman Tibbot on a regular basis to vent. Eric was there to listen, but he had enough on his plate with constantly worrying about me when I went out on patrols. The first few patrols we went on were hard on the Wolverines and me, but we pulled through it and were slowly becoming functional again.

I had visited my mother shortly after the battle, but not until my face was completely healed. I didn't want her to worry about me being at Anguish. Eric, of course, went with me and my mother absolutely loved him. I was beginning to question whether she loved him more than me.

War Advisor Jennings called me into his office quite frequently to talk, but not to talk about Anguish. We just talked about random topics and had a few drinks. Eric wasn't too fond of me drinking with his father; however, he dealt with it.

Things appeared to be finally getting back on track, but I refused to think they'd ever be the same as they once were. Nothing would ever be the same, again, here at Anguish…at least not for me.

Chapter One
New Wolverines

The graduation hall was quiet while War Advisor Jennings passed out orders to a group of graduating trainees, but wasn't quiet when he announced their regiment. Each regiment cheered loud and accepted their new comrades. So far, the Wolverines hadn't received anyone and I had a feeling we wouldn't. We were probably considered cursed in everyone's books. I was debating on ordering my regiment to leave and go have down time, since we had a patrol in two hours.

"Parson, Locks, Jeffrey, Truman, Guthrie, Schmidt, Richards, and Cunningham front and center," War Advisor Jennings announced. The group he called was the most mischievous trainees of the entire graduating class. I could hear other commanders grumbling, hoping that their regiment wasn't called. I could only laugh at their distress.

The eight trainees fell into formation on the platform next to War Advisor Jennings. War Advisor Jennings ran his hand through his hair, shook his head and laughed.

"I hope you all have lots of stamina, discipline, hard work, and a lot of heart. Not to mention a room at the infirmary because you will probably get your ass handed to you, once or twice." War Advisor Jennings said laughing. The commanders were all pointing at each other, hoping the other one got the group. "It is with great honor that I announce that you are now Wolverines."

All eyes were on the Wolverines and me. I was waiting for the trainees to run off the platform and out the door, but much to my surprise they started doing the Wolverine battle cry. The Wolverines and I were on our feet and doing the battle cry with them. The trainees quickly jumped off the platform and made their way over to us. They stood in front of me at attention. The Wolverines fell quiet.

"Welcome to the Wolverines," I said grinning. "Take a seat."
They quickly sat down. I saw the other commanders and they
were all pointing at me and laughing, including Eric. I rolled
my eyes and went back to looking at War Advisor Jennings,
who was also laughing. Soon he wrapped up the graduation
and we were out the door.
We quickly got the new Wolverines into their rooms and
situated. I caught Dimitri walking down the hall.
"Hey, do me a favor," I asked walking up to him.
"Sure. What do you need," he asked? I leaned over to him.
"Will you keep an eye on the new Wolverines?" He raised an
eyebrow. "I'd feel better if they stayed back for this one. I'll
take them out on the next one." Dimitri nodded his head.
"They can come hit the mats with us."
"Thank you," I walked down the hallway and called out all
their names. They stood in front of their rooms along with a
few veteran Wolverines. "I need you eight to follow
Commander Aiyetoro. You will be training with him and the
Cobras." They groaned.
"Ma'am, why can't we go with you," Jeffrey asked.
"I'd feel better, if you went out on the next one. Please, don't
question my orders. Everything I do is in your best interest."
Edwards stepped further out of his room, fully geared, and
glared at Jeffrey.
"Question our commander one more time and I'll personally
bury you," Edwards snapped.
"Not necessary, Edwards," I said laughing. "You think you're
ready to go out on a patrol," I asked staring at Jeffrey. He
hesitantly nodded his head. I laughed. "Fine, all of you gear
up," I announced.
"Ma'am," Edwards asked. I grinned and faced Jeffrey.
"You're with Edwards, Jeffrey." Jeffrey's face paled as he
looked at Edwards, who was grinning. "You all have five
minutes to be fully geared up."
They ran into their rooms. I looked at Dimitri, who was
shaking his head and laughing.

"Maybe I should have just babysat them, because now they are being fed to the sharks," Dimitri said laughing.

"They'll be okay... for the most part," I said winking. I faced Edwards. "Five minutes. Not a second more. Have them at the Guardian Gate in six minutes." He nodded his head and I walked off.

At exactly six minutes, all the Wolverines met me at the Guardian Gate. We grabbed our weapons. The new Wolverines were nervous and fumbling with their weapons. Allen, Smith, and Croteau took them under their wings and attempted to help the new Wolverines. The rest of the Wolverines growled as they walked passed them. We found our way to the depot and waited for the truck.

"Armistice," Eric growled coming around the corner. I just grinned, as he began walking through the Wolverines, who quickly moved out of his way.

"Yes, Commander Trials," I asked sweetly. He rolled his eyes and walked over to me.

"Just like that?"

"Like what," I asked grinning.

"Just going to go out on patrol without saying anything?" He crossed his arms.

"You and the Vipers were busy tossing each other around on the mats," I said laughing. He shrugged his shoulders.

"You could have interrupted."

"You guys need all the practice you can get," I said grinning. A few Wolverines began laughing, but quickly stopped when Eric glared at them. He turned and faced me.

"You think the Vipers are weak," he asked trying hard not to smile.

"No, they aren't weak. Just not as strong as my Wolverines," I said looking around him and the Wolverines, who had cocky grins on their faces. "Or as fierce." I looked back at Eric and he finally laughed.

"We will talk about that later. Did you forget something?"

"To say 'goodbye'," I asked and he shook his head. I began thinking of what I could possibly have forgotten. Finally, I shrugged my shoulders. "What?" He leaned down and kissed me. The Wolverines were snickering to themselves. Eric and I slowly pulled away. I could feel my cheeks burning from embarrassment. It was the first time Eric had kissed me in front of people.

"Next time you interrupt my training or I'll kiss you again in front of your," he looked over his shoulder, "Wolverines." The Wolverines were laughing. Eric looked at me again and smiled. "Be safe."

"Yeah, yeah. Now that you have me all flustered," I whispered. He laughed and put a hand on my shoulder.

"I mean it, be safe." He wasn't laughing anymore. I nodded my head.

"We will be." The truck started up. "Load up!"

"Yes, ma'am!" They began climbing in to the truck.

"I didn't mean to embarrass you," Eric whispered and I laughed.

"Sure you didn't," I rolled my eyes and he laughed.

"Just be safe." He gave me another kiss. "I'll see you when you get back." I nodded my head and walked past him. Him saying, 'I'll see you when you get back' had become his motto in a way, which he'd say to me before I went out on patrol.

We were on hour five of patrol and things were quiet. I kept doing headcounts every half an hour to keep everyone awake. Patrols could get boring and soon you found yourself drifting to sleep.

"I got movement, ma'am," Harlan announced and my heart began to race. I couldn't handle losing anymore Wolverines. We had lost too many already.

"Identify the target," I said calmly. I wanted to scream for them to get out of their tower and run. I didn't want any of them to die. "Is the target identified?"

"Negative, ma'am," Harlan said. "Still trying to identify target, ma'am." I began scanning my sector even more thoroughly in case there was more than one group of Fritz' troops. I was ready to give the order to retreat.

"Have you identified the target," I asked again. I heard Harlan laugh. "Harlan?"

"Sorry, ma'am. It is just a bear." I let out a breath and laughed. Damned bears.

"Good call. Stay alert."

Chapter Two
Neva Forgive Me

The remainder of the patrol I was on pins and needles. Even though Harlan had only seen a bear, it didn't mean no one was out there ready to attack us. Dimitri and his Cobras came and replaced us at the sixth hour. I briefed Dimitri on the bear, which he laughed about, and then we were on our way back to Anguish. I leaned my head against the wall of the truck and closed my eyes. I was a nervous wreck. I was so scared that something bad was going to happen to us out there, especially with my new members in tow. The Wolverines were laughing and joking about the bear.

An explosion went off in the distance and made me sit up. I heard the muffled sound of gun shots being fired behind us. I quickly pushed the Communication hi-fi button.

"Driver, turn around," I screamed to the driver and truck made a sharp U-turn. I looked at the Wolverines, who looked terrified. "I'm sorry. You are welcome to stay in the truck and I won't think any less of you. Understand?"

"Yes, ma'am," they said and began readying their weapons.

"This time," I said, they all looked at me, "send them all to their archangels. I refuse to go to any of your memorials. Understood?"

"Yes, ma'am," they said. The communication hi-fi was already filled with chatter.

"We need back up," Dimitri screamed.

"The Vipers, Widow Makers, and Knights will be to your position in fifteen minutes, Commander Aiyetoro," command base announced.

"Fifteen minutes," Dimitri shouted. I pushed the communication hi-fi.

"Dimitri, the Wolverines will be there in less than a minute," I said.

"Negative, Kaitlyn. Not you," Dimitri said. "Get you and the Wolverines back to Anguish. You don't need to," I heard an explosion ring out across the communication hi-fi for several seconds.

"Dimitri," I asked, but he didn't respond. "Driver, command tower first."

"Roger, ma'am." I wasn't ready for this. My heart felt like it was pounding out of my chest and I felt that at any moment I was going to hurl. "Almost there. Thirty seconds, ma'am." I stood up and began opening the back of the truck. I grabbed explosives off the wall of the truck and began tossing them to the Wolverines. I placed five of them in my vest and then looked at the Wolverines. They were just as scared as I was.

"First in," I said smiling.

"Last out, ma'am," the veteran Wolverines said standing. The new Wolverines stood up and took deep breaths.

"We go out as an entire regiment and we come back as an entire regiment along with all of the Cobras. I can't lose any of you." I was on the verge of tears. "I'm proud of all of you."

"Always an honor, ma'am," Edwards said placing a hand on my shoulder. The doors fully opened.

"You're up, ma'am," the driver announced. The truck slowed down but didn't stop. I quickly hopped out of the truck, lost my footing and ended up combat rolling until I stopped. I was quickly on my feet and running up the stairs to the command tower. It was in rubble. I made my way to the far side of the tower and it was completely blown out.

"I'm at the command tower and don't have eyes on Commander Aiyetoro," I announced. Bullets began whizzing past my head, flattening and ricocheting off the walls. I crouched down and began returning fire. Everything inside me told me to run. Time seemed to crawl as my rifle spat fire into the forest beyond the tower. War was scary regardless if it was in the dark of night or the light of day.

"We need a status report, Armistice," War Advisor Jennings said over the comm. I continued firing, while trying to count the number of Fritz troops I saw.

"Minimum of fifty troops and, at least, ten vehicles advancing toward the wall, sir." They were only advancing down the center and nowhere else on the wall. "They are trying to ram a salient through the center of the wall."

"Get out of there, Kaitlyn," War Advisor Jennings shouted.

"Towers three, four, five and six make your way down to towers seven, eight and nine. Do not go to past tower ten. I repeat, do not go past tower ten. Light up anything that moves. I don't give a rat's ass if it's a damn bear. You shoot to kill."

"Yes, ma'am," they shouted over the communication hi-fi.

"Towers twenty-three through thirty, you make your way to towers fifteen through twenty-two. Light up anything that moves," I continued firing on moving targets. "Towers one, two, thirty-one, and thirty-two they don't seem to be coming in your directions, but be ready just in case. Announce," a bullet flew past my head and I felt my heart skip a beat. I took a deep breath. "Announce any movement." I said with my breathing ragged.

"Yes, ma'am," they chimed.

"Kaitlyn," I heard Dimitri say faintly on the communication hi-fi.

"Dimitri," I said hysterically. "Where are you?" I continued firing and dodging bullets.

"The bottom of the tower," he was wheezing, "outside the wall." My world shattered. I took up position in a corner and began peering over the edge. I couldn't see him. I scanned further out away from the wall. Finally, I saw a leg. I jumped to the other corner of the tower to get a better view. I could see him. He was bleeding and covered in rubble a hundred feet or more away from the wall. None of the rubble appeared to be big parts of the wall; just blast pieces from the explosion.

"I have eyes on you, Dimitri," I said in a hushed breath. I began looking around the command tower. There was barely anything left of it.

"Leave, Kaitlyn," Dimitri said. His breathing was getting worse.

"War Advisor Jennings," I asked.

"Yes," he said.

"I need the command codes."

"Command codes?" I was already running down the stairs and to the wall door.

"I need to open the door," I was out of breath.

"Don't you dare do it, Kaitlyn," Eric growled over the communication hi-fi.

"War Advisor Jennings, please, give them to me now, before Eric gets here."

"Don't you give them to her," Eric yelled.

"If you don't, Commander Aiyetoro will die," I pleaded.

"Martin, get to my location now." Martin was the closest one to me.

"Yes, ma'am," Martin said. I could hear him running.

"Just wait. We are ten minutes out," Eric stated. I slung my weapon on my back.

"Sir, he doesn't have ten minutes. I need the codes now," I asked.

"No," Eric growled.

"Five, three, two, four, six," War Advisor Jennings whispered. Eric began going off on his father, but I didn't have time to deal with either one of them.

"Towers eight, nine, fifteen and sixteen I need smoke in front of the command tower and lots of it."

"Roger. Smoke coming your way," Edwards announced. I could hear the shots being fired, a short series of staccato thumps, and the impacts hitting in front of the wall.

"Let me know when the sector is covered in smoke," I readied my fingers on the key pad. Martin was now by my side. "Martin, do not open this door back up unless I call it over communications, okay?" He looked at me with terrified eyes. "Okay? Do not come out after me."

"Yes, ma'am," he finally said.

"You close this door, immediately, behind me." He nodded his head. "Five, three, two, four, six. Can you remember that," I asked him? He nodded his head. "If you forget just ask War Advisor Jennings." He nodded his head again.

"Kaitlyn," Eric said calmly.

"I'll see you later," I said holding back the tears. I was scared beyond disbelief. I was living my nightmare all over again. I should've walked away from Anguish after the first battle and returned to Neva, but I stayed. I stayed for the Wolverines and I stayed for Eric.

"You're good to go, ma'am," Edwards announced and I was already punching in the code. The doors opened and I quickly slipped through and began making my way to Dimitri. He was just shaking his head and gesturing for me to go back. The closer I got the more frantic he became about me leaving him.

"I'm not leaving you," I said finally reaching him.

"Go," he said faintly. "Save yourself." I could hear the vehicles getting closer and the shots getting louder. I didn't know how much longer the smoke would hold.

"Buy me some time. Explosives, now," I said beginning to remove rubble from the top of Dimitri. Loud whistles filled the air and soon the ground shook. Flames burst throughout the tree line.

"Cover yourself, ma'am. Firing another round of smoke," Edwards announced. I leaned across Dimitri's face.

"Clear," I said and the ground shook and the air filled with smoke. I was moving as fast as my arms could go trying to remove the rest of the rubble. I wrapped my arms around Dimitri.

"Just go," he said staring at me. I just shook my head and a tear slid down my face. I began dragging him towards the door. An explosion went off a few feet from us, showering us in dirt and grit. I screamed without thought.

"Kaitlyn," Eric shouted over the communication hi-fi.

"I'm okay," I said panting and continuing to drag Dimitri. The door was a lot farther than I thought. I continued dragging Dimitri, who seemed to get heavier and heavier. The battle was getting more and more intense. I could hear the Fritz vehicles growing louder. They couldn't have been more than a half mile away. I had to do something fast. "Jennings?"

"Yes, Armistice?"

"Patch me through to Neva," I said and stopped dragging Dimitri.

"Okay." He didn't even question my reasons.

"Neva command center," I heard a voice say.

"This is Princess Kaitlyn Armistice of Neva. Launch the squadron to the North wall of Lynx, and permission to fire on anything north of the wall," I said. Neva was a canton of peace, but had an entire squadron of fighter jets, who were proficient in air-to-ground combat.

"Princess, we are in a time of peace," the voice said.

"Not anymore. Neva is now at war status; authorization code ten, fifteen, twenty-two, five."

"Roger. Pulling the squadron from training exercise and inbound to requested position now. Estimated time of arrival one minute," the voice said reluctantly. I would ask my mother and Neva for forgiveness for getting them into a war, but without them, Lynx would not survive this battle. The wall would crumble and hundreds of Lynxans would be killed. I began dragging Dimitri once more.

"Wolverines and Cobras, cease fire," I heard all shots cease on our side of the wall. "Now, gather up any injured Anguish and get the hell out of the towers now. Run towards Lynx and do not stop running until you can no longer run," I shouted. "Trucks inbound to the Northern wall, stop and hold your position."

"Roger," I heard a voice say.

"Negative, we are on our way to you," Eric screamed.

"Sir," I asked hoping War Advisor Jennings would back me up on this.

"This is War Advisor Jennings all trucks cease movement and hold position until told otherwise," War Advisor Jennings hesitantly said. Nothing that came out of Eric's mouth was pleasant. He wasn't just yelling at his father, but he was now yelling at me. I could hear the squadron nearing our location and began dragging Dimitri faster towards the door. I was struggling to pull Dimitri and couldn't seem to catch my breath. I pushed my communication hi-fi to Wolverine frequency only.

"Martin, I'm going to need you to run towards Lynx," I said out of breath.

"Ma'am," Martin asked. His voice was shaky.

"I need you to go now," I said firmly.

"I can't leave you," he said softly.

"I know, but you're going to have to. I need you to help the others. Now, go. We're almost to the door. You can open it once the squadron leaves." Dimitri looked up and me. We still had at least a hundred feet until we would reach the door and I was beyond exhausted. I looked over my shoulder to make sure Martin had obeyed me.

"Princess, thirty seconds. What are your orders," the Nevan command center asked? I switch back to command frequency.

"Orders are to destroy anything to the north of the wall," I said laying Dimitri down.

"Roger. Squadron leader, did you copy," the Nevan command center asked.

"Roger. Princess, we're inbound to your location and will destroy anything north of the wall," the squadron leader said proudly. I dragged Dimitri over against the wall, as close as I could get him. I looked at him once more.

"Just go," he said. I shook my head, ran a finger down his face and leaned over him. He tried to move me off him, but he was in no condition to fight me. I easily overpowered him.

"Armistice, are you on our side of the wall," War Advisor Jennings asked. I couldn't lie to him. "Armistice?" There was a pause. "Armistice," he asked softly.

"Yes, sir, I am," I finally said.

"No, she's not, sir," Edwards said. "She ordered Martin to leave her. She's still on the other side, sir."

"Princess, is that true," the squadron leader asked. "We can't fire with the chance of hitting you."

"You have your orders," I said as firm as I could.

"Roger. Weapons are going hot. May the Nevan Guardians be with you," he said.

"May the Nevan Guardians be with you, as well," I said. There was silence across the communication hi-fi.

"Armistice, talk to me. Why aren't you on our side," War Advisor Jennings asked.

"I'm not leaving him, sir."

"Kaitlyn," he said. The tears began pouring down my face. "Kaitlyn, I am ordering you to get behind our walls. Stop being stubborn for once in your life and obey an order."

"Sorry, sir, I can barely hear you. I think the squadron is interfering with our frequency." I pushed the button turning off all outgoing transmissions and did the same thing to Dimitri's.

"Kaitlyn," War Advisor Jennings asked.

"Kaitlyn," Heat shouted. I didn't respond. I just cried and listened to the incoming squadron.

"Kaitlyn, answer us, right now," Eric shouted. His voice was distressed. I didn't respond because I didn't want to say 'goodbye'. I knew they would all just tell me to leave Dimitri and get to safety.

"Mission still a go," the squadron leader asked. I quickly pushed the button.

"It's a go," I said.

"Roger, targets in sight." I held Dimitri against my body and I felt the walls shake from the Squadron. They were coming in low and fast. I didn't look up, just kept my head down and held Dimitri. His arms wrapped around me and he held me against him. The tears were streaming down my face as fast as the squadron was moving. "Firing."

Whistles filled the air. The atmosphere turned hot and dry, howling wind accompanied by earth-shattering impacts. I held on to Dimitri as tight as I could, while the ground shook and rubble fell on top of us. The whistles and explosions continued. I heard the squadron fly over us.

"Going to make a second pass," the squadron leader said. I didn't respond to him. I just held Dimitri. He had always been kind to me and over the months at Anguish became a good friend. He stuck up for me numerous times and was always smiling. I couldn't just leave him, even if it meant my death. He wouldn't die alone.

"Kaitlyn," Eric said. His voice was shaky. I couldn't answer him, because I refused to let 'goodbye' be the last thing I said to him. "Kaitlyn, please, sweetheart, say something." I heard the squadron bank around and they were inbound once more. I held Dimitri as tightly as I could.

"Ma'am, please," Edwards begged. "Say something. Let us know you're okay." Again, I said nothing. I knew if I said anything that they would come through the door to protect me and we didn't need any more Anguish lives lost. Dimitri squeezed my arms and I looked down at him. He didn't say anything, just looked at me. I smiled at him and he smiled back.

"It has been an honor, ma'am," Martin said. I could hear the sadness in his voice and hear that he was crying. I began crying more and saw the tears slide down Dimitri's face as well. I kissed him on his cheek and leaned over him one last time. The squadron flew back from Fritz canton and fired everything they had left. Rubble rained down on Dimitri and me. My ears rang from explosions practically on top of me. My back felt like it was on fire, and the screams that tore their way out of my throat left my body limp. More tears fell from my eyes. I was in excruciating pain, but refused to let go of Dimitri.

"All targets destroyed. Returning to base," the squadron leader said. The squadron flew over the wall.

"Armistice," War Advisor Jennings asked. I couldn't speak. The tears no longer ran down my face. I just laid across Dimitri's body. "Anyone, give me an update on Armistice," he yelled.

"The last thing I heard was her screaming after the last explosion, sir," McKenzie said sobbing.

"All trucks get to that door," he ordered.

"We're already on our way to the door, sir," Edwards said.

"Get it open, now," War Advisor Jennings growled. "Get them out of there."

Memories began flashing through my mind. Memories from my childhood all the way up to this moment. The two people I was going to miss were my mother and Eric. I would miss the Wolverines as well, they had become family.

I heard the door opening and footsteps running towards us. My body was rolled off Dimitri's and Edwards was standing over me. His face was frozen in a twisted mask of horror.

"We found them, sir," he said turning his head and covering his mouth. He turned back to us. Martin, Hess, Oden, Allen, and Smith were standing over us now. They all went pale.

"Status report," War Advisor Jennings whispered.

"It's not good, sir."

"What is it," War Advisor Jennings asked. "Are they alive?" Edwards bent down and felt my pulse. Allen felt Dimitris' pulse.

"Commander Aiyetoro is alive, sir," Allen said.

"What about Armistice," Eric asked.

"Barely, sir," Edwards said bending down to pick me up. I shook my head and pointed at Dimitri. "We have to get you out of here first, ma'am." I shook my head. "Sir, she won't let us move her, until Commander Aiyetoro is out."

"Then hurry up," War Advisor Jennings snapped. Martin, Oden, Hess, and Allen picked up Dimitri and carried him off. Smith and Edwards bent down and picked me up.

"Easy, Edwards, she's burned pretty bad," Smith said.

"Burned," War Advisor Jennings asked with his voice shaking.

"Yes, sir," Edwards said, carrying me with Smith. A truck was already waiting and Dimitri was loaded up. I was next to be loaded. I laid there with my eyes closed. I felt a hand touch my arm. I turned my head and opened my eyes. It was Dimitri. I smiled one last time and darkness consumed me.

Chapter Three
Nevan Archangels

I slowly opened my eyes. I could see a bright light shining
through the crack of door in front of me. I slowly sat up. I was
sitting on a bed in an all-white room. I looked around the
room. There was just the bed and me. I found myself standing
up and walking over to the door. I was wearing a white
hospital gown. I grabbed the handle and it turned with ease.
The door opened and the light shined brighter.
"Kaitlyn," a soft female's voice called out to me. "You're safe
now." I found myself walking further into the light. Warmth
filled my body and I continued walking. "You were so brave.
You saved many lives." I nodded my head.
I reached the source of the light. Before me was a tall, pale
woman with long red hair. She was wearing a white gown
that covered her feet. She was smiling at me.
"You have a heart of gold and the soul of a warrior," she said.
I nodded my head and looked around me. There was nothing
around me but whiteness. I looked back at her. "Do you know
where you are?" I shook my head.
"You are where all Nevan Warriors go," a dark-skinned
female in a white gown said stepping out from behind the first
woman. "You are in the Warriors' Bliss."
Warriors Bliss was where all Nevan warriors went when they
died. It was said to be a place of honor, where the warriors
could finally rest in peace and look down upon all of Neva.
They were the guardians of Neva. I now knew who the two
females were. They were Camilla, the pale skinned female,
and Dina, the dark skinned one. They were Nevan archangels.
"Warriors' Bliss," I asked. They both smiled and nodded. I
looked around me once more. "I'm not ready to be here," I
whispered.
"Don't be afraid," Dina said.

"I'm not afraid," I said shaking my head. "I'm just not ready to be here."

"You have fulfilled your destiny," Camilla said. She extended her arms open. "You are home, now, Kaitlyn."

"I will trade anything to go back," I whispered. They stared at me, in silence, for a long time.

"Anything," Dina asked. I nodded my head.

"Are you willing to go to Volos, if you are to perish again," Camilla asked. I thought long and hard before I answered. Volos was where all damned souls were sent. It was said to be a place where all our fears and demons came alive. Volos was painful and there was no returning.

"Volos is not a place I wish to be, but if it means going back and doing some good, then I am willing to damn my soul," I said with my held head high. They both smiled.

"You truly are a warrior, Kaitlyn," Dina said. They both turned their backs to me and began walking away.

"Wait! Where are you going," I shouted running after them. "Please, don't leave me! Please! Why are you leaving me," I shouted, still continuing to run after them? No matter how fast I ran, they just got farther and father. Soon they were out of my sight. I stood alone, surrounded by whiteness and began to weep. Now, I was all alone and scared. I didn't have any of my loved ones, no archangels, no one. The white faded and I found myself standing in darkness. I had damned myself to an eternity of empty solitude.

Chapter Four
Simple Wish

The lights flashed on and I screamed. I began frantically trying to run away.

"No, no, come back! Don't leave me," I screamed. "Please! Come back! I don't want to be alone!"

"Kaitlyn," a voice said. "Kaitlyn."

"Please, don't leave me," I said and the tears flowed down my face. "Don't go." My head hit the pillow.

"Kaitlyn," the voice said again, this time recognizable. It was War Advisor Jennings. He was standing over me. He held my hand and squeezed it gently. "You're okay."

"Is this Volos," I asked. He shook his head and laughed.

"You're in the infirmary. You've been in an induced coma for ten days," he said smiling. "We thought we lost you. You flat lined a few times, but came back seconds later. We weren't sure if you'd pull through." I nodded my head and looked around the room. It was an all-white room just like the one I had just been in.

"Dimitri," I asked looking at War Advisor Jennings.

"He is fine, thanks to you." He patted my hand and smiled. "You really are stubborn."

"I know," I said rolling my eyes. "How come I'm awake?" He shrugged his shoulders.

"Not too sure." Right then the doors opened and Doctor Thomas walked in grinning. I rolled my eyes and he laughed. "Just can't stay away. Can you? You know, I'm going to have to start charging you," Doctor Thomas said.

"Bill War Advisor Jennings," I said. War Advisor Jennings laughed and let go of my hand.

"I'm going to give you some privacy while you talk to Doctor Thomas," War Advisor Jennings said. I nodded my head and he took his leave.

"How bad is Dimitri," I asked Doctor Thomas. He shook his head and laughed.

"You wake up from being in a coma for days and the first thing you want to know is about someone else," he asked. I nodded my head. "He is fully recovered and back to his regiment." I felt a weight on my shoulders leave. I nodded my head.

"Good." I just laid there.

"You, on the other hand," he said. I waited for the bad news. I had asked Dina and Camilla to return me to this world, but I never specified that I wanted to be in one piece. A tear slid down my face. "Hey, it's okay."

"Nothing is okay anymore," I said sobbing. He pulled the sheet back and I looked down.

"You're in one piece. We healed you a week ago." I looked my body over. "We had you in a coma to ease the pain. Your brain waves were off the charts."

"Oh," I said feeling more at ease. He laughed and shook his head.

"Oh? You really are my special patient."

"Job security," I muttered and he laughed more.

"That's true. As long as you are around, I will always have a job." I swung my legs off the bed. "Oh, come on. You can't be serious. You were shot, burned, and nearly blown up and you want to get up out of bed?"

"Should we start arguing over my discharge papers now," I asked grinning.

"You are so stubborn," he said walking over to me.

"Seems to be the general consensus," I said chuckling to myself. He began unhooking the monitors and looking me over.

"I'm going to give you a shot and some medication. If you have any symptoms, any at all, you come straight here and see me, okay?"

"Yes, sir," I said saluting him. He rolled his eyes and then helped me up. My legs, like always it seemed, were shaky. He wrapped an arm around to help keep me steady.

"We'll take it slow." I stood for five minutes with him supporting me. Then we practiced walking around the room. He kept suggesting a wheelchair, but I refused. He was growing annoyed by my stubbornness and, honestly, I couldn't blame him. Dealing with me had to be the biggest challenge for anyone here.

I had started life off so timid and never questioned anything. I just went with whatever was said. I was a puppet to the world. Now I was the puppet master, so to speak. I didn't take orders that weren't justified and I stood up for anyone who needed me. I proved time and time again that I would stand by my word and loyalty. I had truly become Anguish.

Chapter Five
One More Thing to Say

Doctor Thomas helped me change into a uniform that was laid out on the chair and we made our way out of the room. War Advisor Jennings was standing there. He grinned and shook his head.

"Somehow, I knew you'd be discharged," he said chuckling. I shrugged my shoulders and began following him. We walked through the empty corridors.

"Where is everyone, sir?"

"They are all in the dining hall. We had a ceremony for the Wolverines and Cobras," he said. I nodded my head and smiled. They all deserved medals for their bravery. We continued walking the halls. "You scared me to death, Kaitlyn." I glanced up at him.

"Sorry, sir."

"Henry."

"Sir?"

"In private, to you, I'm just Henry." I smiled and kept walking. My legs were slowly gaining back their strength.

"Well, I'm sorry, Henry." He smiled and patted me on the back, it was uncomfortable but the medication kept me from feeling most of it.

"I can't be mad at you. I would have done the same thing. I just wished that it could've been preventable."

"Everything happens for a reason."

"This is true." We stopped in front of the dining hall's doors. The dining hall was the quietest I had ever heard it. I looked up at him. "Think you are up to it?"

"No one knows I'm awake?" I asked. He shook his head.

"I didn't bother telling them, in case something went wrong." I nodded my head. It would be harder on them, if I didn't survive. I took a deep breath. "You don't have to. We can just wait."

"It's okay," I took another deep breath and he opened the doors. All heads turned towards the door and the room became even more silent.

"Look what I found in the hallway," War Advisor Jennings said laughing. We walked further into the room and Dimitri came running over to us. He picked me up in his arms and held me. I heard a noise and it was him sobbing.

"I thought you were going to die," he said against my cheek. I laughed and held on to him.

"Can't get rid of me that easily, my friend." He set me back down on my feet and looked at me. He was smiling with tears flowing down his face. He wiped his face.

"I owe you my life." I shrugged my shoulders.

"You would've done the same." I said with a tear sliding down my face. He nodded his head. "I'm just glad you are okay."

"You were the first thing she asked about, Commander Aiyetoro," War Advisor Jennings said. Dimitri frowned and then laughed.

"I am well and back to the Cobras," Dimitri said gesturing to the Cobras. I smiled at the sight.

"Good. They need their commander," I said nodding.

"As do the Wolverines, ma'am," Edwards said. I hadn't realized the Wolverines had walked over to us. A few of them had tears in their eyes, which made the tears run down my face. I smiled.

"I'm glad to see you guys," I said wiping my eyes.

"We're glad to see you too, ma'am," Martin said giving me a huge hug. I hugged him back and he began to sob. "I'm so sorry I left you." I laughed and pulled away from him.

"You were following orders, Martin. I'm proud of you." I looked at the others. "I'm proud of all of you," I said wiping the rest of the tears from my eyes. "Now go finish eating before we hit the mats."

"Yes, ma'am," they said laughing. War Advisor Jennings, Dimitri and I walked over to the commanders' table. All the commanders gave me big hugs. I looked around and Eric wasn't there.

"Where's," I swallowed hard, "Eric," I asked War Advisor Jennings.

"He pretty much hasn't come out of his room, since you were hurt. He comes out long enough to do his duties, go on patrols, and check on you. Occasionally he eats, but very rarely," War Advisor Jennings whispered. I frowned at his words.

"Well, that crap's going to stop," I growled and they all laughed.

"Yes, ma'am," War Advisor Jennings said laughing. He pushed his communication hi-fi. "I need an order for Commander Trials to come to the dining hall, it's urgent."

"Urgent. Commander Trials, report to the dining hall. Commander Trials, report to the dining hall. Urgent," the announcement said. We all stared at the doors and no sign of him. Finally, he ran through the doors and looked around.

"What's the…" he stopped dead when he saw me. "Kaitlyn," he asked. I barely heard his words. I nodded my head.

"Hey," I whispered. I felt myself getting choked up. He looked like death. He was still muscular but he had lost weight in the last ten days.

"You going to just stand there, or are you going to come kiss her," War Advisor Jennings shouted. The dining hall filled with laughter. In a few long strides, he was in front of me and holding me against him. I wrapped my arms around him and cried into his shirt. He kissed the top of my head.

"She comes back from the dead and all she gets is a kiss on her head," Conner asked laughing. Eric looked up and growled at him. "Easy. I'm just messing around… kind of." Eric laughed, held me tighter against him.

"Does this mean you're no longer mad at me," I asked. He pulled me away and looked at me.

"I could never stay mad at you, sweetheart." He leaned down and kissed me. The entire dining hall began cheering. Part of me was embarrassed at the public display of affection, but the other part of me didn't care. I needed Eric more than I needed my pride.

"Alright, you two, breathe," War Advisor Jennings said clearing his throat. Eric and I pulled away. I laughed against his chest and he rubbed my back.

"You'll be lucky if I let you out of my sight," Eric whispered into my ear. "Ever again." I chuckled to myself and nodded.

"Fair enough, sir," I said looking up at him and laughing.

"Kaitlyn," he warned. He smiled and turned me around. "Now sit down and eat." I frowned and the commanders' table laughed.

"Oh, come on. It has to be getting better," Walter said grinning. I shook my head.

"I almost died and you guys are still trying to poison me with your gruel," I asked crossing my arms. They all laughed and Dimitri stood.

"Allow me to have the honors of retrieving you some soup," he said. I smiled and nodded.

"Now that is a true gentleman," I said grinning.

"He's like, forever in your debt. You might as well consider him and Eric your shadows," Milton said laughing. Dimitri grinned and so did Eric.

"Oh, come on, I don't need two babysitters," I pleaded. I looked at War Advisor Jennings and he just nodded his head. I rolled my eyes and he laughed.

"It's either that or we put you in a room, tie you to a chair, lock the door, and throw away the key, so we can keep you out of trouble," War Advisor Jennings said in a fatherly tone.

"Oh, like that would stop me from getting into trouble," I said smirking.

Chapter Six
I can't breathe

A week after everything, I made a trip to Neva to see my mother and ask for forgiveness for entering Neva into a war that was not theirs. Much to my surprise, she was not angry with me. She said I did the noble thing. Another peace treaty was drawn up between Neva and Lynx. Both cantons pledged their allegiance to one another. My mother declared that the squadron was at Lynx's disposal and Lynx declared that the Anguish was at Neva's disposal.

Two weeks had now passed and I was still recovering. I was able to command, but I couldn't hit the mats just yet. Eric and Dimitri were serious about babysitting me. When one couldn't be with me, the other one was. Everywhere I went with the Wolverines either the Vipers or the Cobras went with us. At first it was annoying, but then it just became routine.

The Vipers and Dimitri were currently on babysitting duty. The Vipers and Wolverines were doing physical training on the mats together, while Dimitri and I sat on the bench watching. The Cobras and Wolverines had a strong bond between them because of that day. Their bond was almost as strong as Dimitri's and mine.

"What are you thinking about," Dimitri asked. I shook my head and laughed.

"Was just admiring all of their friendships," I said. He turned his attention to the mats, nodded and smiled.

"The battlefield has a way of bringing people together," he said making me look at him. "I owe you my life. My family owes you for my life."

"Nonsense."

"You are modest, but this is not something you should be modest about. You risked your own life to save me."

"I couldn't let you be alone, Dimitri," I whispered and he nodded.

"I know. When you ordered Martin to leave and you refused to leave, I knew what you were doing. The odds were not in our favor, yet, you wouldn't leave me." A tear slid down both of our faces.

"I'd never leave you," I said smiling. He smiled and nodded his head.

"I am honored to call you my comrade and friend." I smiled more and gave him a hug.

"As am I, as am I." I sat back up and we watched the Wolverines and Cobras go at it some more. It was finally time for dinner. We formed up and made our way to the dining hall. The Cobras and Wolverines sat with one another, while Dimitri and I found our seats at the commanders' table. Eric was already at the table and I was sitting across from him. He smiled when I sat down.

"How long are you two going to babysit her," Milton asked laughing.

"As long as the sun shines and night falls," Dimitri said. I rolled my eyes.

"We're in a compound with no windows. I think I am safe," I said laughing. They were all staring at me and frowning. "Oh, come on, you guys. I was ordered in to the simulators, water tank… "I tried remembering the other things. "Oh, and I volunteered for the electric lashings to save my Wolverines." They all rolled their eyes and shook their heads. "What," I asked laughing.

"You're going to be the death of Eric," Covington said pointing at Eric, who nodded his head.

"Why can't you just go back to your nice quiet self who first showed up to Anguish," Orion said. They all looked at me and I shook my head.

"Not happening," I said crossing my arms. Orion shrugged and laughed.

"I tried, Eric," Orion said looking at Eric.

"She doesn't listen to me either," Eric huffed.

"I allow you and Dimitri to babysit me," I said, pointing at him and then Dimitri.

"Allow," Eric asked frowning. I laughed.

"Yes, I allow you both to babysit me, because I don't feel like hearing your whining." I growled. They were both frowning and staring at me. The rest of the commanders couldn't believe I had said that.

"Wow," Franklin said and I busted out laughing.

"Should've seen your faces," I picked up my spoon and began eating my soup, while they just stared at me. Finally, they laughed and went back to eating. They all small talked and I just sat there eating my soup.

"Armistice, front and center" War Advisor Jennings yelled. I dropped my spoon and rolled my eyes.

"I can't even eat in peace after getting blown up. I didn't even do anything," I grumbled. The table was laughing at me.

"Sometime today, Armistice," he said. I quickly made my way over to him and stood at attention. He looked around me.

"Trials, don't think you're getting out of this so easy. You get over here too." This really couldn't be good. Eric stood next to me.

"Sir," Eric said.

"Well, either one of you have anything to say," War Advisor Jennings asked. I tried recalling the day and anything I might have done to get myself in trouble. I couldn't come up with anything, so I shook my head.

"Negative, sir," I said. War Advisor Jennings looked at Trials.

"What about you, Trials," War Advisor Jennings asked. I heard Eric take a deep breath. I looked over at him and he was down on knee. My heart began to race. I looked at War Advisor Jennings and he was grinning. I looked at the commanders' table and they were all grinning. I looked back at Eric. "Well?"

"Kaitlyn, I know you hate attention," he said looking around the room and back at me, "and I'm sorry. I also know that you will never leave your command. I have accepted this despite the fact it is likely to give me a heart attack." He chuckled. He dug into his pocket and pulled out a small box.

"Oh," I whispered and Eric laughed.

"You always choose that word whenever it's something sentimental, Kaitlyn," he said looking at me and removed a ring from the box. He set the box aside.

"Sorry, I whispered. He shook his head.

"Nonsense, it's one of the many things I love about you." He hadn't ever told me that he loved me, and now he was saying it in front of all of Anguish. I felt my eyes swell up with tears and butterflies fill my stomach. "Even though you are stubborn, ornery, backtalk quite often, don't listen all the time, and are a spitfire," he began and I frowned. He grinned. "I wouldn't change it for the world."

"Eric," I whispered and a tear fell down my face. I wiped it away.

"Would you give me the honor of calling you my wife?" I felt all my walls crumble. I stood their speechless. "Kaitlyn?" Eric was now terrified, and probably regretting his approach. He ran a hand through his hair.

"Yes," I said faintly.

"Yes," he asked with his eyes wide. I nodded my head and smiled. He slipped the ring on my finger and the entire dining hall was on their feet clapping. Eric stood and kissed me like there was no tomorrow. I held his face with my hands and kissed him like there was no tomorrow for me either. We probably would have kissed for quite some time, but War Advisor Jennings cleared his throat. Eric and I stopped kissing. I couldn't help but laugh as I faced him. He was smiling and held out his hand.

"Congratulations, Armistice," he said. I began to shake his hand and he pulled me to him. He gave me a huge hug and leaned over to my ear. "Welcome to the family."

Chapter Seven
Ever After

Eric and I moved upstairs and settled in to our new quarters. It was made for a king; plenty of room to walk around and enough space if we needed to get away from one another. We had a galley so I could make my own food, but still sat at the commanders' table and watched them eat.

I became closer with all the commanders', since the day Dimitri and I were stuck outside the north wall. They still gave me a hard time about my stubbornness, but they opened up more about their lives. They even allowed me into their families' lives. I never knew it, but big bad Lance Bruce was a father of two little girls. He was the complete opposite around them. He would roll on the ground and play with them without a care in the world.

I saw Councilman Tibbot almost as much as I saw the Wolverines. I filled his ears with my rants and issues. He never complained, just sat back, listened and occasionally nodded. I don't know if he was really listening to me, but it was nice just to get stuff off my chest. War Advisor Jennings, well Henry, and I frequently retreated to his office after a long day. We sat back in our chairs, shared stories, laughed and indulged in spirits. He often shared embarrassing childhood stories of Eric for me to tease Eric with later. I truly couldn't have asked for a better father-in-law.

Eric and I visited my mother once a week. They would stay inside and talk, while I walked around Neva, greeting those people who I had freed from my father's tyrannical madness. Of course, Dimitri followed behind me with the Cobras and Wolverines, but even that didn't stop me from spending time with the Nevans.

The relationship between Eric and I had grown stronger with each passing day. I fell in love with him, all over again, every time our eyes met. How could I have been so foolish and not seen him in front of me from the first time we met? Whatever the reasoning for me being blind to him, I was grateful that I could finally see. He was now all I could see.

The dining hall was filled with conversations and laughter, as was the commanders' table. Lance and Conner were currently out on patrol, so the table wasn't filled with their bickering over who had the better regiment. Today, Dimitri and Eric were disputing over which one of their regiments was the best. At a minimum, ten minutes had gone by and finally I burst into a fit of laughter. They stopped arguing and the whole table looked at me.

"What's so funny," Eric asked frowning.

"You two are fighting over who has the best regiment," I said pointing at them both.

"Okay, who do you think has the best regiment," Dimitri asked looking at Eric and then at me. I just shook my head and laughed.

"Kaitlyn, you can be honest," Eric said pointing at himself making the table laugh.

"Okay, if you really must know," I said leaning in closer to them. All of them leaned in closer to me. I sighed. "Really want to know?"

"Yes," they said in unison.

"I do," I whispered and sat back up. Their faces were priceless. They just stared at me in disbelief for a while and, finally, Covington broke the silence with his laugh.

"She does have a valid point," Covington said laughing more.

"We should never ask for a female's opinion," Eric said grinning. I balled up my napkin and tossed it at him. He laughed and began to throw it back at me.

"Commander Trials," War Advisor Jennings, Henry, shouted. The entire room went quiet. Eric grumbled and began to stand. "Not you, the other one!" The whole table looked at me and grinned. I rolled my eyes and began to stand.

"What'd I do now, sir," I said in a groan and the entire room filled with laughter, including Henry.

Dear Reader,
Thank you so much for purchasing and taking the time to read, *Train to Anguish*. I hope you enjoyed it, as much as I enjoyed writing it. If you have the time, I would be ever so grateful, if you could leave a review on Amazon. (*Smile*)

Come find me:
Good ole' Facebook →
www.facebook.com/monsterinthecookiejar
My Blog →
monsterinthecookiejar.wordpress.com

Again, thank you so much for your purchase and for reading, *Train to Anguish!*

Happy Reading & Lots of Love,
S. E. Isaac

Made in the USA
Las Vegas, NV
05 October 2024

96336589R00142